T0197108

THE ★ HOUR
OF ★ LEAD

THE ★ HOUR OF ★ LEAD

A NOVEL

BRUCE HOLBERT

COUNTERPOINT | BERKELEY, CALIFORNIA

Library of Congress Cataloging-in-Publication Data
The hour of lead : a novel / Bruce Holbert.
p. cm
ISBN 978-1-61902-550-9
1. Ranchers—Washington (State)—History—Fiction.
2. Families—Washington (State)—History—Fiction. I. Title.
PS3608.O48287H69 2014
813'.6—dc23
2014014411

Jacket design by Michael Kellner
Interior design by Elyse Strongin, Neuwirth & Associates

COUNTERPOINT
2560 Ninth Street, Suite 318
Berkeley, CA 94710
www.counterpointpress.com

Printed in the United States of America

For Holly, Natalie, Luke, and Jackson

Caliban's nights are full of teeth

—JOHN WHALEN
Caliban

PART ★ ONE

This is the hour of Lead—
Remembered, if outlived,
As Freezing persons, recollect the snow—
First—Chill—then Stupor—then the letting go—

—EMILY DICKINSON,
from poem 372

★ PREFACE ★

IN 1918, SPANISH INFLUENZA KILLED seventy-five million people worldwide, though not the Romanovs, who were instead murdered in their palace basement by Bolsheviks. The same year, on the eleventh hour of the eleventh day of the eleventh month, World War I closed with the Treaty of Versailles. No one was awarded the Nobel Prize for Peace.

In that year, for the only time in the century, America's population shrank. One hundred one people perished in Tennessee's Great Train Wreck. May 20 in Codell, Kansas, tornadoes leveled every building, just as they had on May 20, 1917 and May 20, 1916. In Boston, Babe Ruth pitched a shut-out for the Red Sox in the World Series, though he hit no home runs.

The Wobblies and AFL crippled the city of Seattle, Washington with a general strike adding fuel to fears of a Bolshevik insurgence. The state initiated prohibition with the Bone Dry Act, and the *Wenatchee World* published the first public mention of a concrete dam on the Columbia River at Grand Coulee.

Yet, east, past the mountains, in the Big Bend and the Basin, on the reservations and the Palouse and the fissured basalt paralleling the Columbia River's deep trough, among channeled scablands and the wheat country and orchards and cattle ranches and dairy farms, horses still powered crude machines not much improved from a hundred years before. Towns of no more than a hundred, many just a grain silo and half-dozen houses that served the railroad lines, scattered over the state's eastern and central portion. Most people resided far even from these skeletal communities, settling in draws with good water or meadows livestock might graze or beneath eyebrows so as not to waste arable acres or at the mouth of canyons that kept the herds.

Far from cities' competing glare and industrial haze the year appeared to pass this country like another cloud in another sky of another day. Its half-dozen papers delivered month-old world and national reports along with fair winners and local obituaries, though people received most of their news through tales added to and subtracted from a hundred times before reaching their ears. Most were good for nothing sensible, just wonder and doubt and the uncertainties attached to them. Nevertheless, alone, behind a plow or aboard an animal or pulling a saw handle or over a chicken boiling in a pot, the denizens chewed and swallowed and digested them until the stories turned as tangible as bone and muscle and tendon.

⋆ 1 ⋆

Linda Jefferson was a cliché and she knew it. Twenty-four, both schoolteacher and widow, she tugged a sweater over her blouse then her husband's sheepskin-lined riding coat. His death the year previous had deposited her in a sad, inevitable season. She weathered it as a dumb animal scratches for summer's remnants beneath the snow, not understanding winter or seeking to, only enduring it. The absence was endless and reasonless; it seemed less a wound, which mourning would have mitigated and eventually closed, than a flaw in herself, requiring constant stitching to keep from bleeding through.

In this country, loneliness was unassailable law. A man weighed his heart by the number of sleepers under his roof when the lights went out and a woman by the number of eggs in the skillet mornings. The distance between souls, however, remained incalculable. Blood made them kin, yet a heart does not beat solace or joy. One must hunt that in others, and others remained few and far apart. Days she entertained a room full of children but a job was no remedy for an empty house.

In the schoolroom furnace, quartered pine ebbed to coal and ash and wind clattered the flue. The weather battered the cottonwood in the yard and clouds clotted and thinned the light. The storm was a relief. A hard wind could perform beautiful things to country, sweep it clean like a new room. Once it let up and the sky emptied to blue, the snow seemed a new start.

As she approached the twins, pressed into desks for which they had grown too large, they hitched themselves a little taller. Clad in a cotton shirt and grey trousers, Luke flipped his book closed with his forefinger. Clothes passed between the brothers and were never a reliable way to tell them apart; still, three minutes in a room, you knew Luke from his twin, Matt, who was bent across his spelling, crimped hand steering his pencil.

She tapped a finger on Matt's paper to identify two words that remained misspelled. He nodded and opened his primer to correct the work. Matt was better suited for practical pursuits. Fall, the boys demonstrated a bent to arrive early and she'd assigned Matt the stove. Each morning, he retrieved the axe from the long covered porch and quartered a couple of aged tamarack rounds stacked at the porch's far end. After, he knocked loose some kindling and propped it across a handful of dried pine needles and a balled page of last week's news. He struck a match—one was all he'd allow—against the paper two or three places and coax the damper draft till the wood burned blue and smokeless. Not a wisp entered the room. All the while, she shot Luke new and difficult words to spell. She felt odd enjoying boys this age. Eighth grade, they recognized a woman differed from them and that they were meant to do something about it. She thought of her husband once more, his broad, callused hands on her shoulder and waist while they danced at the Fort Saturdays, not pulling her, just steady and there. His nails, yellowed by cigarettes, the hair dark and wiry between his knuckles, the same hand that dangled from the sheet as the logging crew carted him from the forest. As his crew recalled, the tree turned on its stump and thrust a wooden blade through Vernon's throat and out one ear. The mortician could do nothing without removing the head entirely, so he appeared like an awestruck child in the casket, marveling at something overhead and slightly to the left.

Wind creaked the building trusses, but it was the winter's first storm and early, likely packing only a skiff of snow and freeze enough to finish the pumpkins and squash. Still the boys ought not to risk a chill.

"You two better get on," Linda Jefferson said.

She watched the boys button their jackets and tug their stocking caps past their ears. Outside, they patted their horse and each took a stirrup and mounted. It left them one-footed until they had purchase enough to reach the saddle horn. Neither asked nor offered the other assistance. Their mulishness struck her as comic and she laughed.

•

ED LAWSON NARROWED HIS EYELIDS and peered toward the horizon as the first strong gusts batted the shutterless window. Flakes no bigger than birdshot and nearly as hard followed. They whirled and rapped the crosshatched pane. He held no rancor against the season coming hard. After, he'd walk his property to scout coyotes or the few cougars left in the cliffs that might harass the livestock.

His wife, though, had been fussing at the window since the cattle had congregated at the feedbin despite half a day till the next feeding. They huddled at the barn door and lowed for Ed to admit them. Eventually he relented and, past them, she watched the horizon swell purple and pulse like blood through an opened vein that spilled across the sky. Winters in this place turned afternoon brief as a heartbeat, and night unraveled over day so thick sleepers dreamed themselves swimming through it to breathe. Day, when it arrived, was little relief. Breaths turned hurried, drawing in more cold than air and expelling a body's warmth until a person was left light-headed and pneumatic. The sun, shimmering behind the cumulous haze, looked as warm as it might to a fish at the bottom of a lake.

A half empty coffeepot perked in the center of the table. Ed Lawson rocked his cup below his mouth and enjoyed the vapors from the moonshine inside it.

"Probably stopped somewhere to throw a ball."

The front of her head disappeared in the glass reflection as she turned to him. "You know it's too cold for baseball."

Ed inhaled over the cup then drank. The window was nearly blank with frost. He fortified his coffee again and joined his wife looking out. Her head swung when she caught the liquor scent. He winked at her. Her face had slackened and too much sun had guttered her eyes. He recalled her profile from their first days, a crescent and white as the moon, and the thinness above her hips that tapered her. He felt no different about the woman now and considered that his greatest good fortune.

An oak crate tumbled past and splintered into the house wall. "Goddamner," Ed said. "This one's got a bad humor."

His wife nodded, still at the window.

"Not supposed to blow like this till January," she said.

Lawson joined her and stared out the glass. "Maybe January in Alaska," he said. His wife turned and watched Ed lift his long duster from the chair back and tug his gloves from the pockets and test his fingers inside them.

"Boil some water. They're liable to be frosty when I find them," he said.

He screwed a hunting cap onto his head and opened the door; cold blasted through, a lamp shook, and light wavered in the kitchen. He waved to her and stepped toward the corral. The light in the doorway became a shadow then nothing, enveloped by the sideways storm.

•

WHEN HE AND MATT WERE left alone, Luke poured moonshine into fruit jars and let Matt dare him into sipping it. That woolly burning felt like Mrs. Jefferson next to him. Luke had tracked his teacher through autumn, hunting her insides under the breathy voice and slow windmill circles her hands spun as she recited poetry, like words were birds she could coax from nests. The best reader and speller in the class, Luke could not fathom where his teacher disappeared when she spoke those words. Each time he recognized her fragrance, he wished to know more.

The horse halted, a three-year-old Appaloosa mare, Mule, named for such moments. The sun, only a smear of white without warmth in the short days, turned memory aside from the shallow, long light lining the horizon. The wind pitched itself into the riders and the horse. Luke stood in the stirrup, dismounted, and twisted the reins, the rawhide frosted white to the bridle where it thawed with the mare's breaths. An ice layer clung to her neck and under her belly, and tongues of snow spiraled around them, sometimes moving up instead of down, or remaining halfway, scouring the boys' exposed skin.

A week later, the papers would report a seventy-five-degree temperature drop in fifty-seven minutes. Four feet of snow, light as down, piled onto the hardening earth in the next three hours, and double that the six that followed, all so far past the almanac records as to render the whole book inadequate. Seventy-year-old farmers from Norway and the Russian North, usually quick to reduce the New World's winters to minor annoyances, when asked about the storm of '18 remained mute and just shook their grey heads. At the river's bank, sheep huddled near the steaming water and eventually waded into it, since it was warmer. Dozens would pock the steely surface as the ice stilled even the fastest waters. Gusts spun the windvanes until the spindles stripped their couplings and the blades and ribbing spun from barn tops to be discovered months later and miles away.

The boys cussed the horse, separate and together. They quirted her face with the reins. The snow piled against their torsos and welled in the lee sides as if they were trees or hills. Wind snapped Luke's hat from his head and it vanished across the road. In his brows the ice thickened. It clotted his hair. Matt pulled the reins hard and Mule lunged forward. She accepted their weight when they mounted, swayed in the wind, and tried another step. The wind shoved the boys' heads into their shoulders and blistered their hands and faces. Luke couldn't clench his fingers over the reins. The twins gazed at the snow, eyes tearing, tears freezing to their skin. The muscles in Mule's chest bunched when she stepped, the hole her hoof punched obliterated before she could attempt the next. They traveled half a mile. Frost reached the mare's chest, ascending past the stirrups. After each step she rested before attempting another. Her breath pressed out in short, dutiful gasps and she ran a half dozen uneven strides until her weight tipped.

Matt expected Luke to act, but when he didn't Matt kicked one foot from the stirrup and hauled Luke clear of the horse's falling weight. Together, they disappeared in the high snow. Matt shook Luke and he rose. In the slanting snow, they watched the mare paw and roll and regain all fours and back away, steam coming from her nostrils.

Matt pushed Luke's shoulder. "Which way?"

"Out of the snow."

"Don't seem likely."

"Give me your hat."

Matt set his gloved hand atop the wool cap. "I got ears to warm, too," he said. Luke nodded.

"Can you drown in snow?" Matt asked.

"I don't want to find out," Luke said. He shoved Matt in the direction of an elm skeleton.

•

LINDA JEFFERSON COAXED THE FURNACE fire. Some coals pinked but most had fallen to grey ash. A hard chill buffeted the room. Heat from the open stove barely pierced it and only for a few feet. She alternated between facing the flames and warming her back with them. The snow and the biting wind had frosted inside the window glass. Outside, the road passing the school and leading to her small house had become indistinguishable half an hour before, like everything else, just drifts and swells of white. Wind hammered the north side of the building. The storm was unlike any she had witnessed or read of. She checked the latch on the window and wondered how simple pine and glass could restrain such weather.

Though no friend of cold, she enjoyed the snap and aroma of burning wood. Winters, the log camp abandoned the woods and Vernon, when he wasn't hired out as a handyman, assigned himself the cooking. She would be treated to apple and berry cobblers and read a book or her students' work, while next to her he tinkered at songs from memory on an old mandolin like temptation itself. Occasionally, she'd turn and kiss his shoulder as he played. If the number of pecks passed three, he was allowed to lead her off to the heavy-quilted bed. Sometimes he cheated, bumping into her lips without her conceding. They would argue until she'd kissed him honestly and ended the squabble. Later, the shepherd dog would climb to the bed foot. It slept with her still. She spoke with the dog often, and at times thought she might be daft, but allowed that being alone granted a person privileges not permitted others.

She approached the window in her reverie and permitted the snow to sketch the steely air, flakes spinning a familiar image then destroying it before she could attach it to a name. She imagined a story the wind was attempting to recount, wondering if it might be prophecy she was seeing. She wanted to prepare. A darkened shape appeared, at first she thought it a shadow, but the ebbing light was too unclear to cast it. The form dangled just outside her comprehension but did not vanish like the others. She squinted to study it. Shoulders and the thick neck of a horse began to appear.

A pair of her husband's wool pants hung in the closet. She tugged them over her pantaloons and under her skirt. Outside, her arms swam in the white air, and flying ice beat her face. The horse belonged to the twins. The frozen saddle was taut against its chest. She touched its jaw, which was rigid as rod iron. The animal's glassy eye did not close. Snow had drifted to its withers.

•

ED LAWSON REGRETTED THE SNOWSHOES in the barn he'd decided against. For half an hour he'd hiked what he thought was the road from the creek wash, but now he'd slogged into a stand of birch he recognized as west of that road. Ed's gloved hand raked the snow from his face. He tipped himself against the leeside of a tree. He could taste his stomach stir: this afternoon's coffee and shine, a couple of eggs from breakfast. He belched once and the pain eased. The pint bottle clanked inside his jacket and he worked off a glove and twisted the cork. His fingers branched over the bottle and the glass seemed to join his flesh. His numb hand raised it a second time. The glove dropped from his arm's crook and skittered away like mice before a plow. Ed acknowledged it as punishment for tarrying and a harbinger to head on. He finished the bottle and wished for the warmth of a cigarette.

•

THE FENCE THAT LINED THE road to the creek was Linda Jefferson's only prospect for locating the boys. The barbed wire pulled her wool gloves apart and the air stung her hands and the cold spread, numbing her arms and shoulders. Snow rose like water rippling for fence posts and trees in its rising current. Like many in similar straits, she only now realized that country could kill a person dead as Jesse James and just as quickly.

•

ED STOOD. HE'D SURRENDERED HIS footing twice, cratering the snow with shapes that seemed unlike his own. He hoped the boys had reached the house. It would be a relief to Helen. She would fret his absence, but less than she did theirs, which is as it should be. He would manage. The time had arrived to do just that and join them at the stove for something hot. He bore straight north. A mile, no more, and he would be thawing his numb feet till they were pink as pigs. The storm shoved at his shoulders and chest, and he tilted his body against it. He busted through a drift. His hips led the way for his legs. Blowing snow pelted his eyes. He angled his gaze down and forward, then, following three steps aided by gravity, floated into the air. His arms circled and the breath in his chest filled him. He thought he would see his ranch soon, the river's wide bend at Gifford Ferry, the Fort, the arc of the earth itself.

•

LINDA SPOTTED THE BOYS BALLED like porcupines midway up the birch tree. They floundered toward the schoolhouse in a chain, Linda breaking the snow, Matt between them squeezing her gloved hand and Luke's. Luke toppled twice. Linda feared they would be required to pack him, but after they changed order and towed him by both arms, he stumbled onward.

Matt spied the schoolhouse shape first. Snow in the doorway had heaped past the knob. He and Mrs. Jefferson clawed at the powder. Luke lay behind them and shut his eyes. Closing them was a relief; they still functioned. His brother and his teacher bent like the humped hills a few feet away. The snow they shoveled floated over him like cottonwood seeds in the wind. Through it, he recognized Mrs. Jefferson's gold hair, dull with ice. He wanted to lift himself and help but couldn't find his hands.

Linda grunted and the snow gave a little to the door. Matt burrowed on until they gained the few inches needed to wedge through. When he turned, Luke's arm raised from under the snow like a grave marker. Matt swatted the snow and found his nose and mouth. Linda pressed her face to Luke's, but through the wind could not make out a breath.

Inside the schoolhouse, they lay him on the floor. Mrs. Jefferson's fingers fumbled to untie his frozen shoelaces, then unscrewed his socks. Luke's yellow, bloodless feet shone in the faint window light.

"Get blankets from the closet," she said. She unsnapped Luke's pants while Matt found the blankets and laid one on the floor. Luke's pants were off. Matt stared at his white undershorts. He looked at the furnace, but felt no heat.

"The matches are in the top drawer," Mrs. Jefferson told him.

Matt watched her roll Luke onto the blanket and use it to drag his brother toward the stove.

The wood crib was empty.

The shape of her face in the light trembled. "Books," she said. "Tear the pages out."

He found math books stacked behind the desk. "You sure?"

"Yes."

He ripped the multiplication chapters from their binding and stacked them inside the stove. His hands wouldn't pinch onto the match. He closed his fist, jammed the stick between two knuckles, and struck the sulfur head against the stove's iron lid. The match flared. He set it to the pages. They lit and curled above the cold ash. He doubled the pile and watched while letters, numbers, whole equations unraveled. The hatchet was in the closet and he hacked the desks, separating the legs and the seat ribbing to kindle the blaze. The flames snuffled the varnished wood, then took. He added a top and seat back and left the door open to give them light.

Luke lay naked on the blanket. "Undress," Mrs. Jefferson said. She unbuttoned her own jacket and wrenched off her gloves. More blankets lay next to Luke's clothes. Matt's underwear stuck to his skin and hissed when he shucked it from his legs. He covered himself with his hands.

"Get on the blanket," Mrs. Jefferson said. He watched her lift her blouse. Her hair hooked to the collar, then fell to her shoulders. Through the burning, he could smell her clothes. She bent at the waist and her skirt dropped, then her pants and pantaloons. Her eyes shut. She reached behind herself with both hands and undid her camisole, then curled her knickers past her ankles. She put herself between the two to warm them both.

Luke awoke to her next to him. She extended her arm across him for another blanket and her thick nipple brushed his chest. Her hair curved, a half crescent to the bottom of her neck. It shone like polished metal, and with her over him, the paper ash fluttering in the apricot light like warm snow, he felt vaguely content.

Linda saw the boy's breathing stop. She tapped at his sternum and set her cheek beneath his nose. The fire's watery heat washed over her spine and ribs and muscles and skin. Matt watched as she opened her mouth and placed it on top of Luke's. He envied his brother the kiss. Air passed from her into Luke. His throat fluttered then quit. She blew into him twice more and then drew back and waited. Luke's tongue lolled in his mouth.

With her thumb and forefinger she closed Luke's eyes. The flesh felt cool and damp, like her own. She was afraid suddenly that she couldn't separate the living from the dead. The wool blanket raked the skin of her shoulders when she turned toward the living boy, who lay on his side, facing the opposite wall. He tensed his legs and buttocks against her cool skin, but as the warmth built between them, his muscles relaxed. He twisted his hips into the space she had left for them. Her breasts parted. He rose to peer past her shoulder, but she halted him with her hand against his chest.

"Let him sleep," she said. She shifted to slide one arm beneath Matt's spindly ribs, then drew the other around to meet it. The boy's breath warmed and dampened her wrists. She could smell his musty hair. She turned one palm and traced his chest. The muscle of his heart opened and closed. His diaphragm dragged in the warm air. His whole body worked. She rubbed his stomach for the friction that would warm him and in doing so, touched his adolescent pubic hair, recognizing the stirring in the flesh it covered below. She felt his heart beat again, when, by some sort of natural knowing, he turned and guided himself into her.

•

DAWN SPLINTERED THE NEXT MORNING. It brightened the west wall of the schoolhouse blue and pink and orange. Matt awoke and gazed at the pure light. His legs ached and semen clung to the thin hair on his thighs. The stove fire had taken all the math and reading books. All that was left were a few encyclopedia volumes scattered in front of their low shelves. He had chopped six more desks during the night. Mrs. Jefferson lay with her arms and legs extended to where he'd slept like a cat. He could smell her, them. Luke didn't move. Matt bent to affirm what he already knew. Luke's skin was cold and tight as animal hide.

Outside the window glass, the sky had blued and cleared and turned so deep he could see the peaks of the Okanogans and Kettles farther, the rock slides where snow couldn't hold and the blue-green sprinkling of pine blown clean by the wind. Steam rose from the river in long columns that danced above the water, and the earth in front of him was all one thing, simple, colorless, and impossible to know.

★ 2 ★

FROM ABOVE, THE COLUMBIA RIVER'S Lincoln County shore-
line appears as if a giant child has dragged a hoe through the land.
The steep banks collapse from the U-shaped bluffs, narrow and less
vertical where the bays and streambeds, fed with spring rains, carve
the rock to gravel each year. The river itself, a half-mile wide, hurried faster than a horse galloped: the boys had thrown in sticks and
raced them with their ponies for proof. They knew no one who had
navigated to the other side without ending up in Keller or drowned.
It was not unusual to row a boat to the current's fringes and anchor
it with two or three large stones, but even the goofiest of the home-
steaders had little inclination to cross.

The river bottom constantly changed with the season's rainfall
and drought. Spring runoff, a thousand uprooted trees might pass
in a week, their starry roots bobbing on the current; some trees,
halved by winds and rot, slowly drowned, needles and all, creating
pools too acidic for fish or fowl. Others spun in the current or sunk

separately and made homes for trout that harbored in the river's slow spots. Still more hung up in the cataracts where they idled for years, unraveling under the constant beating of water and rock like obscure sagas absent a necessary listener, occasionally providing deadheads, hazards for the four ferries that shuttled soldiers and Indians and farmers from one bank to its opposite. Each spring, snowmelt lifted the waterline. The fortified current pressed the winter's silt from the graveled bottom, readying it for the Coho, Sockeye, Steelhead, and Chinook spawn, when the river shallows would teem and boil with red salmon, days from expiring. Their tails and dorsal fins puckered the water's surface in the river's bays and inlets. Like the old Greek said, you could never step in the same river twice, but anyone in this country recognized the long view, that the river's change was its constancy, like the turning Earth itself.

Above, the basalt gorge appeared to have stood since the primordial epochs, sharp bluffs and talus slides exposed and last disturbed by ice age floods. Though sagebrush and ponderosa pine and birch and larch pocketed the river banks and descending grades, in the rich loess beyond the cliffs stretched wheat and barley by the square mile, not native to this country but graceful enough, whether whiskering the plowrows spring or early summer or rocking in the midsummer winds, cresting and falling like the river's surface, and even when threshed and gleaned to stubbled loops, it smelled like wet dough in the evening dew.

Summers, the sky, held in place by the high barometric pressure, looked an azure sheet for weeks at a time, deeper than any lake or sea, muddied only by the occasional plow's dust plume or a wildfire's ashy billow. Falls began gently with cirrus clouds and corduroy skies that filtered the sunlight to cool and colorless. Later blustery; nimbus and cumulus clouds blossomed in the thinned light and delivered rain then winter full on, which alternated between clear and cold freezes where a man could hear a footstep five miles off, and blizzards that stacked snow upon the river country until the spring, which delivered more blue and less grey, and the occasional mile high thunderheads, shattering the quiet with thunder and the sky with brutal electric streaks that split trees to the trunk and occasionally exploded houses and outbuildings and twice farmers who were late finding cover.

Here, Eugene Lawson, Ed's father and Matt's grandfather, took over an abandoned half section, then bought another five good crops later, then turned to beeves, accumulated a thousand acres of scrub grass to graze them, and here Ed Lawson was reared and never entertained residing elsewhere. Indeed it was here he had finished his earthly turn, though his son remained not inclined to accept it. The hours that took his father and his brother and delivered Matt to an adult woman before his time—and, it appeared to his conscience, the former a punishment for the latter, and his brother and father and mother casual innocents of a wrathful god's broad blow—loomed over him like a six-month arctic night. Yet Matt found no fault in the country from which his tragedies sprung.

Like anything in nature, a child's notion of the ordinary depends upon the ground in which he was sown. Born in dirt crannies, trees split basalt cliffs and the heartwood and cambium and protective bark reach for sun and rain in all sorts of unnatural geometry, knowing nothing of vertical and horizontal.

Ed inherited the place entirely. His twin brother, Willy, offered no argument. Willy possessed less interest in raising crops than he did space flight, and Ed lived for it—not because he worshipped the work and not because he loved sacrifice. From a distance a farm appeared rote, a season to plant, another to cultivate, a third for harvest and the last for prayer. But inside that ordered hoop each day differed so that every minute inside required attention, and it was this that made him a farmer.

•

CARDS ARRIVED AS WORD OF their tragedy swelled throughout the county. Mrs. Lawson had contracted pneumonia in her grief. Entire days she inclined over a steaming water kettle. Matt boiled her clothes each night and warmed canned vegetables and apple-sauce for their meals. Days, he battled the weather to keep the cows and pigs in fodder.

Between Sundays, the church's women's group delivered gro-ceries the congregation donated. The women never talked of Matt's brother—stowed in the barn as the ground was too frozen to shovel—or his father, still not recovered, and Matt's mother did not press them for news from the Lord on their fates.

When her fever broke, she asked Matt to harness the team and deliver her to church. The preacher perched them in the front pew. They were his accomplishment: a family whom in their grief he'd returned to the Lord. Yet, Matt's mother dismissed the words, not standing or sitting or singing with the congregation. The choir's voices swam to her like song snips from her school days, tuneful, but meaning nothing save the stir of memory, which was as reason-less as weather passing.

Matt's mother closed her eyes the entire service and Matt squashed his shut, too. His head thought nothing; he stared into blackness and listened to words that had torn loose from meaning and become only sounds a man made, no different from the barks or grunts from animals.

On the way out of the sanctuary, though, he would allow the light through the stained glass to warm him. He pinched his eye-lids shut and stopped in the aisle, and, for a moment, the other parishioners would look at him strangely, as if he might be taking the whole exercise more seriously than he ought.

Matt prayed every night. His mother followed and, when he shut his door, tarried outside and listened. The boy pushed prayer further than a person should, wrestling with God for his soul.

She missed Luke terribly. Secretly she feared parting with Matt might've left her less grieved. Matt was like a good skillet, dull and duty-bound. But it was Luke who stirred a person up. Having both had spoiled her. The church had offered up prayers for her perseverance and Ed and Luke's eternal salvation. But, she realized, no one had prayed for the living boy. The deaths made such a crater in their lives. She'd be filling it the rest of her years. He would, too, but he had a longer life coming.

Later, she entered his room. He slept soundly. Wind sawed at the window's frame, and he'd made a fist of himself under the blankets. Like a balled animal, he sought his own warmth. His pillow held only the top of his hair and one hand, which shuddered then stilled under her touch as if his skin recalled her mothering. She stroked his fingers and remembered it herself. She hadn't mothered the boy in a long while, she knew, longer than before the storm. That it was still in her to do it gave her some courage. She wanted to love him as much as the other, and she asked God for the power to do so. It was as generous a prayer as she could summon.

•

BETWEEN STORMS THOSE BITTER WEEKS the neighbors did their best to find Ed Lawson, but with only frostbite to show for their labors, they returned to their own homes and chores. Matt, however, continued. His mother suggested he hunt the draws and canyons between the ranch and the school. Instead, Matt hitched the team to the sled and headed to Peach, the nearest town. Hope

without cause is the last great mystery; it is beyond nature's accep-
tance of what is and man's reason to predict what will be and
memory of what was. In the religious it is simply faith the absence
of explanation and the proof of God, and a great comfort. In those
uninclined to churches and good books, however, such hopes still
occur, certainties born from fear, desperate, stubborn, full-pitched
battles against truth and time. In Matt's mind, too, such a force
resided. His will battled horror with the one truth he still had some
use for: his father had not been found and he believed, though he
could not speak it to another or explain it to himself, that if he
could pull that stitch his other troubles would unravel as well.

He inquired at each house in Peach. Almost no one had escaped
injury from the storm. Children lost pets, houses windows and roof
portions. Several ranches saw thousands in cattle and horses disappear; farmer's barns collapsed against the wind or under the snow's
weight. Windpump blades contorted their pistons beyond salvage.
Some trying to limit their damage lost fingers and toes to the cold.
None outside the Lawson ranch, though, lost people. So they listened politely and shook their heads and answered in the negative
when he inquired if they might have run into his father. Soon he
was a sad joke at coffee or breakfast for the locals. Some townsfolk
refused to answer his knock at all, but lonely old-timers fed him
and pressed him into conversations that went nowhere.

At the near end of the town lived the grocer, Worden. His oldest
daughter, Wendy, was a grade behind Matt at the school. Matt
often ended his search there, where she would inquire after his
mother while her father would box day-old bread or rolls and other
odds and ends he thought his mother might make use of.

After two such stops, the girl inquired if he desired company,
and, when he could devise no polite protest, she joined him.
Aboard the wagon, she arranged her bundlings. Settled, he could
still hear her easy breathing. She rode the buckboard as simple as

a man. There was little proper about her, which was what generally set him off girls. The tip of her nose was red. She blinked her long lashes, recognizing his attention and batted a mittened hand at her breath cloud. It vanished and she laughed, trying to meet his eyes, then puffed a breath his way. He had been a long time without play, even if he was inclined, but he felt warm in his blood and smiled despite himself. She seemed satisfied to return it, and he clucked the horses forward.

She waited while he knocked on the doors of one block of houses after another. The horses trudged and halted from house to house. Matt listened to the hooves squeak the snow. They continued like that until sunset, when Matt returned her to the grocer. She asked that he wait while she hurried inside and returned with a warm honey-filled roll and a handful of carrots she split between the two horses. The animals nodded and snuffled appreciatively and she rocked her head as if in conversation with them.

The next Sunday, he made the rounds and Wendy joined him once more. The pair repeated the same route as the previous week. Wendy had prepared a basket beforehand, loaded with vegetables for the horses and cinnamon rolls for the two of them. Grey clouds filtered the warmth from the bleak sunlight. Since the blizzard and a week following of twenty below, dull, colorless skies had draped the country horizon to horizon in all directions and the temperature lingered in the mid-twenties. The snow had turned dingy with grime and ice. The whole of the place seemed the color of cigarette smoke. Matt labored from the buckboard, his mind in the same straits as if he'd breathed in ash. Wendy began to hum, to herself at first, as if to pass the time, then with enough heft, she knew he would hear. He didn't know the song's name and didn't ask but listened to the tune, taking pleasure from her husky feminine voice.

When she stopped he was disappointed, until she commenced upon another. He thought of the songs he knew; they were few and incomplete and he only recognized words, pitch tone nor key, not music, and he considered the memory required, and the capacity to shape one's throat for a sound, and the diaphragm to funnel air, and the lungs to release it in time so that one sound began another like water climbing stairs.

He didn't tell her he enjoyed the song and she didn't ask one way or the other, yet she continued. His head lightened and he thought nothing, and soon he could not hear himself inquire at each door nor the answers from the houses. All that was left was the music in his head, and when he deposited Wendy at her door, he said, "Thank you," and she smiled at him and waved. She turned in the doorway and waved again, her silhouette in the doorway's glow the only sharp lines he had seen all day.

Wendy joined Matt the next Sunday. She did not sing or hum. Instead, she perched on her seat bent and rocking slightly and impatiently sucked her lower lip in and out of her mouth through the first half dozen stops.

"Can I ask you a question?" she inquired.

Matt nodded.

"Do you miss your brother?"

Matt halted and knocked on a door. No one answered. He mounted the wagon seat and she handed him the reins. He recognized the subject hadn't been dropped.

"I was never without him."

"Is it being twins that makes it hard?" she asked.

"I never been anything else," Matt said. "I'm still twins. My brother is just gone." He shrugged. "I've still got Mother."

"Is that the same?"

Matt was quiet awhile. "No," he said finally. "But it's not different, either."

He banged at a new door and thanked a woman for a cup of warm cider, though she had no information. Matt clucked the horses forward to the next house and stepped out. She watched him rap on the door until he was convinced no one would answer. "They go to Reardan some weekends," she told him. "They got a grandma there they tend to."

He hit two more houses. Someone offered him a piece of buttered bread. He split it with Wendy.

"My father says you're the best man in town," she told him.

His face reddened and she smiled at that. "You want to know my feelings on the matter?" she asked.

Matt shrugged. "I suppose I'm going to."

"I told him I thought you might be, but you got no imagination for the search."

"That's true enough," he told her.

She took the reins from his hands and stirred the team to walking. At the next house, she undid her blanket and labored down the high step. Matt watched her knock and speak to the young livery hand inside.

"I guess you aren't so quick either," he told her upon her return.

She wrapped herself. He took the horses.

"They'd get word to you, you know," she said. "If they'd seen him, I mean. It's not necessary to continue."

He was still staring far off. She realized he hadn't looked at her the entire ride.

"My looking's what's stupid?"

"No," she said. She saw she'd hurt him, and it wasn't her intent. "It's looking in the same place. Maybe someone in Creston or Lincoln might know more."

He rattled the reins and the wagon began.

⋆ 3 ⋆

THE NEXT SUNDAY, THEY INVESTIGATED the southwest third of the county, encountering still only shrugs and warm coffee for their efforts. They passed farmers and their families traveling to or from Plum or Lincoln or Creston or Sherman. Fathers nodded; mothers and their blank-faced children stared. Others, fellow wanderers, appeared at odds and ends with reality, as well. Canadian war veterans aimed south to try and clear the shells and trenches from their minds, aimless Indians travoising a deer carcass and badger skins or hauling a wounded man to a Nez Perce healer rumored near Clarkston. Town ruffians leered at them like prey until Matt lifted a rifle from beneath the wagon seat and levered the bolt. Alfred of Coffee Pot Lake was dressed in ragged gingham trousers and a drab T-shirt and a long buttonless duster he closed with a knotted rope length. Seven dogs and two cats followed him, the cats at a leery distance, the dogs, tongues and tales awag, happy as full-bellied apostles in a land of Not.

The prophet lifted his pork pie hat, revealing a bald head and two storms of swirling hair above each temple. The horses fussed as Matt tautened the reins. The prophet smiled. He offered his name and explained a prophet's moniker is determined by his birthplace rather than a surname, as prophets spring not from the loins of man.

Wendy nodded at the animals. "Are these your pets?"

One dog cocked his head in question. The cats had scurried for the ditch grass.

"Apostles. The cats come and go. Agnostics, I believe."

Wendy opened her basket and offered him a sugar cookie and the remaining buns. The man accepted, first offering a prayer about Coyote delivering fire, which seemed sensible as dogs would have no interest in a sermon that concerned something differing from them as much as humans. The dogs waited, silent. Alfred bent to one knee. He opened his hands, a portion of biscuit in each, careful to protect the bulk. The dogs rushed him and wrestled for their morsels. The prophet batted the more aggressive dogs' noses until each had a share, leaving the leaders the dregs. The cats remained uninterested, capable of fending for themselves.

Two hours later, they found a Model T in the road, a pair of legs splayed beneath. Metal clanged until a crowbar slipped causing the legs to flop like fish on a stringer and a litany of curses from underneath.

"Are you all right?" Wendy asked.

"I'm not," he said. "Henry Ford put cars on this earth just to vex me, and every person buying one is an accomplice."

"It's not your car?"

"I wouldn't want one. It'd be like marrying."

He'd been in the war, he said and learned to fix most anything to avoid the trenches. Now he claimed it was all he was good for that paid.

"You killed others?" Wendy asked.

"You going to scold me over it?"

"No," she said.

"I shot at them same as they did me. Wasn't much chance or reason to check the damage you did. No one had any idea what they were doing. Especially the generals."

A bolt screeched, then gave. Matt heard a part drop. The man asked for a hand and Matt stepped from the wagon and joined him beneath the automobile. The man extended his hand and offered his name: Harlan Miller. Matt gave his and Miller asked him if he was the boy looking for his father. Matt nodded. Harlan directed Matt to manipulate a fuel pump so he could drive the bracket bolts and cinch a hose. Harlan whacked his hands together to knock the grease free. "Well, let's see if we can get these horses to travel another mile."

They both pressed themselves from beneath the automobile. Miller handed Matt the crank and demonstrated how to engage it. Miller unclasped the winged hood and primed the carburetor with a gasoline-soaked rag. When Miller circled a finger, Matt spun the handle until the engine caught. Harlan hustled from the car's seat and whisked the rag, which was aflame, from the carburetor and stamped it into the damp dirt. He adjusted the choke until the idle settled and the pistons and plugs and crank fell into a rhythm they could maintain without sputtering on a mixture too rich or too lean.

Miller glanced to Wendy and the horses. "She your girl?" he asked. "She's her own self," Matt replied.

"Most of them are," Miller said.

Miller shook Matt's hand once more. "I am in Davenport and if I can be handy to you and you do not call I will be disappointed. Same to you, ma'am."

Matt and Wendy thanked him and, after he puttered the automobile east over a hill, Matt offered the reins to Wendy. She enjoyed driving and roused the horses the opposite direction. They spent the rest of the day in silence, aside from inquiring at the houses. Wendy realized this was true of most of their time spent together and was surprised to discover the quiet did not make her uneasy; quite the opposite, it quieted her on the inside, as well.

Upon their return that evening she hugged Matt and when she relented and he thought that was the end of it, she pulled him tighter for a moment. Her hair, which smelled something like her but like itself, too, brushed his face. Matt had never felt anything akin to it and wanted to again.

•

A WEEK LATER, WENDY CONVINCED him to cross the river and search the San Poil portion of the reservation. They waited at Keller Ferry with two automobiles while a gasoline engine hummed and gears wheeled to drag the barge toward them along a thousand yards of cable. Arriving, the captain and his assistant secured the craft with chains and dropped a grated ramp. Cars and riders and horses exited and, after the assistant circled his hand, Matt encouraged the horses forward along with the others waiting. The animals rode the ferry nervously, enduring a headwind and were happy to bolt with the clank of the ramp. They barreled halfway up the grade like Pegasuses, before relenting into a pace they could hold.

Above the incline, Keller, back then, was a town of two thousand. The San Poil River bordered it, clotted with logs boomed to tow into the Columbia and its mills. Tenders poked and rolled the tree lengths to keep them soaking evenly. Matt and Wendy rode through a busy main road. The churches had let out, but the locals dawdled at a market with winter vegetables and salted meat and steer testicles on a spit. Wendy appeared ready to sample one, until Matt related its source.

They traded sitting with the horses and inquired at doors about Matt's father. The population was mostly San Poil and Nespelem Indians. The few white men managed the hardware and livery and a small sawmill. The Clouds, a San Poil family, had constructed a community grain silo the few Indian farmers employed for storage.

Most comprehended English well enough, but had not heard or seen a man lost in the November storm. Many offered fried bread or dried fruit to the travelers and one a hot coal in a tin can to warm them. Several inquired if he and Wendy were part of a tent-toting evangelist family rumor put descending from the north and east where the Republic and Curlew churches had hosted them.

At the Cloud mill, the saws screamed over planks of raw timber until the operator switched off the planer and overhead blade. The man promised to inquire about Matt's father.

"Others tell about you," the man said.

It was a compliment, Wendy explained as they left him and climbed the grade from the river. The wagon passed small tin hovels and others constructed with unfinished logs, a few not much beyond lean-tos, one an army tent converted into a tipi that belched grey tamarack smoke. Cattle and a few sheep and goats dotted the bald hills and scoured the bare places for fodder.

At the ridgetop, they circled a butte and came upon a small shack, smoke climbing out its tin chimney. A gangly German Shepherd pup staked to a chain circled a dirt yard. The dog cried and woofed and dug in a trench that marked his limits until a man who appeared not much older than Matt emerged through a curtained opening and began whipping it with an axe handle. At first the dog bared his teeth and growled, but following the first blows all it could manage was to cower and roll in submission and whine. Wendy cried. Three hours later, as the sun descended toward the coulee's eastern breaks, their return route passed once more the dog at his stake. Matt halted the horses and jumped from the wagon. From under his seat, he retrieved his rifle then set out toward the dog, who eyed him until Matt took the opposite arc of his circular path, and eased to the stake where he unlooped the chain from the rod keeping it.

Matt returned to the wagon. The dog studied him without reaction. Matt clucked and the horses made for the ferry. They heard the jangling chain before they saw the dog loping the road behind them. It halted before the wagon gate. Wendy threw a bread piece into the bed. The dog sniffed the air but didn't move. She tossed another over the endgate and the dog devoured it. The dog whined in confusion. Matt lobbed some jerky and the dog could not help himself. He leaped into the wagon and ate all they could feed him. By the time he'd finished their scraps, the wagon rode the ferry, mid-river. The dog looked at the water on both sides, and recognized jumping made no sense and simply lay against the wagon floor watching Matt and Wendy.

When the ferry landed, the dog leaped onto the firm earth and jogged from sight. He appeared several miles later, halfway to Lincoln. The dog loped next to them and Matt halted the wagon. When he descended the dog growled and cowered, though he allowed Wendy to unlatch his chain so that if he bolted once more, he could at least avoid snagging himself on the sagebrush and rocks that pocked the hills.

After the dog took the last bite of the jerky, it jumped from the wagon, though it paced with them into Peach, where Matt stopped at the Worden house to return Wendy. The dog looked at her and whined. "Go on," Matt told him, but the dog instead labored into the wagon. It tipped its head and met Matt's eyes a moment, and Matt saw the animal's bewilderment, a sort of permanent vigilance, a vast fear prodding the sentry in his head to maintain its watch, but also a glimpse of doglike faith, too, a trust that comfort exists despite knowing the contrary. Wendy turned and disappeared into the lemony light of her parents' house. Matt stirred the horses, and they moved toward home. After a time, the dog joined him on the bench seat, curled into a ball, his head opposite Matt's thigh for a quick escape if it came to that. Matt covered him with the wool blanket.

$\star$ **4** $\star$

MATT'S DAYS DIFFERED FROM WHAT they once were. Two months of a man's ranch duties had added twenty pounds of ropy muscle to his frame. He'd shot up four inches. He felt no anger for his burden, and once the dog joined him, he rarely was lonely.

That first night, Matt watched the dog make water then permitted him into the house and fed him scraps from the dinner his mother had prepared. At first, the animal cowered in a corner. Finally, Matt carried the dish into his bedroom and coaxed the dog inside. The dog curled at his bed end but avoided the plate, though morning, the food was gone and a careful circle of feces reeked at the edge of a throw rug. The dog watched Matt from the bed as he scraped the scat into the empty pan, then scrubbed the woven carpet to erase the stain. Finished, he looked at the dog, "Come on, then. Chores."

The dog uncoiled itself and tracked Matt all day as he foddered the animals and harrowed what earth had thawed enough to break. Like most ranchers, the Lawsons maintained a barnload of cats to kill rats, and when Matt slid the door loose the cats flew into the light, saw the dog and scattered. The dog stood taller and his ears tipped forward, but he remained still.

"Good," Matt said. He treated the dog to half his sandwich.

From that day forward, the dog repeated Matt's steps and maintained a polite vigilance. Nights, he didn't appear to sleep past a doze. He rested, silent, eyes aglow, reflecting the moonlight that trickled through the window glass. Even when Matt rose in the wee hours for the peehouse the dog was to the bedroom door before Matt's feet hit the floor.

The ranch duties Matt favored most required strength and little forethought. Throughout December and January, he leveled a birch copse for wood and another half acre to plant. When each tree creaked or rocked, he dealt it one more blow and hurried clear. The fallen birch showered him with bark and limbs. He sawed the trunk and central leader into rounds and after sheered and split and quartered them and the biggest of the branches into arm-length posts. Their sawdust oranged the brisk sunlight.

Matt tolerated the farm's half-dozen cows only on his mother's bent for cream and butter. They didn't care to be milked and employed blunt and common tricks on his sleep-dulled mind. He'd look at the milk trickling across the straw and flex his toes stunned with pain and wonder at the thick mind that gives way to such blockheaded creatures.

The first of the year, a heifer so angered him, he hacked her hamstring into mop-shreds with a blow from the maul. The animal bawled all day and night, and the next morning he shot and butchered it, though he had only a vague notion how to cut steaks from roasts so ground most into hamburger. Covered in blood, he offered the scraps to the dog. The dog accepted them nervously and hauled the bones into a dark portion under the loft, then to the brush beyond a hill knob.

Matt's brother's form darkened the barn rafters above the hay-loft, and each instance he gathered tools and fed the stock, his brother's blanketed shape hung over him, though his labors and weekly searches had seemed to lessen the heft of his brother's and father's absence. Of course that was not so. The loss appeared smaller, but so does a freight train in the distance, though up close its wheels will slice an automobile in half like a blade cuts warm butter.

Matt attended school only in spotty fashion. On one of the days he arrived late, he walked into the room during a recess as Mrs. Jefferson sat at her desk alone next to her stacked papers. She glanced up at him and began to cry and so did he, and Mrs. Jefferson lifted her forefinger and touched his face where it was damp with tears for a moment, then retrieved her hand and put her wet fingers to her own cheek. Otherwise, she seemed to neither note nor miss him; his being at all stumped her.

As for the children, once a schoolmate mocked him until Wendy gloved her hand and rubbed a fresh horse turd into his face, after, the others circled wide and let him alone. They seemed to be following some code to adulthood that he himself only had rumor of. Though he recognized the rituals required to participate and responded as fittingly as he could he did so with a wooden self-consciousness that kept him in fear of being found out. The one thing he possessed that equaled their knowledge was muscles stout as cottonwood root and a capacity for work that appeared bottomless.

One evening, the dog curled himself into a comma at Matt's feet. Matt scratched its ears and it sighed in a manner unfamiliar and melted into the wood floor, asleep, finally willing to trust the world a few hours. Matt wondered if he, himself, ever slept with such certainty. He envied the dog and patted his head half hoping to wake him, but instead the dog's chin sunk between his paws farther and he breathed deep, regular breaths that seemed to Matt how a creature ought to breathe if things were right with it. It did not shift its weight with Matt's mother's footfalls when she retired or his own as he made his way to his bedroom, but Matt left the door ajar and some time after passing into sleep himself, the dog climbed next to him and traced his shape, and, when Matt woke, it stirred only a little and stared into Matt's face, its tongue lolling over its jagged teeth.

The first week in February, his mother decided she could bear Luke's body in the rafters no longer. Matt stoked the barn furnace to white hot, then forged two spade faces into a single horse-faced blade. An inch under its skin, the earth turned bone, but Matt's newly thick arms separated it like time itself.

Matt climbed the ladder into the barn rafter and found the ends of the wires holding the blankets over his brother. He unwound each and lifted his brother. Years before when their parents left them alone, his mother ordered Luke to tend Matt and Matt to mind him. Matt was sixteen minutes older, but Luke read first in school and wrote in neat, tiny letters Mrs. Jefferson admired. When they fought, Luke wrestled him in new, unexpected ways, and Matt would have to give uncle. He had worried he'd misplaced something vital when they were babies and Luke had found it and learned whatever there was to learn before him. Now, Matt understood he'd lost a fine rival, and, over time, he determined that that was worse than losing a good friend. His chest rippled and his biceps and forearms bore Luke's weight easily and Matt couldn't help but believe half his size undeserved.

He set Luke into the simple coffin his mother had asked the mill to cut. The box was too large. He thought a moment, then stood him on a hay bale inside it. The team was already harnessed. They gazed at his labors lazily. In the shed, Matt cut a rope in equal lengths and wound them around each end of the coffin and tied them off. He made a loop of the opposite rope ends around the horse's neck and dragged Luke and the casket to the open pit. Two planks lay crosswise over the grave. He slid the casket across them. The planks whined and bent with the weight. He could smell nothing leave the dusty straw. He opened the lid. His brother's face startled him.

When the horses shifted and the boards under the casket creaked, Matt knew he'd tarried too long. He threw himself over the casket and gripped its edges. The board holding Luke's feet popped. The rope jerked, held, then gave, as the surprised horses were yanked backward. The coffin's foot slammed the graveside and clattered to the bottom. The end keeping Luke's head slid from its plank to the top edge, putting the coffin upright. Above, the horses whinnied. Matt cursed himself. He looked at his brother. He could imagine his laughter. His memory rang with it, until Matt wondered if maybe dying was just another way for Luke to pull one over on him.

He climbed the graveside and tried to scrape the mud from his pants. The horses were out of whack. He coaxed the team until both ropes were tight and the casket level against the hole's edge and backed them toward the grave.

When his brother was again lying flat, Matt dropped himself to him. Above, the stars had commenced their shining, and though he couldn't hunt up any of the constellations his father had taught them, he tipped Luke's head so his eyes could get a look. The weight of Luke was, he knew, the weight of a child and the thought left Matt happy for his brother. His own new sinew and raw bone had all but swallowed him. He kissed Luke's open mouth. His lips felt like cold wood rubbed smooth. They tasted of nothing, though the smell reminded Matt of butchered beef. He pushed himself backward and blew a cloud of breath into his brother's face and watched it break up, then closed the casket and nailed it shut.

He went inside and warmed himself. His mother sat crying silently, sorting through her bible for a passage she thought suitable. She could find none and rose with Matt when he opened the door, bracing herself against the cold with a shawl and a heavy sweater and Ed's duster. She stood at the opened grave, the dirt mounds rich and black and fertile; a gas lantern dangled from one hand and rocked with the breeze and the trembling of her arm and cast shadows and yellow glare across the scene.

"Ashes to ashes," she read and Matt missed the rest, studying instead the casket's construction and regretting the hickeys he'd left in one corner with an errant blow.

•

THE DOG SOUGHT HIS APPROVAL, and for a kind word and a pat between the ears he would herd the dairy cows into stalls and nip their hind quarters if they stirred while Matt relieved them of their milk. The dog attempted to organize the cats, as well, though they paid little attention, and upon discovering his benign nature, rubbed their backs under his belly and chest and purred, and when he bent his head, they met his nose as equals.

The dog rode the wagon and learned to speak when Wendy coaxed him with a cookie. Occasionally, he leapt from the bed to pursue a badger or rabbit but always returned a few minutes later to perch on the seat between them.

His mother ignored the animal, as she did Matt. Her day's chores kept her inside and his labors out of doors. He rose before her and breakfasted on bread and butter and filled a lunch can with meat and more bread, then, outside, levered the pump until his water jug filled. Evenings in the house, each arranged their paths to avoid one another. They occupied opposite ends of the dinner table and in the parlor ignited separate reading lamps and hung them from hoops situated to leave them in separate, buttery universes.

The dog hooked himself under Matt's feet. It recognized Matt's mother's disapproval, though she never spoke to it and selected places to lie where it could watch her and exit the room if she appeared to anger.

★ 5 ★

ONE MORNING NOT LONG AFTER, Matt rose to the dog whining in distress. Half dressed, he stormed from his bedroom to find the animal cowered into a corner, his mother over him crying and swinging a mop handle.

"Mother!" Matt shouted. She turned to him. The dog used the pause to bolt into the bedroom and under the bed.

"The animal has no manners," his mother said. "It stares at me."

She wiped her face with the back of her hand and replaced the mop in the mudroom. In the kitchen, she hacked at the chicken on the cutting board.

"I'm not myself," she said. "You should not have brought that animal into this house when I'm not myself. It was unkind." She spoke with her back to him. "You are hurting me," she said. "Do you know that? Marching that poor girl here and there on this folly. Have you once considered my feelings?"

"I don't know what you mean," Matt said.

She wiped her hands on a towel and turned to him. "I loved your father, too," she told him. "I want to see him at peace."

"Like Luke is at peace?"

"Yes," she said.

"Then why don't we feel better?" Matt asked.

She returned to the chicken and her knife.

Matt hunted the dog who growled and whimpered and would not leave its sanctuary until he began to dress, when the dog scrambled past him into the living room turning mad circles until Matt's mother opened the door and the dog bee-lined into the yard, past the corral for the brush behind the barn.

Matt watched from behind. His mother turned.

"I'm sorry," she said. "I'm not myself."

"Me, too," Matt said, though knew which not half of the statement he was agreeing to.

The following days, the dog looped wide to keep clear. He studied Matt's work from under a tree or in high grass, but refused lunch. Once, he managed to kill a rabbit and chose to remain in the yard with his prize rather than follow Matt inside at the day's end for the nightly dinner scraps. When Matt opened the door later to offer him a roof, the dog remained in the darkness. Matt returned with a lantern and turned in a slow arc to reach the shadows, but saw no sign of the dog.

The next day, the dog returned in the daylight, hulking in the hill brows, apparently grown hungry enough to resume house living. Matt finally resorted to scraping the dinner dregs into a tin pie plate and depositing it next to a water trough. Soon, the dog disappeared for days. The animal lost weight and his coat turned ragged. He tore part of an ear off in some sort of altercation.

Matt considered him nights when the coyotes pitched their voices at the moon and owls hooted in reply. He didn't sleep, though neither the owls nor the coyotes nor the dog was the reason. Work occupied his day, body and mind, and negotiating his mother's illnesses or moods amply squandered the evenings, but after she retired and he had read as much of a book as he could and blown back the last lantern, his thoughts awoke and flew at him in the silence.

The dog continued with Matt and Wendy on their Sunday outings though he had no interest in the wagon. They encountered the prophet Alfred several times and once he halted on the hill above Matt's home to lead his congregation in a memorial prayer. The dog yipped with the rest of the canine choir. Another instance they discovered him at Miles Junction along with Harlan Miller and a transmission in a wagon driven by two haggard mules.

"You're acquainted with each other," Wendy said.

"This man broke my nose in grammar school," Miller replied. "We've been friends ever since."

Alfred said, "Faith or not. We beat on each other in our youths and didn't hold a grudge. That's a blood bond."

Alfred's dog following had increased by half. Matt recognized his own at the boundary of the pack, sniffing and being sniffed. His hackles tautened and so did a few others, but the animals arrived at some agreement that didn't require submission or dominance and soon his dog sorted the group as if a member.

The subject of the revival rose. Alfred seemed unimpressed.

"It seems you would be pleased to see the country go toward Christ," Wendy said.

"This man has no credibility," Alfred said.

"Because he doesn't preach to dogs?" Matt asked.

"You've got to start simple. Dogs, they don't have human sense, but they have dog sense and loyalty and they can be brave or cowardly, depending upon how they're treated. They are simple but mighty."

Miller nodded. "A man that starts with people is in too big a hurry."

"Dogs don't have money," Alfred said. "Or heathens and atheists or pagans or machines to make gods."

"Good," Miller said. "Because I'll be damned if a god who let the automobile into the world gets my patronage."

"That's excusable," Alfred said.

"I don't need excused."

"I didn't mean it like that."

"Doesn't matter how you meant it. I'll think what I want."

"It is America," Wendy said.

"Damned right, girly," Miller replied.

A terrier bit a collie mix and a tussle ensued until the collie found his adversary's throat and pressed him to his back. The terrier rolled and the collie eyed him hard, but relented, and the melee went quiet.

"Well you got the soldiers to give him what for," Wendy said.

Matt rustled the reins and the horses tugged the wagon forward. After a mile he wrestled in his pocket for a pipe and tobacco pouch. It had been his father's. He had never smoked it, but enjoyed its fragrance and the weight and smoothness of the ebony bowl. Now, though, he hooked his finger into the pouch and tamped tobacco into the pipe, found a match in his possibles bag and struck it. Burning tobacco popped in the wind. Matt looked onto the land that was his father's and his grandfather's and before that no one's. He gazed at the mottled grass in the few spots the thaw had uncovered, and at the sky so deep and blue he felt lost in it.

He once again wondered at the hours that took his father and his brother and delivered Matt to an adult woman before his time—it loomed over him like the constant arctic night, though he could put words to none of it. Luke had always been calmer over the turning of the world. Even when Matt bowed his head and cried real tears over a scolding, Luke could let things be. The knowledge served him as well as it had his father. They had given into the cold and let it take them, while Matt had stayed too long alive, when dying made the most sense.

"Where's the dog?" Wendy asked.

"He must have stayed," Matt said.

"We can retrieve him," Wendy said. "Just turn the wagon back."

Matt shook his head. She took the reins and clucked to reverse the horses.

Matt batted her hands and the rein. "No, goddammit."

Tears shined on his face in the twilight followed by deep sobs that frightened Wendy, as she was unsure he could manage a breath between them. His chest heaved and he could not speak. Wendy replaced her hands over his, perhaps because she had once seen or felt her mother do such a thing, perhaps for no reason other than the beauty of instinct, which even the fiercest animals will offer one another, or perhaps because a thing in him moved a similar thing in herself. She took his head between her hands and held it, then moved toward him until her face was all he could see.

"I am tired of looking."

"Your father, he's not returning," Wendy said.

"I know it," Matt said.

"I'm sorry if that's cruel."

"Just the truth."

He watched her eyes blink and an emotion quiet the muscles in her face. "Sometimes the truth is just plain mean." She put her forehead to his and released her hands from his chin.

"We can return for the dog," she said.

Matt shook his head. "He's got his reasons."

She blinked her eyes and feigned a pout for him. He stirred the horses forward toward the buildings and clustered light of Peach, but she demanded the reins and steered them another direction, eventually to his ranch. Matt was surprised at how well she maneuvered him through the rocky draws of his own land. From a bluff that overlooked the big river bend, he could see Hawk Creek, and the Columbia and where they met. Below was the house and barn and, above, Fort Spokane north and east, and farther, the reservation village, and south, Peach. Past that, the Okanogans, stripped of their snow, stood like a fence waiting on paint.

Wendy spread a blanket in the well of a bull pine cleared of snow by the tree's canopy and prevailing wind. He watched her draw a long knife from her basket and divide a hoagie sandwich. Crickets rattled in the closing day and the sun skimmed the couleed horizon and purpled the rolling snowy fields beyond it. She patted for him to sit and he did and she bent to one knee with him and it was like wind shifting. Her shoes were within his reach. He wanted to clean them with his handkerchief. He turned his face to hers. She said nothing for more time than he thought a person other than himself could keep still.

"You always brought me something to eat," Matt said. "You always bring something to eat."

The night was mild, but he collected brush in a pile and ignited it with a matchstick from a box he was never without. Together they watched the fire crack and burn. She bent and kissed him and erased the sky. He kept himself as still as he could, not wanting the moment to pass him. Her skin was orange in the firelight. She closed her eyes and her face turned blank as a piece of paper waiting for his writing. He outlined her jaw and chin with his rough palms and felt the wispiness of her hair.

She lolled in his fingers, and he held her there, pleased with the weight.

"Can I kiss you?" he asked.

He did, and their lips met awkwardly. He let off to stoke the fire. He coaxed it to a blaze. The heat made her face shine. The darkness past looked like a piece of overworked metal with dings and nicks of light. He wondered when it would wear out, when day would tear clear through. They kissed again. Her tongue dabbed his lips.

"You're better at this than me," he told her.

"I read a lot," she said.

She kissed him again and after let her face rest on his shoulder. He gazed down at the clear part in her hair and the white skin and her forehead and nose underneath. He'd never looked at anyone so close. She turned her head up to his. This time he set his lips to hers carefully. Matt leaned back to where he could see her better.

"You learned this from books?" he asked.

She rubbed his arm and watched the hair stand on end. Her eyes blinked hard and her face twitched. He looked at his belly. He half expected it to be bleeding. "I'm disappointing, I'm sure," he said.

"No," she said. She took one of his hands and laced both hers over it. He clamped her wrists and pulled her toward him until she was stretched enough to kiss. When her eyes opened, they stirred him like fever, chilling his flesh and burning his floating mind. A bead of sweat collected, and fell onto her lip. She touched her finger to it as if hushing him or tasting something and reckoning its contents. He felt her breath dampen his arm next to her and knew he'd come to the end of himself. He waited to die, to be broke from her and this earth like a tree limb on a too-strong wind, and he understood that he had stopped hunting his father a long time ago, that each Sunday he made the trek to Peach and waited in the wagon for Wendy to notice him through the window and gather her heavy coat and a blanket and appear in the doorway and climb the step to sit herself next to him for the bulk of the day for an entirely different reason.

★ 6 ★

WHEN THE EVANGELIST FENNIMORE JENKINS and his indigent family, along with the devotees whose fervor survived the morning's Jesus hangover, prepared to leave for old Fort Spokane at the confluence of the Spokane and Columbia Rivers, they sought a jackpot of sorts. The army had seized the tribes' children and delivered them to the fort where priests and nuns instructed them in civilized behavior with the rod and the whip, and in response the Indians converted to Catholicism almost whole hog, fearing more efforts to enlighten them. The surrounding ranchers were Christian as there was little else to be. Together, they made a receptive audience—the natives primed by guilt and despair and the stoic ranchers by their devout wives and their own superstitions, mostly regarding weather. The good Lord could turn handy in a dry spell.

Sunday, after services, Wendy joined Matt in the wagon once more. They traveled the country the evangelist recently cleared: Hunters, Fruitland, Cedonia, Emerson Road, and the Naborlee Camp. By evening the bluffs and hills above the Spokane's rocky crease glowed with lanterns and firelight, even ten miles off. As they neared, the crowd's rumble left quail skittering through the wild grass and the doves flitting brush to brush. Starlings abandoned their mud-bank nests and flung themselves into clouds of gnats and early mosquitoes, and hawks and one eagle coasted in the winds that sprung from the Columbia evenings, too uneasy to perch their nests. Anything larger lay in thickets and hollows bending for the rivers or in burrows and warrens under that same earth.

When Matt and Wendy skylined at Reservation Ridge, they saw the fort grounds boiled with believers, would-be and genuine, gawkers, and anyone a long time between beef in a meal. The chatter turned din with talk and hymns and shouts of hosannas or hallelujahs.

Fennimore Jenkins, like his namesake, lived in a narrative dream. In the county's two taverns he drank nightly, whiskey not beer, and after imbibing mounted hundred-foot trees and lit them afire from the top, then watched the flame follow the sap to the taproot. Once, at a Keller inn, his meal had angered him so that he axed the beams, and the place's porch slid into the river along with diners and drinkers and chicken dinners. He cited scripture against fornication and railed of a modern Sodom but also surrendered his honor to women who sought comfort for loss or shortcomings or their own sinful nature.

But he preached like a house on fire, and being a sinner just seemed to add to his credibility. His shock of wild black hair left him looking like he was constantly surrounded by his own stormy weather. With his oblong, cleft chin, he reminded onlookers of a better-crafted Lincoln. His lips and nose didn't protrude so dramatically, his brow didn't hood his forehead with brooding. His appearance wasn't as contemplative as the Great Emancipator; he looked instead heroic, and his voice boomed, yet rarely lacked clarity, and, when before a crowd, it dropped and rose with emotion like a church organ.

Matt and Wendy had met him on the road a month before, when the snow had yet to clear the lee side of the draws. He was limited to two wagons then—he'd added two as his reputation gathered— and they seemed a humble group as they lumbered toward their Gifford Ferry appointment between heathens and the Lord.

A quarter mile away, two riders broke the horizon. One stopped and lit his cigarette—the orange flash painted his face, then the cherried ash. The man offered it to his companion and struck another for himself. He wore a bowler and the other was hatless, the last of the sun blackening his unkempt wiry hair. They surveyed the scene below several minutes before directing their horses to Matt and Wendy's wagon. As they closed, Matt recognized Harlan Miller, the mechanic, and an Indian who was a ferry hand.

On the ridges above the gathering it remained quiet enough to hear the thaw trickle from the high ground and lee hillsides as gravity tugged the groundwater toward the big river through the draws and cuts and seasonal streambeds. The soft, vernal months the ground plowed like warm butter, and automobiles' rubber tires and wagons' iron-rimmed wheels cut the roads axle-deep until the county or frustrated farmers filled them with highway department sand. It was weather that, July, the country rarely received, though March and April, they saw little else.

Matt studied the preparations: the fires smoked, voices hollered commands, others laughed; some hummed gospel songs; a few told stories between swings of a sledge or the rhythm of pulling on the ropes, like slaves in Egypt lifting obelisks before Moses cut them loose. The believers labored like insects constructing a hive. Some cut and trimmed timber, another group split long pine rounds into seats. Others hammered stakes to anchor the canvas tent and more propped poles to support the folded oval from which the fire's exhaust could escape while its warmth comforted the faithful. Outside, a whole beef turned on another fire, this one straddled by a crudely welded spit; on the other side of the flat a pig was in the same predicament. Wagons and chugging cars arrived regularly, and nervous horses danced at the occasional backfire from a worn exhaust. A brother believer waved a lantern in one hand and circled the other this way and that to direct each to parking areas. Others anchored horses to a long rope snubbed to two trees; another still manned three water troughs to support failed radiators. It was a synchronized, unnatural order: lurching starts and halts. Matt had witnessed deer in a field harassed by barnstormers: they employed no method, but were not without order, in fact the opposite. They behaved as a single body, each animal responding to those with him not like soldiers marching but like organs pumping blood and oxygen and the rest of it to and from the necessary muscles. They turned as one, leapt as one, doubled back as one, and even scattered into the rocks as an organism that comes apart, in order to return to its whole when peril passes.

"Quite a circus," Miller said.

Matt nodded.

"That beef down there has nearly drove me to worship, though."

The Indian ferry hand nodded.

Wendy offered them the last of her sandwiches. Miller offered his thanks, as did the Indian. The men ate in silence. Wendy and Matt swapped a canteen, having lunched late enough in the day to sate their hunger.

"You children can keep close," Miller said, "Never know when a man can use a hand. And I meant children only in terms of years. I've grown to like you two. Don't ever purchase an automobile, though." Miller nodded at the opposite bluff a quarter mile off. "That's a wild card I'd like to see played."

Across the wide maw that opened to the river, Alfred of Coffee Pot Lake stared into the melee, aboard a horse, which contradicted a sworn oath to the dogs never to employ an animal for labor.

Another rider paralleled him fifty feet away and between were at least thirty dogs, Alfred's entire congregation. Matt could see Alfred had constructed collars for each and tethered them to a rope. He imagined the cats were serving reconnaissance. The air had cooled and stringy clouds rose from the dogs' mouths, together gathering into a fog that made them look like demons in a moor. Some barked and others howled; still more nipped one another in their anxiety. The cooking meat stirred their stomachs and they leaped to break the ridgeline, stout horses and good hemp rope knotted on a pair of saddle horns all that held them.

Some below glanced at the animals but dismissed them. Animals were drawn to a meal that didn't require the effort of killing. They would all be scavengers if circumstances permitted. People differed little, Matt realized: most would eat a beef steak or chicken leg, skinned and plucked and cut and papered and piled into their freezers or root cellars rather than kill and butcher for themselves. For a man civility seemed the ladder out of the melee; otherwise, like his animal brethren, a man only survives. Straight up killers seemed more moral, though. They turned lives into food knowing the flesh their teeth ground and their tongues savored and their gullets swallowed breathed an hour or a day or a minute before. They recognized their own existence was constructed upon slaughter, and the debt they owed their victims could never be repaid, simply owed. It seemed to Matt, though the meals arrived on porcelain and cooked, the scene below was no less savage.

Those below seemed somehow humiliated, as if their hallelujahs and amens and heartfelt confessions and impromptu baptisms evoked ancient fears and uncertainties akin to the Neanderthals, who spent centuries drawing the stars into something other than scattered light though more constant than winds and rain and the shuffle of tectonic plates.

They could not address their fears with a plow or a strap or loyalty or deceit, and the knowledge bent their knees, rattled them into
prayer. The dogs pawed the earth. Their minister, Alfred, and his
companion continued to restrain them. Animals knew no guilt, no
death, only avoided it to dodge the pain each might predict with the
few wits they could direct past here and now. They didn't ponder
the impractical like what happens to smoke when it quits being
smoke.

Below, a whistle sounded and the crowd, spread like water
on a flat rock before, headed for the canvas tent. A few women
remained to tend the spits and coals and stirred pots of baked
beans and boiled potatoes and onions. On the stones wrapped in
towels were baked rolls and loaves that required only to be warmed.
The women labored with a resolve Matt envied. Such certainty
rarely had visited him. Service, Matt had heard repeatedly from
the pulpit, was a human being's highest calling, though it seemed
to Matt one ought to at least consider for whom he worked. And
this Jenkins appeared to be an unusual kind of master. He paced
outside the tent, his hands holding a black bible behind his back,
clothed in a black shirt, black pants, a black long duster, and a grey
newsboy cap, nervous in a way his reputation did not portend, yet
his steps were measured and equal. Matt imagined the rhythm like
a clock ticking.

The choir, robed and collected from those that followed the
revival along with any newcomers who thought they could hold
a note, assembled on makeshift risers constructed from 2 x 8s and
cedar rounds staggered in height. A woman leading them tooted a
pitch pipe, and each voice arced or dipped to match, while a boy
tinkled scales on a pneumatic accordion.

In tune, they began, "Be Thou my Vision," a lyric Matt enjoyed,
as it encouraged listeners to act some way after hearing it. The
next hymn, which he did not recognize, seemed the opposite,

inert, contemplative. The choir leader's arms dropped. The audience beneath them lived under good roofs and between stout walls along with husbands, wives, and children. They owned ranches and cattle or worked permanent jobs, yet they remained lonesome. Matt hunted the crowd for his mother. She was a dutiful churchgoer, but he did not see her. Perhaps she waited in the kitchen for him to return and wagon her to salvation.

The accordion wheezed and went silent. No introduction ensued. The minister hiked slowly up the steps and to the pulpit in the same rhythm he awaited his cue.

Neither Matt nor Wendy nor the two joining them on the bluff heard words, but they recognized the audience quiet their hands and their papers and the bibles they held and curtail their whispers and scold those who did not. Finally, the quiet baritone voice become audible beyond the tent.

The minister read, then paused.

"I don't recall that verse," Matt said.

"It's a poem," Wendy told him. "Emily Dickinson. Mrs. Jefferson taught it."

"Must have missed that class, hey little brother?" The Indian said.

"I missed a lot of school."

"Sometimes even when he was in attendance," Wendy added.

The minister stated that a poem, a beautiful poem such as this, was true as scripture. Such poems have a nebulous and ever-smoldering center, weighty enough to bend time and space and compel planets to mind their proper ellipses; a poem steers every line, every word, every syllable into circles held by the gravity of an idea beyond the speakable as is God. People circle the Lord's presence; his power is in the circle we turn. Our lives are evidence by the sense in them, the repetition in them, birth, death, seed and earth and sprout, then harvest and tilling and the undoing of the stalks and their return to feed in the season that follows.

He paused. "Aside from a sidewise glance or a reflection in a window, you can't look at the sun. It will burn your eyes out. So you look at shadows and blue sky and faces, and that's the evidence it is day and the sun you can't look at exists. And when night falls and you can't see these things without a lantern or electric light that, too, is evidence of the sun. Its absence proves its presence."

"The man has a silver tongue," Miller said.

"White isn't black," The Indian replied. "That's not Jesus talking. Sounds more like Coyote."

"Maybe they're kin," Miller said.

The preacher broke for a silent prayer, and each head within the tent bent while the woman outside continued spinning an animal at the spit or stirring salads or toasting muffins upon the rocks encircling the cooking fires. One dipped a paintbrush extended with rake handles into honey-filled buckets and striped the baking pig with it. The choir commenced "Onward Christian Soldiers," which started as dirge, built to a march and finally turned a cry for war that left the accordion player's white shirt clinging to his sweaty skin, a kind of pink mottle as they finished.

It was a startling reversal from the pensive to the fervent, and when Matt turned to Wendy, she appeared shaken to witness it. He took her hand without thought, and she his. She stared at them, joined that way, as did he, and it was as if they had joined every other way, as well. Past sex and ardor and lust, all of which they were vaguely conscious, past anything they could imagine and only equal to the simplicity and innocence adults could recall in their most wistful moments of awkward, sincere feeling.

Matt gazed at those beneath, tucked in the tent, hushed, awaiting their marching orders or outside daubing the braised meat with condiment. Like drunks entering a tavern or soldiers going to war, they had enlisted individuals but turned gears in a larger contraption and now could not be separated unless to undo the whole machine. They smoked cigarettes and nodded their head, songs and philosophy fixing one to the other a sloppy, messy paste, but adhere they did to the sway of the hymns and the minister's voice as, refreshed by water and a biscuit, he lifted his god's standard and continued.

Wendy squeezed Matt's hand. He wondered if she was seeing what he was and thinking his thoughts. He had never been alone; even the womb he had shared with a brother; they bobbed and breathed the same fluid and tapped the placenta's feed tube in unison, hollered their first cries together, shat their first diapers. Their fights often seemed to him to emanate from a particular kind of vehemence, one rooted to separation. In anger, they returned to a single furious entity at least until the blows commenced, when each felt his own pain separately.

Wendy squeezed his hand again, and he looked up at her face. She was smiling with a devilment that eventually interested him. She nodded to the opposite ridge, now nearly a blank against the sky. The dogs' racket had increased. One or the other rider had loosed the rope, and the dogs instead of a line turned a crescent, then a half moon, then a broken charge as one rope end was freed. The animals hurtled toward the spits like a prairie fire with a tail-wind and leaped upon the beef and hog, ignoring the women batting at their haunches and shoulders. The cooks' screams along with the spits collapsing into the fires distracted the congregation from its preacher. The dogs darted to and from the flames and yipped and howled and scrapped for their treasures, their paws and undersides singed.

The Indian and Harlan Miller galloped their horses for the melee. Wendy laughed and Matt snapped the reins and steered the horses and wagon onto a game trail with an angle shallow enough to keep them upright. The horses shuffled the slush for footing and the wagon flung Matt and Wendy hither and yon. The prophet Alfred hurtled through the assembly's aisle toward the minister, Miller right behind. The Indian cut a pork shank slice with his hunting knife. He ate and laughed. Alfred's horse drove through the risers and collapsed the podium stand and herded the preacher, Jenkins, through the back tent flaps up the hill behind and into the darkness. Meanwhile, the stunned congregation stared at its meal, half scorched against the coals, the other half torn to ribs and vertebrae by the dog pack, which had organized enough to drag the carcasses from the fire.

A few men tore tent poles from their moorings and swung them at the dogs, which proved too lithe to be dissuaded by such tactics. Others laughed, and soon most of the gathering had joined them. The whole group appeared to be enjoying the scene until they parted and the returned preacher burst between, shotgun in hand. His first blast tore beef from bone and sent half a dozen dogs backward stunned with buckshot. He reloaded and raised the gun for a second go, this time directing it at the hog and, Matt realized, his own dog. He leapt from the wagon and barreled between the dog and the pig and the gun. The dog ended up underneath the pig shank, eyes oddly untroubled. Matt lay atop them both. The buckshot's sting peppered his shoulder and drove a howl from him. He rose. The preacher reloaded the breach, but Matt delivered him a blow to the head that separated gun and man and man and jaw and kicked three ribs into his lungs. The man gasped and hacked blood that blacked his teeth. He tried to spit and Matt dragged him by the ankles through the fire. His skin spat on the coals, not unlike the cooking pig and cow before. He screamed and attempted to twist free, but Matt whacked his kneecap with a quartered round and lifted him into the trough. When the preacher rose gasping, Matt held his head under with both hands until he felt a blow against his wounded shoulder. Wendy was hammering him with an axe handle. She shouted his name over and over.

"Stop," she said. "You're torturing him."

Matt shrugged.

"The dog is fine," Wendy told him.

Matt glanced at the dog, who stared back, then licked the hog shank.

"Okay," he said. He retrieved the preacher from the water. The man sucked at the air and moaned. The other combatants gazed at Matt. After a long while, some turned and made for their wagons and automobiles; soon the rest followed. The dogs began again on the meat. Matt's dog joined the feast, tussling for all he could gather.

Matt drove the wagon on the main road following the tire-worn grooves, as the evening temperature had not yet reached freezing. Miller and the Indian nodded, but Alfred refused to look his way. Wendy mopped Matt's cheek with a handkerchief. When she drew it away the thin material was peppered with blood. She began on his jacket sleeve, but it smeared like oil and justed clotted the wool.

Matt shivered in his damp shirt. Wendy withdrew and huddled in a blanket at her end of the wagon seat. He wanted to say he had not heard; it wasn't that he wouldn't listen to her. He was not certain that was true; however, he only knew he had not enjoyed beating the preacher, unlike some who fought for pleasure or to win. The event had humiliated him worse than losing could have. He said none of this, of course, and drove the horses in silence until, finally, Wendy spoke, suggesting he hunt the open country for his father's body, the same place his mother urged, but he only shook his head and clucked the horses.

"Don't you want to put an end to it?" she asked.

"Sounds as though you do," Matt replied.

He didn't speak to her the rest of the trip, and she knew, bringing it up, she'd betrayed him, though she didn't know to what extent.

He dropped her at her door, and after she collected her things, she leaned toward him and set her cheek next to his own. Matt felt her tears warm his cold face but did not respond.

The next day, the dog reappeared and followed Matt from the house to the wagon. In his mouth was a human hand. The dog dropped his prize between his forefeet and ran northeast. Matt unharnessed the plow horse and followed the general direction to the east property line. He discovered his father two miles away minus skin and a hand and eyes and nose, yeasty in the thaw, decomposed beyond stink. Matt roped the corpse and dragged it to the house. He wheeled the body in a hay cart to the knoll where the grass stubble had already begun to grow over his brother. There, he started the second grave of spring. The ground split for his spade and he managed six feet deep and long in forty-five minutes.

His mother again brought out her bible and this time read from a line or two from Luke. Which of you fathers if your son asks for bread would give him a stone? How much more will your heavenly father offer those children who ask?

Wendy arrived the Sunday next, dressed in a long calico skirt and a sweater against the still chilly morning. Matt wore his work clothes, split at the knees and elbows, where he had grown most; a bandage patched his shoulder. She stood on the first porch step and he in the doorway. His eyes blinked at the rosy early morning.

"My father's dead," he told her.

"I reckoned that when you didn't come to the house," she said.

"He was right where you said, goddammit."

"I didn't put him there," she told him.

"I didn't either," Matt said. "But there he was."

She looked at her shoes.

"So I guess you're shed of me," Matt said.

She looked up.

"No need to look for someone planted in the backyard."

The dog stood next to her and she patted its head.

"It's what you wanted wasn't it?" Matt asked. "To put an end to it. Well, it's done, isn't it?"

He stepped past her toward the barn and the dog followed. He sharpened the cultivator tongs and patched a hackamore until he was certain she had gone.

★ 7 ★

CHURCH GIRLS GENERALLY LOOKED AFTER the widows, so, later that spring, Wendy assisted Mrs. Lawson in opening the house. Matt made himself scarce. She visited into summer, as well, but cultivating occupied Matt from dawn to nightfall and he saw her only on their dirt road, arriving or departing. His mother, though, sorted closets for fabric enough to construct a quilt for her. She insisted Matt line it and he succeeded in trapping enough coyotes to make a thick padding. His mother presented it to Wendy in a dress box. She unfolded the tissue as carefully as inspecting a wound, and sat, wordless for a long time, stroking the tanned hides. When she turned it over to examine the stitching, she could see it was constructed from Matt's brother's shirts and trouser legs, along with a few things of his father's.

Wendy didn't remain long that day, just enough to thank Mrs. Lawson for the gift before she mounted the grocery wagon for the ride back to Peach. Two weeks after, Matt, leveling a frost slide above the barn, drew rein on the plower. He'd almost convinced himself it was only a funny wind that stopped him, until he looked toward the graves. Planted where he imagined the heads would be were two rose bushes in bloom, fertilized with steer leavings. Roses didn't take easy in this country, and over the season he would glimpse Wendy pruning them off and on, or nursing them with water buckets until midsummer, when they were a thicket of color. Both were red, the color of blood, he knew, but the color of love, too, Mrs. Jefferson had declared in her poetry talks.

●

HE SAW IN PASSING ALFRED, too, who recognized the new grave and paused with his animals to offer prayers. Miller, he met briefly on the town road, navigating a clanking Ford toward his shop, the Indian in the passenger seat beside. Each waved in the ocher dust the machine raised. Two weeks later, he encountered the men again, this time on horseback, and he assumed better humored. Matt had thought talk of him might have halted after word traveled that his mission was finished and a failure; however, the citizens in Peach and Plum and other nearby towns had not forgotten him. According to Miller, he remained news, though the balded preacher, who spoke only when necessary in light of his waylaid jaw, was now the subject of the tale. The preacher had tried to press the law for an arrest, but his public saw the charges as pathetic, seeing he had brandished the gun, and the authorities could discover no one impartial to witness, though they had not spent much time on the inquiry, Miller reported.

Autumn, girls at school were old enough to fill their dresses past skin and stuffing. Some girls flirted with him, mostly the ugly ones, with bad teeth or fathers poor enough to hope to draw easy land. Wendy he no longer spoke to, and soon he stopped attending altogether. At the farm, he cleared a brushy quarter, fresnoed the bowled edges and rodweeded and harrowed the ground for spring and seed.

He worked if there was light and sometimes beyond by lantern in the barn, when the equipment required attention. The dog remained his shadow out of doors, but in the barn or the house, he mirrored Matt's restlessness. The dog would not eat indoors, rather preferring even to spoil a piece of meat and its gravy in the rain. He refused Matt's bed and instead made a nest near the stove from the old blankets Matt's mother deposited for him. In the barn, when a nut would frustrate Matt and he belted it with the wrench handle, the dog would race to the door to be put out or belly into the hay and remain there until Matt departed.

Winter, once he had sharpened the blades and replaced failing parts and organized his tools, little was left to occupy Matt's time. His mother had improved mightily after interring his father and at meals attempted conversation, but when he tried to listen, his mind would leave his head and the room, though where it went, he was unsure.

He read some of his father's books and the few magazines his mother had saved in a box and taught the dog to fetch sticks, though he learned so quickly Matt figured it had been in him all along. He had less luck with teaching him shake or roll over, and as the dog rarely made any sound, he didn't attempt to make him speak as Wendy had. They walked hours each day despite the lengthening freezes, and his thoughts traveled in wide loops that encircled all he'd witnessed or forgotten or remembered or dreamt and bent them into smoky spirals without order and so thinned they broke apart before him. He did not attempt to make sense of them with thoughts or words; they were not of that nature, though if they were, and if he could add them like numbers in a book, he knew the sum would be different each time until the idea of addition and numbers turned ash.

On one of these excursions, he encountered Alfred again. His congregation was down to two spaniels, and neither he nor the dogs looked like they had eaten in a good while.

Alfred gazed at him. "Coyote names the thickets in creek bottoms Woods of Her Private Hairs because water is desirable, but to retrieve it without tearing yourself on the brambles, well, it is beyond Coyote."

Matt nodded as if he understood, though he did not, and he wondered if Alfred, too, was perplexed by his own words, as if the tongue of this strange god had entered his mouth without the sense in his head to stand between. The long nights that followed, Matt considered his own mind, which seemed, opposed to Alfred's, all thoughts and no words, though they did eventually move him, as he lumbered through December and January, idle as seed beneath the snow.

At the north edge of Peach a towering knoll rose out of an otherwise level alfalfa pasture belonging to the grocer. Wendy and her sisters swathed the field summers to fodder the delivery nags the grocer drove twice weekly to service the invalids and bachelors who'd quit on town for one reason or another. Straw and dirt had accumulated under the rocky promontory until it looked a part of the country, but Mrs. Jefferson had told the class a volcano near the ocean had spewed it across the state. February, when the Chinooks began to loosen winter, Matt ended a horse ride at the place. He tethered his mare to the spindly locust behind and hiked to the crest. There, he tucked himself behind the sharp-edged rock.

He let his mind unspool once more that evening, waiting for truths he suddenly felt he required. Swimming below him was the town, all light and motion. Horse hooves splashed the damp streets and children darted in and out of the house glows like birds in the dawn. Full dark, he heard a mother call and then another. An hour past, the lights slipped out. A couple spooning on a porch split the quiet with a laugh, but the night stitched it over like something he'd dreamt.

From his knoll, he saw the pendulum Wendy's arm made when she swept a broom or the rock of one of her legs crossing the other while she read. He became almost giddy with her and, when the light of her window turned the lawn lemony and warm-looking after all the other lights had been blown dark, he crept to the edge of her window's glow on the lawn and put one hand inside it, then one leg, and studied himself lit. Finally, he dared to get his whole body aglow and felt weightless and bold, like he might just walk to the door and knock, until he heard a chair shift inside and dove into the well of a raspberry thicket.

★ 8 ★

FOR YEARS, LINDA JEFFERSON HAD watched parents hunt themselves in their little ones. Pawing mothers and distant fathers both hunting some track that would lead them back to themselves. They would say to their children "You've become a little man," or "the boys will be calling soon." These were one-sided conversations. Children did not answer such silliness. Of course they would turn men; of course boys would call for the girls. It was inevitable as the next daybreak. The children recognized their awkward arms and high water pant legs and new hairy places were nothing except natural. Their parents, though, seemed shocked at such developments. Soon the children realized that when adults spoke about their growth in such a manner, it was in the same bewildered tone they saved for death, which, also, they did not understand.

Poplar trees on her property had grown twelve feet in her lifetime, and, in a field behind her house, the wind had flung pollen and seeds, and the bees hovered over them summers, and the deer and an occasional elk browsed the grasses and dropped pellets, and rain turned their leavings grit, and the grit fed the seeds, and the sun shone, and the clouds rained, until she had seen a patch become a meadow, and, finally, strained by the years and thinned with daily, mundane duties, her tragedies, too, seemed to turn natural.

She drew no comfort with seraphim and a heavenly patron. People who believed in such absurdity in her opinion lacked education and the fortitude to face a future of their own making. However, she fancied herself too possessed by the muses to heed Darwin, whom she found dull and brutal, as she did most science: an appropriate discipline for destructive little boys and men who took pleasure from spreading animals asunder to see how they functioned. The finest knowledge could not be gutted and cleaned like mule deer or river trout. Instead, she thought the world possessed its own order, without explanation, cruel or kind.

Watching the twinless survivor flounder through simple long division and sentence parsing children four years his junior had mastered, she worried his rescue from the storm did him no favor. He made his marks only through graceless effort, an inadequate boy in so many ways. She was concerned the children would tease him—despite his size, he was not intimidating—but few ventured a word one way or another. They admired his resolve and they were frightened by it.

She had joined him at that portal through which men must pass to be born and pass again to be men. The boy had cut the loop too abruptly, she realized, returning to nature so swiftly after leaving it, he'd not forgotten enough of the first to uncloud the second and her living body lay between them as if reason itself.

Over the years, she found herself assigning her classes whole books to read or an impossibly long series of problems from the primers then setting a teakettle on the stove. From her desk, she sipped her porcelain cup and made each child a study, shifting from one to the next wordlessly. If they met her eyes or shied and fidgeted, she would loosen her gaze a moment then return when the child had forgotten her. Often, as the children walked or rode horseback along the paths and roads leading them to their families, she found herself weeping, and those nights she'd lie on the schoolroom's hard floor and stare into the beams until her eyes blurred and she could conjure and scrub clean the faces of the children, and search for any crumb of herself that might allow her a share in them.

Linda had thought it silly, any adult putting so much stock in something impermanent as a child. Such vanity begged the stars to differ. Occasionally, she believed she had not considered the twins and the storm in years, but realized, each time, in doing so, as with things truly tragic, she had recalled the event every day. She was no seer, but, in the images she found filling her thoughts, Linda recognized her own face rising. Like taming her reflection in a pond, the harder she looked, the stiller she became, until she felt steadied and almost right, then something she couldn't say roughed the picture, like a wind or duck landing, the stirrings distorting her likeness until it went monstrous, and she marked that twisting as in herself, and understood, finally, the wanting of another past just company, if only to offer a face to stare into that belongs to you but is not your own. She bore this strangeness through the winter and spring following and, when school let out for summer, she visited the empty building anyhow, smelling for the children and leafing the primers for their grubby fingerprints and scratchy letters.

Mid-June, she was called upon at home by the new superintendent of county schools. The man dismounted and trudged the porch steps. His prominent stomach unfolded beneath his chest, and his shoulders stooped from decades of bearing the girth. He knocked a pipe against his pantleg, loaded it, and struck a match. His face, slack as a bulldog's, pinked as he puffed and exhaled.

The man's name was Superintendent Harrison, and he insisted on being addressed as such. She filled a bucket and watered his animal while politely allowing him to prattle his opinions on the keeping of schools. He inquired, finally, if she would be requesting textbooks or desks. The school board had replaced those lost in the storm a few months after. She told him they were holding up well.

"You are a relief," he said to her. "Most of the others are clamoring for them."

"I am in need of your assistance," she said.

She stood and began unbuttoning her blouse. His eyes flew to her face where she met them. Deflated of smoke and color, they sagged farther, and trembled with his breaths. She shrugged her undone shirt down her back.

"I would like a child," she told him.

Historically, men courted with flowers or jewelry, but weekly Superintendent Harrison trekked the dusty road to her home carrying a new desk or box of colored chalk or lined manila tablets for handwriting exercises. By midsummer, the inventory of his largesse included a microscope she couldn't operate and twenty-three plaster-of-Paris likenesses of the presidents.

Upon spying his poor horse clearing the bend, she would undress and wait. He'd deposit the most recent offering on the steps, and, inside, disrobe as well, folding his trousers and jacket to elude scandal. She placed herself on all fours before him, facing a side window from which she could see the yellow rose bush she favored. He would couple to her like a train car, and spit and wheeze like its great locomotive firing. From the little she'd discerned of such matters, he was unusual in size, and, occasionally, his girth would drive a cry from her. Mostly those minutes, though, she would gaze at her flowers past the glass pane. The petals, closed in fisted buds through spring, had unbound. In them, she could make out handsome profiles and she would imagine them inside her heart, blooming finally.

By late summer, she was six weeks without menstruating. The last time Superintendent Harrison arrived, she greeted him on the porch, dressed. He remained aboard his horse. Her clothed body was unusual to him, and somehow more arousing than her nakedness. She recognized this and let his gaze float over her to remind him that what he had had wasn't her at all, but only some unclothed cavity that feels for him no more than a breeding heifer does the neighbor's bull.

•

WHAT REMAINED OF THE SUMMER, gardening consumed her. The perennials bordering the house required only an occasional trimming but the vegetable rows she nursed daily, shooing aphids and tomato worms from the new leaves and piling the stalks with a pungent mulch she'd prepared with spring grass clippings or steer manure wheel-barrowed from the neighboring pasture. Her aging dog followed her through the day, sulking like a jilted beau.

September, she bartered ten droppable acres for a pair of dairy cows and swapped a dated encyclopedia to a well-off rancher who filled her barn with fresh alfalfa. She downed three dead birches and split wood enough for two winters and, after felled a third living tree to season. Evenings, she canned the garden and filled the cellar shelves with mason jars and lined them on the floor beneath.

October, she locked the dog inside and set out a salt lick in the garden. Until midnight she kept motionless on the porch. Lanterns hung in the trees, but she heard the two mule-eared does that had robbed her garden all summer long before she saw them. They warily descended from the rocks into the stubble behind her house. One bent her neck and Linda heard its rough tongue on the salt. The other joined it. Linda lifted the Winchester and pressed it to her shoulder. The deer glowed like light itself in the sights. The first shot stopped the nearer of the two. She levered the bolt, ejected a shell, and refilled the chamber. The second doe hopped twice, then checked herself. Linda eased down the trigger. There was no sound, save her own ears ringing.

In the garden, amongst the autumn husks, she butchered both deer by lantern light. Her bloody clothes clung to her until she pulled them off. She puffed out the lanterns and started a fire. Morning, when the coals burned low enough, she lay green birch atop them, then strips of venison rolled in rock salt. At the pump, she filled a bucket and washed. Her scattered clothes lay about like a skin she'd shed. She set them in the fire. She was frightened at her happiness and tried to swallow it, to save it like good luck come too soon.

•

NEAR CHRISTMAS, SUPERINTENDENT HARRISON RETRACED his path down her lane. Grey snow and a grey sky kept the light ghostly. The muddy road had spattered his horse's legs and worn suit clothes. She realized it was the only apparel she'd seen him in, and perhaps all he owned of fine wear.

"The school board has asked me to give you your notice," he said.

She took the envelope he offered.

Superintendent Harrison shook his head. "Should I tell them the truth?" he asked finally.

"I would deny every breath of it," she told him.

★ **9** ★

THE FIRST PRESENT WASN'T WRAPPED and no ribbon garnished it. The leather-bound cover had the writer's name impressed upon the spine and her own in the right corner, both embossed gold. Wendy closed her eyes and rubbed the cool skin, tracing her finger on the letters of her name until she would have recognized it if she were without eyes.

The poems were untitled, kept apart only by numbers plain as those attached to the county prisoners. The poems startled her; cropped as a manx tail, many seemed scarcely thought at all. Like birds flitting from tree to tree, their purpose would alight in her mind and she'd know it, then she would not. Some were so dismembered by hyphens and misplaced capitals they appeared butchered as spring lambs. They compelled her as one's own wounds demand exploring and finally led Wendy to realize that, without using the word, they were about love and the holes it thrust in you.

The next day, she woke to her sister Amy's shouts. She approached the door. On the walk was her name again, spelled in polished river agates.

Wendy collected the stones. One was turquoise. The dawn had warmed it. She rubbed the smooth edges across her forehead and the bridge of her nose.

"Who was it?" asked Amy, who was thirteen and boy-crazy, but Wendy had no desire to discuss it. She only knew it was her name printed with the rocks and her name cut into the book's leather. Someone was taking some trouble over her, and she was pleased.

•

A MONTH LATER, MID-MARCH, MATT allowed himself to dally past the sun's rise and watch Wendy discover an embroidered hair band he'd laid upon the porch rail. She lifted the heavy cast hex nut he'd cleaned to anchor it, then rushed to her room and twisted her hair until it met her liking. He remained while her family ate, listening to silver clack the porcelain and later studied her and her shadow and reflection gliding through the rooms in a routine he'd committed to memory. When she left the house, she battled the mud-thick roads to the grocery, her skirt-bottoms bunched into her fists, but the goop still spattered them, and at the store she was forced to find a flat rock to scrape the bottoms of her laced boots. For a moment, she stared in frustration at her sullied clothes and hands.

That afternoon, Matt rode to the Fort and bartered an old single-shot 30.30 to an Indian for a two-year-old gelding. The Indian guaranteed the animal saddle broken, but simply leading the horse turned contentious, and Matt worried he'd been bested in the bargain. Home, he took two hours washing and currying the animal's tangled mane and dirty coat. The gelding darkened under the water and soap, but came up red. Matt stopped and admired the color like rich earth with the sun on the wane.

The next morning, he bridled the horse and trooped him around the corral. The gelding reared after one pass and Matt fought him down. The horse snorted and made a step for his toes. Matt hopped clear. He jerked the lead rope and the horse settled. Two rounds later, they repeated the contest. Five hours every morning, it remained their routine. The gelding kicked slats from the fence and blew snot at him. He crow-hopped so viciously, Matt had to cut a longer lead to keep it from jerking his shoulder from its socket.

At the end of that second week, the gelding kicked him. The lead was long enough and Matt had let himself drift behind it. He dusted himself and tested his leg to see if it was broken. When he found it wasn't, he snubbed the lead rope to a post. In the barn, he found a shovel. He carried it to the corral and there, beat the horse senseless. Each swing the horse screamed and Matt leaped clear of its flashing hooves, crying out, too.

He left the horse panting and shivering in the livery. It had long ceased being a shadow in the corral, but he could hear it step and paw the roughed ground. The night was cold and steam rose from its wounds. He had nothing for his ride this night. It would be a mean trick to leave off Wendy now, but a meaner one to stick her with himself, even if she was inclined to accept him.

His mother stood behind him. It was her breaths he heard now, burdened with another winter of pneumonia. He remembered nights she would sit and read him and Luke to sleep with the King James. Luke could quote scripture when he was five. Matt just liked the sound of its poetry. Like the river and the creek, it would still him. His mother had tried to read to him alone afterward, but without Luke holding down the words, he felt compelled to double-duty. He found little sense in most of the stories, and in yielding to reason's call, lost the poetry, too. Finally, after a month, he sat below her chair to listen, and she set the book aside and stroked his forehead and the tiny lines the storm had left. Her hands were rough from kitchen work and worry, but through the calluses, as she brushed his scalp, he felt her hunting that old wordless hum he loved, trying to offer it back to him.

"You are not the kind of man who beats an animal."

Matt glanced about. The dog had barked and bit the horse's bouncing hooves when Matt began their struggle, but had retreated outside the corral fence where he paced staring, eyes flashing in the glow from the lantern his mother held.

"Will that horse mind better hurt like it is?"

Matt did not reply.

"If I beat you would you be right?"

"I am not right," Matt said.

"Nor me," she said. She glanced toward the dog. "But he had nothing to do with it and he never did a thing to me. I was wrong. So are you."

Matt nodded.

"Now come in and eat a meal with me and let that horse be."

He followed and she fed him and spoke to him, and he managed to attend to her words but they meant less than her voice itself, going on in a way he recalled and did not, maybe the same as you recall breathing without the need to remind your mouth and lungs and diaphragm to do their duty.

Late that evening, he walked to the barn and loaded the trough with oats. He opened the corral's gate and barn's swinging door. The horse stirred and skittered at the sound.

He hooked the lantern then hid in the shadows. The gelding crossed the barn and ate. Matt watched his throat tremble. Welts mottled his ribs, and the bleeding wounds were matted with straw and hair. He found ointment and eased himself to the gelding's side. The horse bolted and Matt let him, returning to doctoring only when the gelding bent his neck again to eat. Before Matt could clean the first wound, the animal retreated once more. The horse's sweat and his own made an odor gamey as venison in the skillet. Matt found an apple and salved every cut, then added sugar cubes to his bribe and applied liniment to each swollen place.

●

WENDY WATCHED THE EARLY THAW stretch into a long springtime. Morning glory and dandelion weeds pocked the untilled garden plot and the lawn's grass was yellowing toward green. Overhead, geese and ducks sliced through the warming sky, headed for the river or potholes in the basin.

Nearly every day a gift arrived. Tiny things much of the time: a scarf, fruit preserves, or jujubes. One morning, she rose to breakfast enough for the entire family, sliced bacon, large boiled eggs, and sweet bread; another she lifted the blanket from a basket containing a tabby kitten with a full milk jug and two fresh trout.

Once Wendy woke to her sisters' squealing. They'd discovered a pair of muddy boot tracks. A few more were in the yard, but they vanished in the rutted street.

"He's ugly," Amy said.

Wendy sighed, impatiently.

"If he wasn't ugly, he'd let you see him."

"You are both insufferable," Wendy said. She led the girls to the house and handed one a straw broom and the other the dusting rag. "This will keep your imaginations occupied," she told them. They complained and she ignored them, preparing herself for the walk to the store, where she had assumed the clerking duties at her mother's insistence. Her mother was at first pleased a young romantic had imagination enough to woo her daughter in such a courtly manner. She had become exasperated by the mystery, lately, though, and pressed Wendy to examine anyone coming into the store for evidence. Each day, she surveyed grocery lists and hunted for indications of it in the gifts she received. But she was left without clues. She'd considered Matt Lawson, speculating that perhaps their history kept with him. He'd stopped into the grocery once, but seeing her had turned him around so swiftly he nearly caught himself in the door's shutting. She'd met his eyes for a moment and recognized only fear. It saddened her until the next morning when a pair of narrow store-bought slippers lay on the porch, red ribbon binding them, and she ceased entirely to think of him.

•

MATT TROTTED THE HORSE RIDERLESS around the corral for a full two weeks, only a blanket on its back. He spoke to it of the girl: what he remembered of her smell, her kindness with the graves, her voice he'd been so long without hearing. The horse grew to cooperate, more or less. There was still the crow-hopping, but Matt, reversing his methods, closed the line slack, allowing the gelding no room, save carrying him into the air. It took more attention, but he'd recognized the chore required it. Afterwards, he fed the gelding well and allowed it to frolic loose in the pasture each evening when he rode to the butte. He ordered a fresh leather saddle from the town livery and paid a middle-aged lady near Lincoln who had some standing in the county in leather crafts to cut Wendy's name in it along with painted roses.

The gelding tolerated the saddle in a few weeks, but threw him six days straight until he snubbed its neck to the sturdy fence post and its hindquarters to another, giving him no choice but to bear him. He repeated this five times a day for a week, though it put him behind in the spring work. To his surprise, the gelding allowed him to ride the eighth day without incident.

Matt saddled and worked the gelding daily, easing his gait and acquainting the horse with the bit and bridle. When he'd tired sufficiently, Matt allowed the gelding to make its own trail back, giving him his head to chew at spring grass or new tree leaves. Fenceposts and low limbs, the horse tried to rub him from the saddle, but any animal with good sense will test a rider; it was more an act of character than revolt.

He mounted the gelding every trip to Peach now and hobbled it close by, where it could watch the house. He'd direct it to Wendy and speak her name like a charm. Late, he'd offer whatever the next gift was for the horse to study. Then, one warm night, he delivered the gelding himself to the porch and tied him to the sturdiest rail.

•

THE GELDING NIBBLED THE GRASS beneath the porch. He lifted his head when Wendy clucked. She patted his warm silky neck. He eyed her, but she was fresh to it. She stroked the reins and the horse chattered the bridle.

"There," she said to it.

The leather of the saddle was whirled into roses, painted red and yellow and pink, her name above them. She patted it gently, then hoisted one leg into the stirrups and swung the other over the pommel. At the street, she coaxed the gelding to full gallop. She felt her eyes crying and the tears dry in her lashes and on her cheek. She reined for a road north that would meet the river. In her nightclothes, she raced and trotted and raced again the beautiful animal the miles toward Seven Bays. There she permitted the horse to drink its fill and, later, deliver her home. She settled on Amherst for his name. It was Emily Dickinson's home.

★ **10** ★

LINDA JEFFERSON WAS NOT TAKEN aback when, after the shock
of her dismissal ebbed, the children visited her home. Fall, she had
arrived at the school to more fruit and wildflowers on her desk than
any year before, and, as each left for the Thanksgiving holiday—
some of the last days she would share with them—she caught herself kissing their cheeks. Even the older boys inclined their straight
backs to offer themselves. They still cared for her, as children will
for anyone who treats them generously, but her awkward condition
hushed them. The boys feared it; the child was a bulk impossible
for them to make. It frightened them to know she could conjure
more than they could.

The girls were much less naive. They only hoped to determine
who had left the seed. Girls were never as romantic as boys. That is
where people were wrong. It was boys who pined for love, and girls
who understood it, and therefore pursued not love, but boys.

The day she was dismissed from her school duties, Linda Jefferson opened an abandoned copy of *Anna Karenina*. It lay on her

nightstand, her place marked with a rawhide strip. She read a few pages each night, preoccupied with Anna's eventual end. Finished, she read it once more with the desperation one devours tragedy. She dog-eared the pages where Anna committed each transgression, as if Linda herself might be able to avoid them. But so many pages were marked finally that the book cover slanted nearly forty-five degrees, and Linda realized she'd marked each page Anna appeared and some where she hadn't and couldn't anticipate the calamity folding over her.

Her breasts were not yet milk-heavy, nevertheless their weight reassured her. She stroked her stomach and spoke to it not with her voice but with the tips of her fingers, where she rubbed her stretching hair follicles and the wrinkled skin line that her elastic undergarment cut and hunted the right place, until the baby, like a fish ascending from deep water, rose to her touch.

When the year turned, Linda harnessed her one good horse and trotted her flatbed up the Peach road. She stopped at the cafe. It was the men's place mornings—farmers drinking coffee by the potful and protesting the weather or the state of their machinery and a few merchants making themselves social like they would at Sunday church. The banker took breakfast every morning at the window table, studying the previous day's market tape, joined by a high-hatted farmer or two.

Seeing her in the doorway halted their banter and gossip, a hush Linda thought nearly visible, all those words collapsing midair, then piling on the floor, quiet as snow. She shrunk until the baby cramped inside her. Small was not a choice afforded her. She nodded at the bank manager, a mustached fellow, whiskers dark where the coffee wet them.

"I'd like to see my money," Linda said.

The man sighed and rose.

"I'm in no hurry," she told him.

"I am," he said.

"Your breakfast will cool."

He looked at his eggs, bleeding yellow eyes where he'd dipped his biscuit. "I'll order more."

"I'll not be a partner to waste," Linda said.

Her baby-heavy belly pressed her distended skin. The banker gazed at it, then back to his plate. The men eyed him. She was in no way his fault, but it was his business that had brought her in the door.

He shoveled his food and chased it with more coffee. Linda surveyed the room, quietly delighted that she'd hoisted her discomfort upon them. The child shifted. She decided after this one, she'd have another.

Finished, she followed the banker across the street. He rotated the doorbolt, spun it the opposite direction, and stepped into the safe. She scribbled out a slip for her balance. It was over seven hundred dollars. He snapped the bills twice and shoved them across the transom toward her.

She recounted them. "I'm sorry," she said when she was satisfied. "Checking others' work is a habit."

She walked the clapboard sidewalks, drawing a few stares. She welcomed them. In the gristmill, she ordered three barrels of treated wheat flour and paid, shucking bills from her stack. She found lead and powder and, on the hardware's shelves, a pamphlet concerning loading. At the mercantile, she bought a pedaled sewing machine and flannel, gingham, and cotton bolts. She purchased several thread spools and an array of needles and a pin cushion shaped like a tomato, before adding yarn and knitting needles, sheets, and fresh wool blankets. The little she knew of clothes-making passed when her mother did, but she had a book and she would learn.

The dime store window displayed a crib. She purchased it and some playthings she could tie above for the child right away, and others, including a kaleidoscope, wouldn't be much use until the child could sit up and take notice of the world.

She ended at the doctor's, a stringy, middle-aged man, fit more for animals than people. His hands were cold and he had horrible gas, for which he never felt compelled to restrain or the courtesy to apologize.

He put the stethoscope ends into her ears. She heard the baby's heartbeat and offered him five dollars for the instrument, but he had none to spare. He pronounced her and the baby healthy.

"Are you friendly with your neighbors?" the doctor asked.

She didn't answer. He wrote a note on his calendar. "When it's your time, I'll send someone around to check."

"That won't be required."

He looked at her for a moment. His glasses shifted. They left sores on his nose and he rubbed them. "Birth is a very violent process, ma'am."

"So is living," she told him.

★ 11 ★

"It's nothing I'm accustomed to, what's going on," her mother told her. Wendy unlatched the cabinet and unfolded a drying towel, then took her place at the dish rack. "It's not normal." Her mother huffed. Her agitated hands stirred the sink to a froth. Wendy passed her the meat platter and watched as she scraped the scraps into a soup kettle for stock.

"It's not love, it's worship."

"Do you think I'm shallow, mother?" Wendy wiped clean a fork. "If I was, I'd keep a regular beau and the only worry you'd have was his pulling at my underthings before we got to the altar."

Her mother's hands quit scouring. "Don't you think they'd want to touch you honey? Don't you want to touch them?" She peeked into the parlor to be certain her husband and the girls were occupied. Her mother emptied the sink and scooped clear the drain, rinsed and filled it once more. She insisted on the hottest of water for fear of botulism, which she contracted once as a child. Her hands went red under it. She sighed and bit her lip and stretched her fingers until they became accustomed.

"Two things worry me," she said. "First, I'm afraid this person who's going to all this trouble will never be able to make himself come for you." She offered another fork for Wendy to towel. "The second is that he will."

They finished in the quiet. Wendy had never brought herself to deliberate on either of her mother's fears purposefully, because she saw them as faithless. But coming from outside her, their freshness stung. She longed for a meeting, but she treasured the anonymity of each gift as well. Maybe, it wasn't the man she wanted but only the idea of one.

Her sisters were prepared for bed, waiting for the family prayer. Wendy enjoyed them both, but felt more cousin to the girls than sister. It was her mother she matched in both temperament and aspect. Their straight-backed appearance and demeanor were derived from pride. They stared at the world and those in it with cold blue eyes, and in them was no patience for fools and silliness or laughter of any kind, which was their most genuine failing.

•

THE NEXT DAY SHE PURCHASED a ring from the backroom of the hardware, where they held a small collection of jewelry. It was simple silver. She had it inscribed: Love Wendy. It cost her savings and credit against next month's pay.

That night, she looped it in twine and dangled it a foot above the porch step. She ran the other end of the string through the upstairs hall and wrapped the loose end to her wrist. Morning, though, the string end hung over the porch where he'd snipped the ring loose, and the next day there was another, this one tied to the balcony beam, twirling in the morning's breeze, a tiny diamond blinking in the sun. Her father scratched a pickle jar to be sure.

Wendy seated herself on the porch step. Off, the ring was an empty hole and her finger one of four digits, and on, the hole was filled and she couldn't imagine her hand had been so bare.

He didn't visit the next day or the one following. She understood as the ring had cost more even than hers for him. The spring stayed mild. Flowers were on the bud and trees fattened with their leaves for the year. Wendy clerked and, at home, assumed the gardening. She relished the lengthening evenings, digging, watering, and plucking weeds. Anytime she felt a jump of doubt, she'd pat the ring and its one diamond. The ring separated her from other young girls and she wanted to remain so. It was her license to ache, to raise the burdens of a life and load them in her heart and pack their weight.

By the fall of a fortnight, though, those aches had grown heavy as lead. She didn't even approach the door mornings, weary of her own expectations. It had been so long, she realized, anything short of he himself standing there would be a disappointment. She began to sleep on the bench below the front windowsill and finally took up a blanket and a pillow and pitched her camp on the porch swing.

Often a breeze would press at the swing and squawk the chains, waking her, and she'd search for stars and planets emerging over the horizon of buildings. She felt she was floating on one great river while staring into another, the one he sailed each night. When Hawk Creek met the Columbia, it lost itself, water against water for a moment, then water with water, then just water.

Approaching sleep, she allowed herself to imagine her anonymous lover's first kiss. It was on the last of these nights that she had a dream. The air was cool, and she could hear forever into the darkness. She suspected every sound was his. Closing her eyes, she dreamed him over her, a simple shadow. She stretched for her bed light but a hand halted her. When she turned, his head was directly over hers, and she waited for her kiss, but none came. She reached to pull him close to her, but everywhere she touched he disappeared like smoke breaking.

She woke bleary and afraid. Again there was no gift from him, no place on the lawn where he had stepped, nothing of him in the light. She rushed through the house, then back onto the porch.

"Where is my present?"

"Honey, there is none."

"You have hid them," Wendy said.

She hurried to the backyard where she'd hobbled the bay. The horse nickered at her. She found him a carrot and a bucket of grain and bent to nuzzle his broad nose with her hand. The horse had never been friendly, only dutiful. She neared him from the backside, thinking she'd spied a cinch sore. The horse's cleaned hoof caught her mid-arm. The kick spun her. Her arm felt warm and she watched as blood hastened from it and spattered the grass. The second kick whacked her shoulder and ear and drove her to the ground. When she looked up, the horse had returned to the grain pail, banging it for the last of the oats.

When her father called to Wendy a moment later, she didn't answer. He worried she'd deserted them completely, abandoning herself to this strange courtship and leaving him a husk of a daughter. When he got closer he was relieved it was only blood, then was horrified at his relief. He lifted her. For a moment she thought it was her man come for her.

•

MATT WAS SHUFFLING THROUGH A saddlebag for jerked venison when the horse kicked her. He was unsure what he had seen and would have fought to believe it, if he hadn't witnessed the second blow. He smacked at his legs and his thighs and got himself standing, but could press no farther. His hands were fists. He could see the black blood on her nightclothes, but he could not move. He found himself sobbing, his chest shuddering for air.

He watched the grocer wagon her to the doctor and, later return with her in his arms. Matt remained and observed all day and into the next night. A lantern in her room winked on. Her father bent and kissed her. In the silhouettes upon the curtain, they looked like lovers.

Very late, Matt skulked to the paddock where they'd left the bay. He carried a buck knife honed as sharp as a strapped razor. The horse nickered and bobbed his head in recognition. Matt patted it and let it eat an apple from his hands. He studied its healed wounds. "Poor boy," he whispered. "Poor, poor boy. I am sorry, my friend."

•

WENDY WOKE TO THE HORSE's throat cut. The straw beneath its body was so thick with blood that it oozed with each of her steps. The next morning, when Matt approached the porch, he fastened the reins of a long-tamed grey to the railing, and stole away. Every gift he'd given her lay on the steps and railing. He touched the lace hair ribbon and the saddle. The slippers were crusted with blood.

The second night, though she'd been generous enough to feed and water it, the horse's lead remained fastened to the post, along with a note she'd nailed to the rail: *You're a horror*, it read: *Take this and go away.*

The third night, at his footfalls a hound bayed and the grocer quick-fired a lantern and put himself to guarding the door with a shotgun.

•

THE DOG WAS WILD, CHOKING at his chain-end. It was trained
to manhunt by the sheriff who had loaned it to her father. Its bay
was a sound like a train passing. Downstairs in the sitting room,
there were whispers and chairs scraping and the up and down of
checking windows. In her bedroom, Wendy covered her head with
a blanket. Rain clattered the roof, then eased. The eaves moaned,
and the roof thunked again with a sound too heavy for water.

Underneath her bed was a small bore rifle her father had sup-
plied her. She leveled it at the window. A hand dropped onto the
frame, then a head, then upside down, swinging, the top half of a
man. He aimed a hammer and tore away the lock and tugged the
window until it gave.

"You killed my horse," she hissed.

"I couldn't abide him hurting you," he said. "He was a bad one. I
should've never brung him. He was so pretty was all."

She peeked over the bed top. "You're not mad?"

"No," he said. "I'd grown fond of the animal."

"Wendy?" she heard her mother call.

"I'll not bother you again." Matt let the hammer go. It thumped
on the lawn below. "I was hoping you would keep the other gifts,
though."

Wendy's door banged open. A wedge of light filled the room.
Her mother peered in, then screamed and retreated to the stairwell.
Wendy rose from her bed and so did the barrel of the rifle. In her
hands, it frightened her. She hated even holding it, and it tensed
her body to think she'd been pointing it toward someone who had
tried to bless her so, and the tension tightened her finger across the
trigger. A powder flash lit the room.

As he tumbled from the rooftop, both hands clutching his side,
she recognized her lover and then he disappeared.

★ 12 ★

LINDA JEFFERSON'S FIRST LABOR PAINS arrived on a full stomach. She studied the applesauce she'd been nibbling for dark spots or spoil. The jar hadn't bubbled nor was the glass cracked. The paraffin smelled sweet enough. The date was October, a late batch, but apples rarely went wrong, and she'd peeled and cleaned each, hunting any sign of worm or bad meat.

Her bowels pressed her to the privy outside. She'd shoveled a fresh pit fall, but spring had thawed the excrement and urine below to a stenchy mush. She vomited before she reached the building and shat herself. The sky was broken with clouds. It still held a veil of light. The days were lengthening she could see, and it disappointed her. She liked them short. Darkness was a solace she could retreat to. Inside it was reading and sleep. Daylight turned another matter. One could only guess what it contained, and guessing was a distraction she no longer had patience for.

The old dog sniffed her dress and licked her leavings. She wiped the vomit from her chin with a clump of cheat grass. The cramping bound her again, but there was nothing to empty in her, and she only shuddered as the pain coursed through her. She had entertained a notion that the baby might remain within and spend its childhood and adolescence—those awkward, horrible times that reduced children to mere people—maturing until, like Pallas Athena, it would burst from her full born, ready for war.

She felt her legs dampen and warm. She stared at the pink fluid staining her dress and began to weep. The child shifted. She crawled to the house and through it into the bedroom. There, she propped herself on the floor with her wardrobe mirror between her ankles. She couldn't see. She lit great candles made with what was left of the canning wax. By dawn, if she peeled her labia mid-contraction, the child's blood-matted hair crowned between her legs. Once it nearly cleared a shoulder, but then surrendered and disappeared inside. Treachery, she decided, was a slow process, and she felt like Othello giving birth to her own Iago. She would suffer as the Moor had. Each pain, she faced with clenched teeth and hands and a contraction of her own to counter the child's thrust. But the child battered her like his father's loins nine months before, only from the other side.

Her light-headedness was close to godly. Death could make people happy; it was guarantee the world was working in their favor. Over coffee in their kitchens and their card clubs, women would determine it was a just as well. They would inter her in a grassy place and mark it with a small stone, her name inlaid. There she'd remain, the child impacted in her womb like a bad tooth rotting a gum.

But the child had no interest in death. It wriggled and pressed at her for hours. She marveled at its strength and, at last, she crawled to the barn. There, she undid a harness and wound a rawhide strap loose. Bailing twine littered the floor. She cobbled eight feet of it together and made a loop, then lassoed an end of a loft beam.

She propped herself on the cart below the dangling twine and waited for the baby to surge forward. When it did, she shoved her hand into herself. Underneath its head, she found one shoulder then another and circled the twine around them until the apparatus resembled a harness. She bolened the leather and twine and took up slack until the contraption held the baby taut. Finally she shoved herself out of the wagon.

The baby dangled above her, coughing. Rope burns bruised each shoulder and one arm. Its tiny penis shook like an accusing finger.

PART ★ TWO

The Soul has Bandaged moments—
When too appalled to stir—
She feels some ghastly Fright come up
And stop to look at her—

Salute her—with long fingers—
Caress her freezing hair—
Sip, Goblin, From the very lips
The Lover—hovered—o'er—
Unworthy, that a thought so mean
Accost a Theme—so—fair—

—EMILY DICKINSON
from poem #512

⋆ **13** ⋆

IT IS STRANGE COUNTRY WHERE a person's behavior opposes his or her emotions. But this country is nothing if not strange. Angered, a man ceases speaking and listening. He is inclined to leave others for his own company whether they are inclined to stir his ire or quell it. Most work themselves to distraction or exhaustion and return to their homes and families or flophouses or work-camp tents, in their stead, and sleep as if stone or earth. Women cleans meticulously rooms otherwise ignored or reorders closets and drawers or hung and beat carpets on the clothesline. If circumstances requires another's presence, both were liable to respond in terse though courteous terms until they have managed the rough water that was other people.

It was perhaps the scattering of people that made them behave so. In the cities people flocked up like ducks in a pen and squawked at one other accordingly. It seemed all tumult, but noise can be as static as quiet and the opposite as disruptive. City boys, west for work, beat at the silence with talk until the locals threatened to hit them with a skillet. And it was clear: the tumult they spat out with talk others just swallowed, and there was peace in neither.

The paradox appeared to multiply in the case of Matt Lawson. He recognized he had passed the frontiers of ordinary when the .22 bullet creased his gut thirteen years before. The fall from the grocer's roof broke Matt's arm, though the bullet failed to damage anything necessary and burrowed into some muscled place within him. He ran like an injured animal, bent, favoring the wound in his side and a broken forearm. Mounting his horse was not as difficult as he anticipated as the wounds were both to his left side. Once aboard, though, he was unsure where to direct the animal. A broken-up fugitive was no way to return to his widowed mother, and Wendy had delivered her opinion. The horse trotted toward the river out of instinct. No one offered chase. He bled from the bullet wound and it lightened his head; his arm buzzed with pain. At Miles Junction he directed the horse north, away from Peach and the family ranch, and nodded into a doze that lasted off and on a day and a night. The horse possessed a shy nature and chose game trails bisecting the highways rather than encounter another rider.

Once he'd ridden far enough into the mountains, he propped the wounded limb in a locust crook and walked his shoulder away until the bones separated. With his good hand, he squared his elbow to his wrist and then, just as slowly, let the bone rejoin.

To lift the arm from the tree required all his strength. When he finally freed it, his wrist was pocked with sap and bark. The break beat pain, though he could feel only numb below it and feared he'd cramped the nerves. He made a fist with the fingers. They answered only when he forced them, which left them useless for even holding a rein. He collapsed against a tall pine. He'd sweat through his shirt. His haunches were too feeble to hold him and he slipped farther until his legs spread before him like clock hands.

He drove a finger from his good hand into the bullet hole, which was raw and burning. The bullet hadn't cleared him. A man often died from less. He'd wandered himself high into the Kettle Mountains; not even Indians traipsed this way until huckleberry season. The Indians believed stories had rules. Once begun, no tale could be uttered twice a season. No less than two could be present aside from the teller, as once a story is loose, though the teller tends it as best he can, like an animal, it owns itself and is not bound by intellect or ritual's restraints and must be tracked to its finish, and the trail required a witness's veracity or the teller could claim it led anywhere he chose. They contained truths past deeds, past civility, past the god preached in churches; they were truths so inarguable they required no faith at all.

He wondered if they happened onto him August—a strange, dead white man, an arm broken and a rib shot—what story they would make of it. Would their tales leave him a god or a wounded devil? Or would he just be a dead man, not fit for story at all? He quit thinking about it. Motion seemed to him an early morning dream. He feared forgetting it altogether. Nothing moved save his eyes. They blinked, and he watched a new world arrive and an old one recede with each flickering, until there were hundreds, all frozen, all the same: a feathered tamarack branch, moss yellowing the limb's underside, a few gnats hovering, and above, blue sky thatched with strings of white clouds. Once a crow crossed.

A day later, he dragged himself to a creek. There, he lay on the gravel bank and lowered his arm into the cold water until, again, the break was without feeling. He was glad for the spring sun. He let it warm his back and shoulders. The horse followed in his own good time, reins dragging in the grass, and the dog, which had followed a few miles behind, gazed, mouth open in a doglike grin.

Sleep came, bright and of no circumstance, but it fascinated him all the same, and he studied himself inside it like a child measuring a rattle the first time he shook sound from it. When he dreamed, he thought it was himself he was watching, then recognized it was not. Luke swam next to him, a baby again, and Matt studied his stubby arms and the rope of blood and veins feeding him. The only sound was fluid when it passed after he moved. It was a fitful doze and he dreamed and woke and dreamed and woke, until the shades between the two were no more than what you'd see between one stalk of wheat and the one next to it.

It was the magpie's flapping that finally stirred him. It marched across his chest, its face and neck feathers tinged scarlet. Its black eye blinked until it drove its beak into the bullet wound and rose with flesh. Matt watched its head turn upward and the neck muscles swallow, then in a single arc his good hand caught the bird, and in another wrung its neck.

Matt propped himself on his elbow and studied the wound, a small, ragged hollow. In a month it would heal, and in two, scar until the Indians crowded him out. He killed a deer and ate roots and kept days on a fir tree, carving a slash for each one. July, he had reckoned for only thirty, so he departed one day shy of plumb.

For the next thirteen years he followed work throughout the state's eastern half, aside from a stretch in Idaho. He insisted upon one rider concerning employment: he must be allowed to work every day. Once hired, he took to any assignment like work was a woman he'd loved and lost and found again. He recognized how best to order a chore, no matter the complexity, and turned iron in the application. Before the lunch whistle, any foremen with sense saw him a bargain.

He'd set grade and paved highways and liked it; he'd driven truck, both long haul and deliveries, and liked it, and he'd braked for the railroads and liked it; he'd skidded logs and set choke chain in forests and liked it, and pulled green chain in the mills and liked that, too. Occasionally, a check crossed his palm, and that was how he kept the months. Days, though, were like trees in timber, one next to the other, and no different unless he studied them closely, and he saw no purpose to. Too soon, though, someone would join his shift who needed talk as much as Matt needed quiet, and he'd take his check and his leave.

He'd grown so large people looking his way saw nothing except him. But it left him bare, too, like a snake shed of its skin, waiting on a new one. He'd heard people say it took a lot to get a big man's goat, but what enraged Matt was everything, all a little and nothing more or less, his belly constantly filling. An outright insult didn't weigh upon it any heavier than the slightest voice. The result was one day he'd take what a man shouldn't and, an hour past, not endure ordinary people behaving in ordinary ways. For thirteen years he tore down whoever crossed him, even those who weren't aware they had done so. He never lost a scrap. When the fisticuffs were finished, another man was likely wheezing or bleeding hard and, for a second or two, his living or dying was up to Matt. He'd seen it in their eyes. Some looked pleading, some looked trustful, and others, they just waited for him to make up his mind. And in that moment Matt just kept getting bigger, though growing was the last thing a big man required. In fact, Matt's size loomed over him so large, that sometimes it shrank his insides to nothing. Matt never knew himself if he would halt, and a roomful of men was sometimes all that kept him from manslaughter. He didn't count himself a brave or noble man and when his jaw tightened and his hands doubled into fists and he closed the distance between himself and his antagonist, it was in disregard of sense and honor rather than a defense of it.

Campfires, Matt listened to stories about whores, some one-legged or hairless, others pretty as porcelain, and one who could twist herself into a wagon wheel and spin on a man's rod like it was an axle. Other tellers recalled devastating wildfires, tornadoes that hurled pitchforks through four-inch beams, dry spells that turned lakes to dusty hollows and creeks damp lines at their channel's bottom. Still more were of men with a blacksmith pyre full of fury, enough gall or ill humor to defy civility and law and good manners. Matt himself had become the subject of many.

He considered his mother or Wendy or his father and brother these thirteen years no more than breathing, which is to say never and always. On occasion they would enter his conscious thoughts. Recalling his mother left him with guilt and Wendy an ache he associated with confusion; only his brother and father delivered him anything approaching nostalgia.

Occasionally he traveled to town to purchase the necessary trappings. Folks would wait on him and take his money and he'd move through them like he was nothing peculiar. He listened to scraps of conversation about dress colors or what riffraff the immigrants were. Soon, though, someone would recognize his eavesdropping and avoid him and others would do likewise, reminding him he was an alien to such human country.

His last job, though, he held for three years. A widow who desired a hand for her cattle took him on. The pay was half of what he cashed elsewhere, but she allowed him a bunk in the barn loft caretaker apartment and left him alone. He warmed to her two boys and trained them in the roping and riding. They threw mumblety-peg between chores and dinner. Christmas, they brought him chocolate candies and he savored them, dispensing one piece an evening so they lasted through spring. He returned the kindness with a stone Indian pipe he'd acquired, and though they thanked him politely, he worried they didn't derive the enjoyment from it that he had from the sweets. He kept on the glean for a gift they might cotton to, but never came upon something fitting. He had departed them the week before, only because the Depression turned even his small wage a burden and the boys had grown proficient enough to mind the place themselves. His last pay was tucked in his pants pocket.

He studied the little family—minus a father—and the pleasure they took in one another and the absence they bore with grace and their efforts to include him and felt his mind rising to him like a fish from the depths after thirteen years of winter. He recognized, though he traveled many miles, he had spun like a calf with circling disease but had collected none of the wisdom required to lift a life past simple existence and little of the charity necessary to turn time into something other than just years. He determined to return home, but with nothing to offer in regards to heart or thought for his absence, he decided he could at least deliver a wallet full of money.

Whitman County remained the only country still flush for that kind of pay, and Colfax was the county seat. The town was situated in a deep cleft the Palouse River tore through the basalt troughs and hills of what was once idle bunchgrass and soft loam. The Indians let it alone and stayed poor, but migrant Germans, Russians, and Norse cut the brush, tilled, then planted and cultivated and prospered. Miles of sprouting wheat sown in late fall greened the softened horizons.

Matt's approach was from the west and above. The farmhouse lights dotted the hills' western portions, where they could catch most light. The larger ranches were in flats between, each with an enormous barn harboring cattle and swine and fodder, and another their implements, and usually a grain elevator, as well. Roads tracked the water flow or property lines: Cherry Creek, Rebel Flat Run, The Big Hole, Green Hollow, Dry Creek, Little Almota Creek, Spring Flat Creek, Palouse River South Fork, Thorn Creek, Duncan Springs or Parvin (Mick and Peter), Banner, Danaher, Hergert, Behrens, Bushnell, Hubble, Biddle, Henning, Wells, Smidt, Smit, Schmidt (the families got along so poorly two sides changed their spelling) and Kleveno, Kleaweno (cousins, who held no grudges). The country's lines were as gentle as his own was stern, arcs and rounded buttes, an ocean of earth. Even the canyon cut by the Palouse River was topped by farm country and the lights of Colfax below followed the water in a shape as lazy and pleasant as the horizon's hills.

The town's major boast was a gristmill. A few hardware stores and two closed banks shadowed its narrow main street, but Matt had come looking for a poker game. Cards and good fortune were too mercurial for him to trust, especially when the best you could hope for was just more of the same the next hand. However, rumor was the big farmers in the Palouse country, those who had work and need for a good hand, swapped cards and discretionary income Wednesday nights in a backroom of a Chinese opium warren.

November remained a week away, but the temperature won the race with the season. The winter's first snow cloaked the fields and floated about Matt and his coyote pup trotting behind. He'd lost the dog six years before and acquired the pup when someone killed its mother raiding the camp garbage.

Five deer browsed a ranch house garden's dregs. Above, sky had cleared and the temperature he estimated had dropped close to zero. His hands ached inside his heavy gloves. A chain of head-lights snaked up the canyon. Most of the country had swapped horsepower for internal combustion in the twenties and many of the farmers managed to keep them running despite the Crash and the Dustbowl. Now midwest clunkers, piled with children and belongings and kept whole with rope and wire and prayer littered the highways, aimed at federal construction projects throughout the center of the state.

Matt permitted the horse its own head descending the basalt. Below he heard jabbering, and at the canyon well where a creek trickled past a cottonwood copse a group of men lit by homemade torches seemed to be arguing with one another.

"Chinese shouldn't be telling an American what to pay in America, Jarms," one wearing a heavy red mackinaw said.

Jarms donned a fresh fedora and an expensive sheepskin coat and clothes not long past a tailor's needle. He wore glasses with wire frames, which made him look intelligent and thoughtful. It appeared he wouldn't know a worry from a snipe den, though his harassers had snubbed his wrists behind his back and tethered him to one of the cottonwoods.

"Can he tell him how much in China?" Jarms asked.

"Not there either." Two others nodded. One smoked a cigarette and tapped his ash into the damp earth. Both were dressed in work clothes. Snow swirled in the orange torchlight like moths made crazy with lanterns.

"Chinese got a right to earn a dollar."

"They can get their living on others, not Americans."

"Jesus, you are a trying bastard," Jarms said. "You know, you shouldn't try and think. It isn't kind. You get a thought in your head and it turns lonely rattling around all by itself. They're in America. That makes them Americans."

"I got a right to think," Pete said.

"Yea, but no talent for it."

"Goddammit, Owen, you can shut up, too," Jarms said to one of the pair listening.

"I never spoke a word," the man replied.

"You think too loud," Jarms told him.

"Ain't you particular," Owen said. "I'll think nothing if that'll please you."

"You got little choice in the matter I can see," Jarms added.

"What makes you the genius?" another man asked. He stood beyond the torchlight and when he approached he held a bourbon bottle in one hand, and in the other his own piece of haberdashery, a fine Texas Stetson that neither labor nor wind nor any other weather had put a mark on.

"Breeding," Jarms said.

The man laughed and offered the bottle to the others. Tied, Jarms went without. He was not inclined to quit his argument, however. "Chinese are from China," Pete said.

"And the Germans are from Germany as your grandpa would tell you when he emigrated this way with a bunch of others who knew no English but lots of work," Jarms answered.

"Chink can't tell an American to do anything anywhere," Pete said.

"Not even in a place they own?" Jarms asked.

"They'd never own it enough to boss white people," Garrett replied.

"Ain't Chinamen eating in Chinese restaurants. It's white people," Jarms said. "Your rules they would never make a dollar. So I bought in and you have to pay now."

Garrett waved a hand in front of his face. "You talk too much. We didn't bring this silly bastard here to lawyer, goddamnit. Get his wallet."

Jarms offered no fight and one of the group pulled a canvas square from his pocket and retrieved the bills. He offered them to Garrett who leafed through them.

"Forty-two dollars," Garrett said.

Jarms nodded.

"Well, take comfort in the whiskey we will drink with it," Garrett said.

"I don't believe so," Matt said. He remained in the darkness.

"Who's that?" Petey asked.

"No one you're familiar with. Just give the man back his money and move on."

Garrett laughed. "I'm not inclined to take orders."

"And I'm not inclined to give them," Matt said. "But you're stealing good money from a man I can't see done a thing wrong but best you in an argument."

"Petey, get the car," Garrett said. "Unless this interloper decides to draw a bead, I'm done with debate for the evening."

"You'll find that a difficult prospect." Matt had circled to their car and yanked the plug wires. He threw one into the light and followed on his horse, the yellow dog in the rear. He held the other wires in his hand.

Jarms laughed. "Sinners meet your reckoning."

"The lord's got no quarrel with me. I'm as much believer as you're heathen."

"You attend the Mass but you don't believe in nothing but your own good."

"The two coincide," Garrett said.

"They're not supposed to," Jarms said. "That's the point. You got to be meek to inherit the earth."

"I don't have to be anything of the kind. No brother this or that or the other thing is likely to tell me what to do. And if the Lord wanted it different it would be different."

"All of that does not concern me," Matt said. He had in the past years taught himself to speak in slow and careful syllables. His intent was to allow time to consider the next word while he was speaking the first, but the habit left him sounding detached and dangerous, which his size could not help but multiply. Matt pressed his back teeth together, until his pulse slowed. Snowflakes clung to his hair and black duster's shoulders. The torches alternated shadows and light over his face and mad, unkempt hair, and he was aware that he was opaque to those facing him and this would push them to add their own well-being to his argument.

"Return the money," Matt told Garrett.

"We'll just rob him tomorrow for it," Garrett said. The others nodded.

"And if I'm not here to witness it, I'll have no complaints. But I am here now."

"You really think you can whip four?" Petey asked.

"I don't believe I will have to," Matt said. "I will break two and the others will see reason. But if need be, we will find out if I can stop four."

"If you knew him you'd take his money and his clothes," Pete said.

"That may be so. But right now all I have is your word on it and that's not ample."

Garrett said, "I will surrender the money to you. What you do with it after, that's not our concern."

Matt nodded.

"You'll return us the wires?" Pete added.

"Yep."

Garrett approached the horse and extended the money and Matt delivered him the plug wires. He watched the four skulk into the darkness and listened as they repaired the engine then started the car, though the motor sputtered as they had not managed the correct firing order.

He unsheathed his work knife and cut the ropes binding Jarms, who, free, built himself and Matt a cigarette each and lit them. They smoked a while in silence.

"They're right," Jarms told him. "You get to know me, you might want to do me worse."

"Well lucky for both of us that's not likely to occur."

Matt tugged the horse in the direction of the car.

"You looking for work, I'm guessing."

Matt halted the horse. One abandoned torch smoldered. A thin flame waned and diesel smoke rose from a blackened rag, which had been secured to an axe handle.

"I got it if you're inclined."

The dog nosed the torch handle. The flame doused against the wet grass. A thread of smoke rose then vanished. Matt turned the horse toward the man.

"Just so you agree. You've been warned," Jarms said.

Matt nodded. "I have been warned."

·14·

Roland Jarms woke to Matt mucking the barn. It was near dawn and he thought the clatter was one of the dairy cows banging the barn latch, anxious to be relieved of her burden. He had to listen longer to recognize the sound as work. He collected his coffee and strolled from his house across the grey yard.

The stranger had already restacked the failing bales that made up the winter-feed and was raking the remains and piling them into the feed bins. The older Jarms enjoyed a smoke and kept his silence. When the stranger finished the bins, he unlatched the barn and steered the milkers to their stalls. Roland tucked himself behind the tool wall as the man and cattle passed. He listened at the gathering of the buckets and the stool and the cisterns, then milk when it splattered the tin.

It had been some time since he'd studied anyone's work other than his own and he welcomed the occasion to. Roland didn't consider himself a more diligent laborer than the next man, or even more efficient, he just supposed he enjoyed the work more. Though he met and married the only woman he'd likely love at North-western University in Chicago, not until he returned her to the ranch and resumed the duties that were in fact more rituals than labors did he feel he'd closed the circle.

Helen saw it differently, he knew. He hoped at first that she would thicken like pine in his country and make her own shape, but came to recognize her form would be grafted to his, his tap-root extended by xylem and phloem to her branches and their leaf or fruit or nut. Over time, however, even that metaphor blanched and it became apparent that her heart was hostage to some other life that he could not imagine, though he waited for its return like any seed he'd planted. However what she endured wasn't a season, it was the country itself and like country, it was endless when stranded amidst it.

He'd hoped family would make a difference. Roland had pulled calves most of his life and figured bringing forth his child would be just one more chore. He met Helen's water breaking with little trepidation. He saw her pain as simple, like that of an animal's.

No doctor was near and even if there had been, snow left the roads impassable. There was not even the comfort of a neighbor woman for her. By the end of the first day, her cries shook him so, that he plugged candle wax in his ears while he saw to her. They didn't speak those hours nor after. Looking back, it seemed to Roland talk between them had lost its consequence. The child would be their conversation, and he longed for it those two nights like he had never longed for anything, not even her in the days of her purity.

When he finally took the baby from her and held her bloody stillness in his hands, he wept. He buried the child alone, on a high place above Rebel Flat Creek. The water ran year long; he vowed she would never hear silence. He chiseled the name Faith so deep into its bark that the tree bled sap from the wound for a year.

Eighteen months later, he did the same, though the child was a boy and the name Elvin.

When Helen told him of her third pregnancy, he bought some timber for a coffin. He'd used scrap to construct the first two and it had since weighed on his conscience. The child arrived easily and like the others was still as a stone. Roland spooned honey and bourbon into Helen until she slept. When her bleeding had slowed, he went to the barn and began the box for the child. He stoked a fire in the potbelly stove and set the baby near it. The air was quite cold and the fire was raging, which made it difficult to keep the baby close enough to warm without scorching it. He found himself breaking from his work continually to adjust the child, then badgering himself for taking the trouble when it would be no better for it.

With the casket finished, he lifted the infant into it. Then, he noticed the child held the fire's warmth even upon the frigid timbers. He watched the steam rise from it. He undid the blankets. The child's ribs fluttered almost imperceptibly and Roland recognized the strings of a breath's vapor over its open mouth.

He touched the baby's cold skin and it stirred. He lifted it from the casket. It was a boy he recalled, though he checked to make certain of the matter. Naming called for more audacity than he or Helen could muster. Still, now it seemed imperative. The only name he struck upon was his own, but he was a junior and had never been comfortable. He recalled an uncle, then spoke his name: Horace.

As soon as the weather was suitable, he bundled the boy into his coat, and together they rode to the cottonwood. Roland thought to begin his formal education that day, and, as they trotted, he expounded on the virtues of summer fallow and putting seed in the ground before the first leaf's turning. But he grew bored with that line of chatter and, instead, took on a story. It turned into Hercules and the twelve labors. Roland was careful to point out that the tale wasn't only concerning a man's muscles. It would wind up the bent all his teaching would follow. He told of the Greeks and the Romans and later, when the boy had memorized those, he traded a winter's worth of straw to a neighbor widow for Malory and Shakespeare's collected plays. It was a mistake, he knew now, filling a child with so many yarns. Horace believed that life itself was only one story following another. It left him no time for working or learning much other than how to spin every day into a yarn.

Roland might have done it differently if he could have. But it had not been in him to. He had recounted the birth in his head daily. At first, he was the hero of the tale, but soon, another version alarmed him. He wondered in his hurry to plant his grief if he'd buried his previous children alive. He'd only found Horace on the boy's own casket floor. His stillness was not unlike the others'; it was in fact like theirs enough for him to take to wood and nails. He summoned from memory as much as he could from each birth but could not recall anything beyond the babies' still bodies. He tried to argue the impossibility of his not recognizing life was in them, but he would remain in his heart unconvinced.

Roland spent so much time with the boy that he and Helen ceased to know one another, and he realized, too, she had ceased to know Horace. He had hogged the boy, taking on the fathering and the mothering, leaving her with something worse than a dead child, one that didn't have much use for her.

She left soon after the boy's third birthday. He and the boy had ridden out to check the stock and they found her absent upon their return, along with her hope chest and the clothes she favored most. Roland saw wagon tracks from a road with many neighbors. It was impossible to know which had colluded with her.

Between cows, the stranger turned and met Roland's gaze with a stone face.

"If you're working off a poker loss, you're free to go," Roland said. "Most everybody knows Horace cheats."

Matt shook his head. "He just said he had work."

"Well, I can see your intent is honest. No one's risen before dawn in this house aside from me in years and even longer to put in a day's labor," Roland said. "If you're in with Horace I have my reservations, however. Most of his friends are shirkers and so is he. He's my son, but he's no friend to sweat."

"I don't know him well enough to say," Matt said.

"We'll see," Roland said. "Come on inside. I suppose I better feed you at least for the morning's milking."

The kitchen window faced east and grew light with the day. Roland hacked two lengths from a rope of German sausage and fried six eggs in the grease. He watched Matt examine the room. The man studied each windowsill and doorjamb, the high cabinet tops and the simple wainscoting. Roland kept no knick-knacks and hung no photos. The walls were scrubbed clean. No bugs dotted the light basins and no cobwebs draped the corners. He was a fastidious man and he inspected Matt like he might a mess that required his attention.

Matt had not spoken, except when answering him. He'd made no attempt at small talk or to ingratiate himself. Most he'd known so scotch with words were sullen and bitter, overall poor company, their quiet as watchful as a deacon's with the same disdain. Scorn, though, didn't seem to be in the way the man carried himself, nor in the manner he sat, slightly bent as if his size were a card he didn't like to play. The whole way he'd put himself together seemed to Roland off center and unfinished.

The dog whined and pawed the screen door.

"That pup a stray?"

The pup glanced like it was inclined to pose a question. "Queenie," Matt told her. "Mind the traps." She disappeared for the barn and his saddle.

"How'd you come to tame her?"

Matt shrugged. "Found her and fed her till she could hunt. Doesn't need nothing from me any longer, guess she just likes company."

"Till she doesn't," Roland said.

Matt shrugged. "Not much different than the rest of us, then."

"No." Roland chuckled. "No I imagine not."

Roland set some day-old biscuits on the table, along with the loaded plates.

"Go ahead," Roland told him. Matt did. Roland fixed his own plate. In a bowl at the table's center was a ball and cup apparatus he'd worked from a stick of soft wood years ago when Horace was small. Matt eyed it through the meal and after and finally reached for the toy. Roland finished, studying the awkward hands flipping and catching. He sighed and shook his head. Here he was seventy and Horace had brought him another child to tend.

⋆ **15** ⋆

IT WAS CLEAR ROLAND JARMS felt morning belonged to him; just as his son lay claim to night and carousing, the old man believed he owned first light and work. The first day Matt had shamed him, and the man woke ten minutes earlier each following until soon it was barely past night when they commenced their labors. Matt slept lightly, and the pup nipped his feet when it saw the house lights lit, then the horses nickered, expecting to be fed, which put Matt in the barn where Roland found him sharpening the scythe or retooling the harnesses. Roland filled two coffee cups from a tin pot. Neither said a word about the hour.

On the whole, this suited Matt fine, as did the man. A yellow notepad remained in Roland's breast pocket except when he paused to scratch a line through a chore, which he categorized on lists titled *dailies, weeklies,* and *seasonals.* Once started, he was liberal with coffee and time to consider what next necessitated their attention. In Matt's experience foremen who headed most crews were little more than workers who'd stuck. Neither better hands nor keener wits than those they bossed, they possessed a narrow view of labor, fixed toward working a man an hour without let-up rather than whether the job he was doing made any sense. It turned men to plodding animals and often left the most important chores incomplete or shoddy. Roland seemed to realize waiting on one end of a job meant not having to rush the other. He didn't speak without a purpose and Matt replied only with a nod unless the work required more detail.

Until noon, the old man accomplished more in an hour than most good hands in a day. He could lug remarkable weights, employing his legs for leverage instead of bulling a load with his back and arms. But after they broke for lunch, he lost steam. He didn't abandon Matt, and, for a time he battled to keep pace, but an hour or so past high sun, he wore down and conceded to supervise, which at first irked Matt—he wasn't accustomed to others inspecting his efforts—though he soon realized the old man was just hankering to participate.

Roland appeared content to live the same day over and over, and working the days with the old man, repeating his repeating, Matt recognized no sadness in his routine, no boredom. Work was praying the same prayer every day, and, as with true believers, it held the calm and certainty of ritual. Roland, though vulnerable to a melancholy spell occasionally, had reconciled those conflicts abundant in a man's conscience. He lingered sometimes several calm minutes over a cleared field or a herd of freshly branded steers, and those moments, Matt understood, were what divided father and son.

Roland never said a word about town and Matt had no interest. They sent a list with Horace, who might get what they needed if he remembered to stop before his card game and whiskey. Those days Jarms forgot, Roland and Matt just toiled at other chores. Jarms's toots typically lasted two days to a week. Matt would notice his horse, hungry and ridden down, before he saw any hint of its rider.

Returning, Jarms slept until afternoon. Evenings he'd wash and shave and deliver them cold beers and half a glass of homemade shine to share while they shelved their tools and hunted what they required the next day. Jarms never drank any himself, in fact did not imbibe at all in the house. He seemed to enjoy watching the old man, though. Roland informed him of the ranch's state: the chores they finished and those that needed their attention. Jarms encouraged him. He enjoyed the discussion of work well enough, as long as he wasn't required to participate.

After a hard rain, though, they required the seed drills straight away. Jarms was two days gone, leaving Matt, finally, to collect them. That night, Matt sat in front of the barn with a bucket of lye and water washing his shirts, when Jarms came to him in the barn.

"You take it easy on him. He tries to keep up by you."

"We don't work past dark," Matt said.

"I'm not talking time, I'm talking what you do in the time."

"I'll keep it in mind."

"Good then." Jarms scuffed the dirt with his boot toe. "Sorry about them drills," he said.

Matt nodded. "Isn't no way to undo it."

"I don't want it undone," Jarms told him. "I want it done with."

Matt hung a wet shirt on a rope strung to dry them. "You find yourself a woman?" he asked.

"I did not," Jarms said. "I ain't shopping, neither. I don't care for them."

Matt said nothing.

"It ain't like that. I just want nothing to do with them otherwise. The boys that tied me up. That was over a woman. Well, it was over me paying the tab at the Chinese restaurant."

"You welch?"

"Nope. Squared the bill in full. That's what made them so hot. They don't believe in paying Chinamen and won't until the law calls and then they only offer half and the deputy tells the Chinese take it or leave it. Well, I got to gabbing with one of them boys and he went on about getting a grandmother and other kin this way from California and I figured our tab would just about foot train fare, so I cashed it out. Then I paid them a thousand dollars for a share in the place. I like their food. That damned Garrett." Jarms shook his head. "He's got more money than the rest of us and is the maddest the Chinese got any at all."

"So what's this got to do with women?" Matt asked.

"They born us, didn't they?" Jarms said.

Matt wasn't inclined to argue and extend the conversation. This did not deter Jarms, who, over the first month of Matt's stay, regaled him with a fog of information that, Matt eventually began to puzzle through. Jarms had come late to town. Roland's books were his studies most of growing up and he figured the ranch's ledgers and taxes for his numbers. For compositions, he penned irate memos to Sears and Roebuck demanding reimbursement for items he'd not purchased. The company sent intermittent checks anyway.

He knew nothing of school until the high grades. The place suited him. He told lies as honestly as most spoke truth and with a good deal more hoots. Teachers thought him backward and wouldn't bend him over for any kind of freshness, requiring only apologies for his ignorance and promises to mend his manners, which were heartfelt and unfelt at the same time. That he could manage both in one sitting was his charm.

Roland enrolled Jarms in the college in Pullman hoping studies would square him to level where he had failed. Horace drank with silver-spoon fraternity brothers and diddled their sisters under frilly sheets. He had no patience for them otherwise; though one, Virginia, a funny drunk, he dated for a semester. She wanted pinned, though, and forsook him for another who would do her the honor.

Being jilted irritated Jarms. He called upon her mother who lived in town and seduced her in the same room he had Virginia, which brought him back to even in his eyes.

Classes, he knew less than the professors and more than the students, who attended university to postpone something Jarms saw no reason to. They bored him enough that finally he purchased Shakespeare's collected, Sandburg's Lincoln, and Milne's Pooh and put his heels to the place.

The years following, he worked and idled and idled and worked and finally only idled. He couldn't say how he'd come to what he was, just that he had. He was not inclined to excuses and not one to crow about his indiscretions, either.

Garrett seemed a black raven circling Jarms's stories, swooping close to chatter before he disappeared, though he seemed to hover always. After his own graduation, Garrett returned to the ranch and, over the next few years, took on much of his father's duties, and, unlike Jarms, embraced the notion of being a rancher. He met a young woman who had traveled from Nebraska to keep house for the Methodist minister's family and, after the appropriate court-ship, married her. He preferred traditions in a manner Jarms recognized but had no map to.

Garrett visited the ranch occasionally. His trimmed beard hairs glistened in the sun and softened his face's sharp lines and pointed chin, but his voice was loaded with more bitterness than Jarms's gibes. The two were sharp-tongued, and they cuffed each other with banter constantly. Jarms was quick, but Garrett bested him at swearing and name-calling, which left it close to a draw. Jarms had a lacking in him, whether it be a mother or just plain empti-ness, and baiting Garrett answered it. When inclined, he'd wrench his neck and tuck his head into one of his shoulders like he was pointing with his chin, then lay a word trap for Garrett, which left him red and stammering.

The tavern gutter dogs, as Roland called them, were steady visitors as well, Petey and the two silent Swedes who turned out to be noted drunks. Petey was pledged to Garrett, but Jarms found Petey's loyalty so funny that he became a running joke. The Swedes remained shuffling hangers-on, enjoying the others like the first row of a circus does a clown nosediving ten feet into a pail.

Near sunset, the sheriff arrived in a Model T that looked to be in fair shape, though, on the rutted road, the frame jostled the cab until his door fell open and nearly spilled him under the wheels. He pulled the brake and hiked the last hundred yards. Roland and Matt patched a feed crib the bull shattered a fall ago. Roland glanced up, then returned to his hammer and nails. Matt stood.

"He knows the way," Roland told him. Roland measured and marked the board for Matt to cut next.

The sheriff was a bean of a man and barely a shadow in the cold winter sun. His badge had torn his pocket stitching and the silver dish faced the ground. He looked a man whose pay alone kept him employed. He eyed the nearly-finished crib. His hand brushed the loose shavings from the rail.

"I come out to talk sense," the sheriff said.

"Well, talk it," Roland told him.

The sheriff sighed and looked toward the house. "I swear, at times I see where he gets it from."

"Surely his mother," Roland said.

"That's what you'd have us believe, Rolly. But the truth roosts a lot closer to home."

Roland dusted his pants.

"He's behind in the card game," the sheriff said.

"You a gambling arbitrator?"

"No," the sheriff said. "I'm just saying what I heard."

Roland nodded.

"They're not fellows you want to owe."

"That all?" Roland asked.

The sheriff nodded and turned for his car. They returned to the crib.

"That pup." Roland nodded at Queen beneath Matt's feet. "She harasses the stock, she'll have to go."

"All right," Matt said.

"I'm serious, dammit."

"She doesn't chase animals except to herd."

Roland nodded and commenced to build himself a cigarette. "You think Horace is a slacker."

Matt shook his head.

"He used to outwork me."

Roland lit his cigarette. Matt didn't reply.

"It turned dull to him," Roland said. "He gets bored too easy. That's his problem. Not the other. Cards, you get a new hand every couple minutes and money changes just as often. Good card player tolerates boredom, lets it saw on others. When the money's right and the cards are right and the players are right, he gambles."

"Horace one of them."

"Nope," Roland said. "Horace is what a good card player counts on. A fellow like him pays steadier than a month of wages."

The old man smoked a little longer, his weathered skin hanging from his face in the orange glow. He ground the butt into his boot heel. He beckoned Matt inside where they ate a meatloaf dinner and made the following day's list.

Finally, Matt returned to the barn. On the hayloft straw, he unrolled his bed. The pup whined and burrowed beneath his arm. It chewed the blanket and Matt batted her nose. The pup gazed at him, eyes flooded with animal figuring, then bedded near his feet, but instead of settling in for the night, it commenced to wrestle with his boot until he was compelled to rap the animal's skull with a coffee cup, which sent it scurrying from the loft to the animals below. So it was an inconvenience to be awakened an hour past to lantern light spilling onto the barn's walls and ceiling. A girl traipsed below him. Her skirt was tired plaid and her legs and bare arms looked sullied and in need of a bath.

"Here's good enough," Jarms told her.

She hiked her skirt and dropped herself on all fours in the dirt. Jarms unhitched his jeans. He hopped to her, his trousers trapped by his boots. She laughed at him. He bent in front to kiss her and she butted his nose with her forehead.

"I told you. My mouth's saved for my husband," she said.

"How do you know I won't marry you?"

"Rich men won't marry me, and they don't kiss me either." She puckered her lips.

"Well, what if I gave you all my money?"

"I wouldn't waste my time with you."

"Most would be thrifty at the other end, darling."

"Every animal in this world bumps uglies," the girl said. "Kissing is the only thing that means something."

"That's just girl wishing," Jarms said, though his voice was quiet and tone tolerant, as if he didn't want to rend the girl's hopes from her.

She took his hand from her face. "I'll wish for what I want to," she said.

"So it's going to be like this?" he asked. "Just one dog doing for another."

"Yes," she told him, and Jarms lifted his leg and pissed on a hay bale.

She laughed and he hopped behind her and plopped his ball sack on her backside, where he dragged his root until it was serviceable.

She didn't cry out with his taking her, just sucked in a lungful of air. Jarms seemed to pay attention to nothing at all, until he found

Matt staring from the loft above. He grinned and played like he had a quirt in one hand and was whacking the girl's haunches.

"Giddyup, there, Pony Express," he shouted. "We gotta deliver the mail."

After, they dressed and he walked her to the barn's door and fired a lantern to light her walk home. Its shadows ebbed and bobbed through the open loft window until it faded to just another part of the night.

⋆**16**⋆

ONE OF THE FEW THINGS Wendy Worden's parents agreed upon was the amount of iron in their oldest daughter's backbone. Her mother thought her impractical and judgmental and averse to any kind of reason once she set her mind. Her father saw her as strong and admired her unwillingness to compromise as much as he despised his own pliable nature. The courtship and its conclusion—the strange gifts from the Lawson boy—had given them both pause, but what followed confounded them completely.

The morning following the shooting, she rapped at the Lawson door. Mrs. Lawson answered.

Mrs. Lawson led her by the elbow inside to the sofa and perched on the cushion beside her.

"Is Matt here?"

"No, he is not." Mrs. Lawson said. "Can I help you at all?"

Wendy nodded. She lifted the ring from the table.

"This came from Matt."

"And you're bringing it back to him." She sighed. "You don't love him."

"He brought me the most wonderful presents. Every day for so long. He didn't speak a word. He just wanted to give me things."

"He never spoke?"

"I never saw him. He hid."

"And you're here now because you've found out."

"Yes," Wendy said. She recounted the rest of it.

"Do you think he's dead?" Mrs. Lawson asked.

Wendy said. "It was a small gun. We found no blood."

"Well," Mrs. Lawson told her. "He's like an animal in a lot of ways. If he's hurt he'll run off."

"You don't care he's gone?" Wendy asked.

"Yes," she said. "I am just not surprised anymore by someone leaving."

"I would have guessed a child would earn his mother's grief," Wendy said.

"And I would have thought a beau deserved better than being shot," Mrs. Lawson said.

Wendy stared at her shoes. "I'm sorry," she said. "I am blunt. It is a failing."

"I have plenty of my own," Mrs. Lawson said. "Thank you for coming. It must have been difficult."

"I'm afraid waiting for him will be just as trying," Wendy said.

"He won't return. I am not that much to him anymore."

"I am." Wendy said.

The next week Wendy arrived in the grocer's wagon, along with her boxed clothes and a tiny dresser drawers that she unpacked in Matt's bedroom, where she settled in to wait. Guilt was behind it, certainly, and perhaps love, too, or as close as the girl could reckon that emotion, but mostly it was the steel arbiter inside her turning her own stern judgment upon herself. Mrs. Lawson recognized the fear in the girl and the misery, too that and the only method she'd conjured to quiet the caterwauling of her conscience was to square it somehow. Shooting him must have been a hard stone to strike upon. Mrs. Lawson had given up dividing the world that way, though, and she was too tired to hurt the girl in the only manner that would heal her. She was an old woman, with a son nearly grown, and faced years alone. Yet here sat the girl. She could not send her away, and here Wendy remained thirteen years later, despite her parents' pleas and her sister's recent marriage, despite fifteen plantings and fifteen harvests, fifteen springs of calving and summers cultivating, and fifteen winters in the small house most waking hours across the room from her.

•

WENDY GAZED INTO AN OPAQUE glass pane that had once been backed with silver paper and served the house as a mirror. Time had undone the glue until only a few strips of herself remained. She appeared clawed, just the line of her lip, two teeth and, above, a sliver of forehead and hair that seemed the consistency of smoke. Last week her anniversary had passed and she entered her sixteenth year on the ranch. She was not sure how many more were left. Her patience had ebbed to a mute desolation, but she would labor here until the old woman passed and likely to her own demise. Despair was her only habit and, like a mill horse, she was trapped by her rut, but knew no other. Progress, however, drew her rein. The Grand Coulee Dam's powerhouses were finished and the river was scheduled to rise for the next pour. The government had purchased any country that would go under and would soon burn the buildings and fell the trees, the Lawson ranch included. A legal-sized envelope arrived a week ago: the address typed and an official icon for a return address, legal documents and a check inside, the first mail in several years to reach the house.

In the kitchen was cake from two nights before. Wendy wet a saucer bottom with milk, and lay a piece on it to soften by the time Mrs. Lawson rose. She set the cake and a coffee cup on the counter, finding her way in the dark and uncorked some shine and half-filled the old woman's cup and her own. Wendy took her eye-opener with cider, while Mrs. Lawson preferred coffee, though she'd been dry for two weeks, after Wendy returned from the field to discover the oven ablaze with a chicken in its own grease and Mrs. Lawson sleeping through it. Wendy stashed the jug in the coat closet, and twelve dry days hunting had sobered Mrs. Lawson mightily.

Wendy lit a lantern in the living room where she alternated between a glass of buttermilk and her fortified cider with one hand and divided an apple with a paring knife with the other. The meal would hold her till supper if she put a few raisins in her pockets. She'd eaten as if it paid her first years on the place. Enormous cuts of beef, whole chickens, and vegetables raw from the garden. When her shirts burst, she began wearing Matt's, which draped past her waist. By the end of that harvest, she could steer horses without jerking and plunge the plow deep enough to furrow and seed the next spring.

After feeding the cattle, Wendy was clammy with perspiration, and she undid her shirt and fanned herself with it until she'd dried enough to tolerate loading the seed bags into the wagon and harnessing the pulling horses, Ebenezer and Uriah, whom she'd renamed on one of her whims. In the Original Eighty, she reined the team and filled the seed bin, then rotated each circular drill until it deposited a treated kernel in the dirt she'd turned two weeks previous. Once she was certain each drill operated properly, she set out. By nine, she rode the drill seat jacketless, lulled near to sleep by the steady turning. The wide coulee remained all shadow, but there was green above and on the water's banks. She was loathe to admit it, but knowing this place, not like a resident or even her merchant father, but as someone who relied on its patterns and whims remained as much solace as she'd likely possess. The day passed quickly, as most had she realized, and evening, she remained lively enough to tighten the cinches that held a loose corral gate.

•

MRS. LAWSON WATCHED WENDY PATCH the gate, then rose from the chair near the window and rattled the moonshine jug from where Wendy had concealed it. She uncorked it and poured herself half a cup of the alcohol.

No meal was in the oven and no sign of one coming, so Wendy found the cake pan in the icebox and carried two plates into the front room.

"This is still my home," Mrs. Lawson told her. "I was here first."

Wendy nodded. Mrs. Lawson lifted her cup. "I'll drink what I like," she said.

Wendy finished her cake. Mrs. Lawson cut a piece from the tray and set it on a second plate. Her finger dabbed the frosting.

"That's just whipped sugar," Wendy told her. "Eat the cake, too." The coals in the stove had ebbed. She added a log. Mrs. Lawson hooked her finger and scooped the icing that remained. "I been swallowing cake all this time just for the little bit on top."

She went into the kitchen and fetched the shine. She filled Wendy's cup, then her own.

"You're doing your contritions," Mrs. Lawson told her.

"What are you talking about?"

"The prayers a person's obliged to say after confession. Hail Marys and Our Fathers."

"I haven't prayed in years," Wendy said.

"Every breath you take is a prayer," Mrs. Lawson said.

Mrs. Lawson peeled the end of the cake frosting while Wendy pulled from her cup and felt the alcohol rise and cover her. She shared the old woman's fondness for it. Drink cropped the edges from pictures and left what she wanted to see. She set her cup on the table and the old woman lifted the shine jar. The old woman filled it once more, her hand trembling not the slightest. She added nothing to cut the alcohol, and the fumes teared Wendy's eyes, but she ducked her mouth to the cup.

"We're going to feel awful tomorrow," Wendy said.

Mrs. Lawson stretched in the light that was left in the room. She had squandered the afternoon considering the coming water. The sky weighed heavy with high clouds, and a person outside this country might see rain in them, but all she recognized was doom. She laughed.

"I already feel awful," she said.

★ 17 ★

THE NEXT AFTERNOON, WENDY RECOGNIZED smoke on the wind. She spotted a grey swell north and wondered if the federals had jumped the chute and started burning houses for the coming dam. She watched the plume double. The smoke blackened, not grain, but seasoned wood burning. Grain made good fuel. With a little wind, fire covered country faster than a horse and rider. You stayed keen for it like a miner watching his canary. She harnessed the team at the barn. Mrs. Lawson emerged from the doorway and perched herself on the bench seat until Wendy finished and pressed the team forward.

They made two miles before the road dropped around a basalt outcropping skirted with shale. Below lay Linda Jefferson's place aflame. After the teacher had grown heavy with child without a proper sire and was two-checked by the city fathers, her students continued to visit. She had been a favorite of the children, more than most realized, and sixteen years past the boys still tied lambs and calves to her porchposts or delivered game salted and cured into her root cellar. Wendy stopped more often than most, as her residence at the Lawson place left them neighbors. They traded novels and, when she noticed a need, Wendy delivered materials from the hardware to patch a roof or caulk a failing window frame. Linda Jefferson asked nothing from anyone and no one doubted she would have soldiered on without such kindnesses.

The house was nearly to the ground by the time Wendy and Mrs. Lawson made the drive to her road. Linda stood near the pump arm, sooty and sweat-stained. She held an emptied bucket. The sixteen-year-old boy next to her looked flushed. The fire had left the house just joists and the door in its brick frame. Linda pushed the pump handle and filled the pail and drank, letting what was left spill and soak her blouse.

From the house came a spitting. Timber jumped and the grass danced.

"Bullets I made," Linda said.

Mrs. Lawson looked at her.

"I learned from a book. There's hundreds down there."

The boy unbuttoned his pants and urinated into a bush.

"My," Mrs. Lawson said. "His pecker is enormous."

"Lucky," Linda said. "Cover yourself."

An explosion tossed three bricks across the yard. One struck the grey in the ribs and he neighed and crowhopped until Mrs. Lawson settled him.

"Do people still live in caves?" Linda asked.

"Not for a long time," Mrs. Lawson said.

The boy lumbered up the hill and sat down in Mrs. Lawson's wagon. His hair was as long as a girl's and his clothes split at the shin and shoulder where he'd grown past them. "Would it be so bad?" Linda asked him, but the boy refused to move.

"Suit yourself," Linda said. "You made this nest, not me."

"What nest?" Mrs. Lawson asked.

"He knows," Linda replied. She mounted the wagon, sat next to the boy and took his hand. He allowed it. Mrs. Lawson drove, breaking the grey into a trot and out of the canyon. When the fire found the bulk of the gunpowder, splintered timber, singed shingles, bricks, and the door whole rose up, then fluttered back to the ground. Ashes rained over them, and heat arrived again in gusts, like strange weather.

•

MRS. LAWSON FOUND THE JUG and uncorked it. She poured two cups and put four kettles on the range for bathing and filled a roasting pan with vegetables and a ham and let them bake. Mrs. Lawson cajoled Linda into the outside tub, a grain trough Wendy had sealed and glued one winter. In the water, Linda's limbs winnowed to muscle and bone; her shoulders and back and ribs secured her to herself, except for her breasts, which were weighty and awkward. Her privates were a tangle, cloaking the cavity under, making it more like something omitted than a mystery. She'd washed her face and her hair and they shone in the sun's setting.

Linda slumped in the tub until her ears were stopped and only her nose was clear of the water. Mrs. Lawson listened to her breaths, then kicked the tub hard enough to make a wave. Linda came up coughing. Mrs. Lawson was already on her way to the house for a fresh jug.

When she returned, Linda was staring at her. "I believe we'll find another to place to stay. If you'll hand me that towel."

"Someplace less contrary?" Mrs. Lawson asked.

Linda nodded.

Mrs. Lawson held the towel in her lap and patted it with both hands. "Most everyone in the county if they find us worth considering at all agree on our peculiarities."

"It's been a good while since I've considered other people's considerings," Linda said.

Mrs. Lawson said, "It's high time to."

"What makes you think so?"

"You're not living in a cave," Mrs. Lawson told her. "The government is damming downriver. There's going to be nothing but water over this country."

She offered Linda the towel, who took it and dried herself. She led Linda to the house and helped her into some of her own clothes. After, she poured some shine into a glass. Linda sipped at it.

"Wendy will be disappointed," Mrs. Lawson said.

"Why?" Linda asked.

Mrs. Lawson tapped her cup with her finger. "I've corrupted you."

•

THE BOY FOLLOWED WENDY TO the barn. Wendy occasionally encountered Lucky and his mother when her duties left her on the north end of the ranch, returning from a hunt. Once, in a travois Linda had constructed they dragged two deer hindquarters, a tattered badger, and coyote pelts, from which Linda made blankets rough as cobs. The boy was toting birds of all kinds, half-plucked, and a dog they'd found hit by a car. Wendy had offered to retrieve the wagon. They declined.

Finished putting up the horses, Wendy filled two dinner plates and returned to the barn. The boy ate delicately as a coon, though he was obviously famished. When he finished, Wendy fed him what was left of her meal and refilled his plate. The weather was cool enough for frost, but afterwards he made his way into the bathtub, still filled with water, and undressed. He was short and stout as a tree stump and bowlegged, each buttock square as the rest of him, and above his back muscles creased his skin as he let himself into the lukewarm water.

Wendy entered the house and rummaged the drawers until she found trousers, a plaid shirt, and a T-shirt. Matt's old underwear were in a box, unused, the only thing of his she would not wear. She set the outfit on a fence railing near the bathtub, along with a fresh towel.

Lucky rose from the tub, the beginning of a chest over his ribs and a ropey stomach and his conspicuous organ between his thighs. The boy dried himself and dressed slowly, admiring the feel of each fresh garment.

"By God," he said.

He held out his arm and admired the T-shirt covering his shoulder. Dressed, he preened across the yard, his hair dripping. He wrung it with his hands.

"You need that cut," Wendy said.

He stood in the yard, motionless. His head turned toward the house.

"Your mother would mind?"

The boy shrugged. "She never said," he replied hopefully.

"Well, then she must not," Wendy told him.

She found the shears in the barn as well as a lantern, a handful of wagon grease, and a currycomb. In the corner was a fresh pan she used for feeding the cats. She set the lantern on the post and gave the boy the pan and told him to watch. She took his hair off like trimming a horse's mane and it fell in fistfuls around a tall bucket he'd picked for a seat. With each rasp of the sheers he grinned, until he was giggling.

His hair was coarse and pleasant feeling, and when she cut it close enough, she combed it with her hands to see if the length was uniform. She put a little grease in it to train a cowlick, and when she finished he looked like any other boy might.

In an hour, the lights in the house went out, and an hour after that, the lantern burned down. Wendy loaded it with fresh oil and relit it and walked the boy into the house where the women had built him a pallet in the front room. With the boy content, she turned in, but she slept hot, and later rose for some air. On the porch, the boy was once again staring at himself with the frying pan lid, the lantern burning the last of its oil, his pants undone, and his free hand tending his erect self like a wound.

∗ 18 ∗

THE FIRST WEEK IN DECEMBER, a month into Matt's second year at the ranch, the sky turned a dark hunk of ice that weighed upon the whole country. Mornings, it was thirty below, the land white and still. Before dawn, Matt constructed fires under the metal troughs—halved barrels—and filled them with snow. He'd busted the creek open with an axe the first three days, but the third, instead of water, all he found was bottom. The cows bellowed from thirst but weren't interested in making even the short trip to their trough. They locked their legs against the cold when he hauled the doors open, and he finally saddled a hardy gelding and dragged the cattle one by one to their water. Each kicked snow over the fires while it was drinking, and he'd have to coax the coals back and add wood.

The chore consumed two hours. Matt's hands, even in lined gloves, couldn't feel the rope by the end of it. He had stirred the last of the cows and watched the steam rise from their backs and wished he could cut one open and dip himself into its warm blood. Milking the heifers should've been out of the question, but he'd discovered the second morning an udder heavy with ice. He examined the others; all were near frostbit from lactating. On the barn stove, he set a pot to heat and dipped his hands into it for as long as he could tolerate, then massaged each tit until he'd drawn it dry. He drove the animals into a manger and forked straw until it covered their udders. After, he covered their backs with wool riding blankets he'd warmed on the stove. Their eyes watered as their tear ducts unthawed and they complained, but they owned enough wits to remain still.

Once he'd tended the animals, he stoked his own fire and watched it blaze. Matt loaded the wood crib and busted kindling for the house while smoke climbed in columns from the chimney into the cold, cold sky.

When the wood grew scarce, Roland directed Matt to a rotted poplar and Matt felled it while Roland watched. The work was the kind Matt favored, muscle and bone, and if you did it properly, you shook thinking altogether and considered only the next blow. When the tree creaked and finally dropped, showering the yard with bark and limbs, he limbed it and cut the trunk into rounds then put diesel to branches and boughs and perched on a fence rail to watch the wood catch and light. The tree burned into the twilight, and Roland sat next to him, content, too, to watch it. Matt was cold and part of him hankered for another chore, but a bigger part was satisfied to sit and gaze at the coals that had started to glisten.

Roland said, "I'll stir a meal up."

Matt nodded and returned to the dying embers, seeing in them faces and objects of all kinds. He looked up occasionally to the white smoke that climbed the bruised sky. It occupied him until Roland brought plates of warmed pork and gravy. They each sat on the ground and took their meals. After, Roland offered him a cigarette and they smoked. What the man was thinking Matt had no inkling. Perhaps he was happy because he wasn't thinking, just seeing. He seemed, like his son, to be a man comfortable. Smiling didn't come so natural to most.

"Nothing like a fire," Roland said.

Matt nodded.

"Not everyone enjoys such simplicities."

"Not everyone's been cold," Matt said.

Roland set out three wool blankets and Matt was grateful for them once he returned to the barn, whose walls were constructed to keep predators out and stock and fodder in; weather wasn't a consideration. Matt stocked the stove with enough wood he worried he'd throttled the flue and was still required to curl himself around the furnace mouth with the dog in the crook between. Even the skittish cats risked cover for light and warmth. The cold required him to rotate position every few minutes like a cook might turn a hog on a spit.

"You awake?" Jarms offered Matt a bottle. Matt's eyes were open, so the question didn't require an answer. Matt shoved the bottle with his hand, but it remained and he finally opened it and drank. It was ice cold and full of fresh grape juice.

"The old man buys this from the grocer and keeps it under some rocks up in Rebel Flat Creek." Jarms rubbed his hands together and put them toward the stove.

"You still live out there in the weather?"

"I've not been in a house to live since I don't remember," Matt told him. "I doubt I'd take to it."

"It's a big place."

"It don't belong to me," Matt said.

Jarms lit a cigarette and smoked a minute.

"All you're going to do is sleep in a room for Christ's sake. You don't need a deed for that."

"Deed isn't the point."

Jarms inhaled and Matt drank more of the juice. The dog burrowed under his arm for warmth.

"You are a stubborn bastard," Jarms said.

"I imagine so." Matt shifted to allow the dog more purchase.

"Old man was ranting about all the work you got to today without freezing solid," Jarms said. "I wish I liked work better, because he favors it so much," Jarms said. "It'd be dishonest to pretend, though."

"Work's dishonest?" Matt asked.

Jarms shook his head. "Pretending."

"You pretending to like that girl the other night?" Only on the last few, coldest nights had Jarms left off the scraggly waif. Otherwise, they locked plumbing steady as stink follows scat.

"You seen that, eh?" Jarms laughed. "That's honest work."

Matt laughed.

"You think I'm fibbing?"

"That girl, she working, too?"

"Making rent for her whole family. They're squatting in the old house, the other side of the ranch. I sent a steer home with her, too."

Matt let that sit. Hard times might mean a girl giving herself up for a roof and meals.

"Sounds like her work."

"That work doesn't get done by one."

"If it's work it does."

"I ain't talking about fucking," Jarms said. "That's a damned sin."

"What was I watching, then?"

"You was watching the bible. Fucking's only supposed to be allowed for one thing, making a baby," Jarms said.

"You're lying," Matt said.

"Which part?"

"That last for sure. Some of the other, too, but I can't pick it clean."

Jarms shook his head. Jarms being born had busted Roland from his mother, Jarms told him, then his growing up left him without a child to boot. It was all he could think to do to square himself with his father. The girl would get a thousand dollars and Roland would get the child.

"As for the rest, I can't tell lie from truth. I can only say I ain't making it up."

Matt finished the juice and rolled the bottle across the dirt toward Jarms, who ignored it. "How come he didn't have more than you if he likes babies so much."

"Did," Jarms told him. "I was all that lived. He was a good father, too. I got watered and fed and cared for like I was in a garden. I just grew funny, I guess. He don't have much use for me."

"He likes you fine," Matt said.

"Nope. He loves me. That's not the same thing."

"He enjoys your company. I can see that."

Jarms sat for a moment. He permitted the idea to settle upon him. It was strange to Matt that Jarms spent so much time talking, when silence was what suited him best.

"I'll tell you something," Jarms said. "I envy them other babies. They never hurt him except when they died and that's easy to forgive." Jarms was right. The living sooner than later disappointed you. He waited for Jarms to speak, but Jarms was in no hurry. Matt had come across more than a few who took to conversation as keenly as Jarms did, and some that stuck to quiet as much as himself. They were all one kind or another, though. The quiet ones found means to mute talk or simply avoided words altogether and the people who made them. Talkers had the same tactics though opposing ends. They either hammered silence with jabber, or left it for noise. There were some in between, of course, but Jarms was not one of them. A man betwixt both was neither, and couldn't carry words or quiet with any comfort. Jarms was able to manage both.

"When my father and brother died," Matt said, "it was cold."

"Colder than this?"

"Colder than I'd ever been."

"I didn't know you lost them."

"I was only fourteen or so."

"Maybe reason to try inside a house."

"Or reason not to," Matt said.

"You miss them?" Jarms asked.

"I don't recall their looks," he said. It seemed to Matt a poor answer.

•

THE FIRST DAY OF FEBRUARY, the weather turned. The temperature remained at freezing but was no longer a danger, just inconvenient. Jarms returned to his project with the girl. Roland, cooped up for a month, demanded a respite from the house and some work with the cattle. Matt accompanied him for the task, but Roland's horse missed a step in a dry creek and rolled up on him. Roland's femur cracked louder than a gunshot. The horse screamed and danced, its forelock, too, broken and dangling. Roland ordered Matt to do for it before tending him. Matt ended the horse with his pistol. The animal wheezed twice, shuddered and expired. Roland had clamped his lip between his teeth and it bled, purpling his mouth. Matt sliced open his trousers. Roland's knee was catawampus, cap facing the sky, even though Roland lay tipped on his side.

"Am I bleeding?"

Swelling had doubled the knee's size faster than bone or gristle breaking. "Inside," Matt said.

Matt lugged Roland to his horse, shocked how little he weighed. Roland nodded north toward a horse doctor a creek away. Matt's horse tried to maintain a level lope, but each step sucked breath from Roland, and after a mile, moans. They both agreed a gallop would abridge the misery, but, reaching the horse doctor, he had gone quiet. Matt worried he'd died.

The doctor loaded laudanum into Roland until he slipped off. The man twisted the leg and aligned the bones then fashioned a splint and cast the apparatus with tape and plaster. He fingered Roland's pulse and pulled open an eye and pressed the stethoscope to his chest, looked at his watch, and did it again.

"You like work?" he asked Matt.

"I can pull my share."

"Good," the doctor said. "Because he's done with it."

"I seen men mend after worse."

The doctor gazed at Roland, who dozed still with the narcotic. "When the older ones get bunged up, I check them thoroughly. It's the only time I see most unless I'm pronouncing for the county." He tapped Roland's chest. "His heart's congested."

"He never mentioned nothing."

The doctor said, "He isn't the mentioning type, is he?"

The doctor fished through his cabinet for some pills. "This isn't a cure," he said. "All it'll do is keep off his dying if he takes one in time."

"You don't have nothing else better."

"This is it. Period," the doctor said. "He's got a son and a hired man. That ought to be plenty. Tell the boy to start eating honestly."

•

ON THE PORCH AT THE house, Matt boosted a bed frame with shortened two-by-fours. He strapped plyboard under the head and mounted a pulleyed come-along on the porch ceiling to raise the whole thing so Roland could watch the ranch's business.

When he woke, Matt handed him the nitroglycerine.

"The doctor said if your chest aches take one of these."

"A long way from my leg," Roland said.

"The other thing's wronger than your leg," Matt told him.

Roland nodded.

"Don't forget."

"Something a man's not likely to, is it?"

Matt warmed a ham portion in a pan. Roland's hands shook with the painkiller. He couldn't direct the silverware from the plate to his mouth. Finally, Matt loaded a fork to feed him. Roland glared at him and knocked the fork to the floor; he resorted to his hands, chewing a ham end and collecting gravy with bread slices.

Jarms returned in the middle of their meal.

"What in hell happened?"

"We were tending the cattle," Matt said. "His horse fell on him."

"I thought the cattle was your job," Jarms said.

Roland set his dinner plate down. "We were working," he said. "You got no say in work."

Matt loaded Jarms a plate and one for himself. They ate in silence, then played some hands of cribbage until the old man began to doze. The night was mild, but Jarms collected a pair of heavy blankets and put them over Roland.

"He's dying," Matt told him.

"It don't take a mean lie to get me to apologize," Jarms said.

"I'm not lying."

"He'll limp is all."

"His heart's filling. The doctor found it when he checked the other."

Jarms squinted like his head ached. He tapped his father's arm with two fingers. The old man's eyes fluttered.

"If he doesn't require those blankets, you can roll them off when I leave." He stood for a minute. "If he gets cold, though, leave them."

Matt nodded.

"I don't want him chilling."

"Me neither," Matt said.

"Well, we're agreed, then," Jarms said.

Evenings, as winter backed off, Matt and Roland took their meal on the porch. They discussed the past day's work and prepared for the one to follow. Matt listened to the man's chest rattle and considered it against his own breathing. He wondered at the motor that living was, fueled more by will than food or drink.

Thirty-two days Roland remained on his back, then reclined, then hobbled. Gimpy and afoot, he pined for horseback until Matt allowed it. Saddled and aboard his mount, Maynard, he rode directly to the thin creek they called Rebel Flat. Matt trailed to mind him. Halting at the tree, Roland hobbled the horse and cripped to the bank. Water barely dampened the pebbles. It would be a short crop without spring rain.

Roland whacked the creek bed with his cane. He sweated through his shirt collar, though it was still morning. Matt watched him stroke the names and dates carved into the tree and unscabbard his buck knife and freshen them. The effort exhausted him. The doctor knew more than horses. Roland was not long for this world.

★ 19 ★

TWO WEEKS LATER, MATT MENDED fence on the property adjacent to the Garrett place. Midday, Queenie approached, her hip catawompus, dragging a hind leg. A bullet had shattered her back quarters. Blood matted the short hair where it entered. He lay her across his saddlehorn and hurried for the ranch. At the barn, he put her under with horse dope, then sharpened a long knife on a whetstone and parted her hide. The sinew and muscle required sawing. Matt worried he'd cripple her further.

"What happened to the queen?" Jarms asked.

"Someone shot her," Matt said.

"You sure?" Jarms asked.

"Look for yourself."

Jarms did.

"Where'd this occur?"

"That knob with the high tree. I was stapling some bad fence."

"Back by Chesik Road."

Matt nodded.

"Goddamnit," Jarms said. "I'm sorry."

"You didn't shoot her," Matt told him.

Jarms approached the dog and patted her head. "I can still be sorry," he said. He tugged one eye open. The milky underside of the lid clouded half the iris. "You patch her up?"

Matt shook his head. "I'm no surgeon. The bullet's still there. I hate to cut her up."

They both stood, studying the animal's breathing.

"Old man's got an encyclopedia. Might have dog anatomy pictures."

"You think we could sort muscle from tendon and gristle and nerves and veins and arteries following those pictures?" Matt asked.

"No," Jarms said. "I do not."

"Me neither," Matt told him.

Jarms considered the matter. "We can't just see how she heals?"

"Leg or rib, maybe. Not with a hip. She'd be bait for anything hungry."

"Well, we're not going to shoot her."

"Might not have a choice," Matt said. "I'd hate to."

Jarms shook his head. "No, we'll take her to the horse doc. He put Roland back together. Well, mostly."

"He know dogs?"

"Got to be better than you and me and a goddamn book."

Matt lifted the dog, which breathed faintly, still lost to the anesthetic, and seated himself in the car's backseat. He laid the dog on the seat next to him. Her head rose a bit and she sniffed herself and tried to comprehend her predicament. He put her head into his lap and she lay still.

The vet owned several hunting dogs, as it turned out, and possessed a soft spot for the animals. He separated meat from bone and found the bullet splattered against Queen's hip coupling. He set the bone best as he could with wire and staples then doused the wound with alcohol. After, he found his sewing kit and a needle and sewed the wound shut with catgut.

In the car Jarms headed them south beyond the ranch.

"You missed a turn."

"You and that dog have earned a damned holiday."

In the backseat, Matt saw fishing gear, a rifle, a bait can, and a skillet along with bedrolls for both of them. The car turned and turned again, before it intersected the Walla Walla road. Outside, the parabolic hills surrendered to grades too steep to farm. The canyon narrowed until the sky stayed only a dim track above each edge. Cattle clung to the steep sides standing or sleeping in the warm evening. The pastures stank. The car passed the lights of a single ranch house and a long barn shadow. At the bottom, the ground turned rocky and the Snake River sliced through, flickering back the sun's glow.

The ferry cut the river water like a trowel. The crossing took ten minutes. Jarms aimed the Mercury through the draw and it hauled them from the valley into the next, a gentler valley, green with wheat and barley shot through the worked earth below. They ascended again and climbed a reach of switchbacked roads. Pavement gave way to gravel, which gave way to dirt logging tracks. They saw gutted rigs, decomposed in the long winters, and solitary houses constructed from what people could salvage from the chuck. As it grew night, starlight filled the sky so that it appeared a new heaven. The road became treacherous enough to demand Jarms's full attention and even he quieted. Matt slipped into a dreamless sleep and woke near first light, still in the car, high up. The bright air had thinned and cooled. The light knew no slant. It threaded through the trees and seemed to puddle on the ground. Grey snow still dotted the lee sides of the hills.

Matt packed the dog into the dewed grasses. She made water propped against a pine. The Tuocannon River stirred near. An old trail was spotty, but Matt sorted a way to the gravel bank. He hauled the dog to his chest and stepped into the high currents. There, he unbandaged and bathed the wound. The dressing smelled clean. Nothing green or yellow oozed through his stitches. She whimpered, but drank when he cupped his hands for her.

Matt re-bandaged her on the gravel bank. He laid her in a sandy stretch to catch the sun. He rolled a cigarette and smoked then put his clothes on a rock and waded deeper. Hurried with runoff, the current nearly lifted him from his feet. It rippled his chest and calmed in the pit of his back like he was only a new stone to be worn into grit. He ached like a bad tooth, but remained. Most everything concerned with home he'd willed from his mind. Water, though, returned it. Drying on the bank, he tossed in pine straw blades one by one and watched them ride the surface before they disappeared or lost themselves in the sun's reflection.

"You want to fish?" Jarms asked him. He showed him the rigged poles. Matt dressed and followed, pausing to turn some earth with a fire shovel and collect worms in a tin can. Upriver he had backed into knee-deep scrub against the water to allow himself to drop his line behind a downed cedar. On a willow switch was a fourteen-inch German Brown strung by the gills.

Matt hunted a place removed enough from Jarms to avoid pressing his hole. A piece of basalt had given way a hundred yards up. He stood on the stacked rocks and baited his hook and attached the weight high enough to drop the worm under without it dragging the bottom. He looped the line into the bend and shallows or puckers where a fish might tarry, but found no luck.

An hour later Jarms shouted, "Turn that rock over."

Underneath, Matt poked at what looked like a cocoon constructed from pebbles. A spidery creature emerged.

"Good bait."

Matt split the crusty insect on his hook. His third cast drew a strike, and after two more, he landed a fair-sized trout then another. He held up the largest, a two pounder, for Jarms to see. Jarms pawed the air, dismissing him. Jarms cast upriver and reeled. The sun bounced on the water and flickered his greened shadow between rows of white light. His eyes were slits, his face clenched, but not like those angry, fisted faces he was accustomed to. This one was simply looking close.

They squandered the afternoon, till the sun spread itself upon the pine and west mountains' edges. At the camp's fire Jarms sat astraddle a peachbox and fried headless trout in a skillet. The hot iron hissed and the fish skin gilded then blackened. The dog's head lay in Matt's lap, eating the skin and meat he fed her.

"Had cats when I was little," Jarms said. "They liked fish fine. Never seen a dog take to it."

"It's the salt," Matt said.

"That animal all you've got for kin? Aside from those passed, I mean."

"I've got a mother may still be alive. She's on the ranch."

"You've got a ranch and you're hiring out here."

"The family's ranch."

"Aren't you family?"

"Only by blood."

Jarms laughed. "There's a middle missing in that story. All I see is a tail and some legs."

"A girl shot me."

"On purpose?"

"The gun was pointed my direction and I wasn't but five feet away."

"You commit some kind of crime?"

"Probably," Matt said. "I wanted to marry her."

"Well unless she was wed already, you should be legal."

"Maybe so," Matt said. "Bullet was just letting me down easy."

Jarms laughed and so did Matt. They began eating the rest of their catch.

"Woman really shot you?

Matt untucked his shirt and showed him the wound.

Jarms said. "That's a rough parting."

"She's probably married with a brood by now," Matt said.

They were quiet a while. The dog's ears pitched when the coyotes began their nightly chatter. A couple of owls occasionally answered and the crickets sawed without let-up.

"You still working on your baby?"

"I am," Jarms replied.

"Even with Roland the way he is?"

"Roland ain't so bad he won't enjoy a child." Jarms paused to fork a bite of trout and separate the bones. "I didn't think it would require so much time to make a baby, though. Way they warn you about it when you're a pup, you'd think each time you matched plumbing with someone a baby would come."

"I wouldn't know anything about it," Matt said.

The next day, the car unwound the breaks from the Snake to the ranch. Water under the ferry, spanked a little by the wind, turned another shade of dark than the trees or the night. The Mercury lifted them from the canyon to the softer hills above and finally toward Jarms's own country. The old man was ready for shut-eye and his own sack, but Jarms insisted on treating Matt to a restaurant meal. The dog would keep in the car.

"I got no money," Matt said. He kept it in Roland's house safe. Matt would've settled for a tally on the notepad, but Roland insisted on counting the bills out to him every month and allowing Matt to place them in the vault.

"You don't need any," Jarms replied.

Matt gazed into the car's side window. It had been years since he'd seen his own face. Flashes of a likeness appeared when he doused himself in the trough, but all he really recalled was the blunt shape of his head.

"They favor you?" Jarms asked.

"One was my twin."

"You know what he'd looked like, at least," Jarms replied.

Matt closed his eyes and squinted into the sun lifting from the bottom horizon. Living alone had left him intuition like a woman. Sometimes it served him well. Others it hardly mattered. Some futures were already put down and he couldn't guess them gone.

"You'll likely be the one finding old Roland when he goes."

"It's not the finding that matters," Matt said.

The road turned onto another on which the county had laid gravel. Jarms hit the throttle and let the engine whine. They opened the windows and the air rushed past, ruffling their hair and tearing Matt's eyes. His chest filled with it. He could see why driving attracted Jarms. It was faster than riding and a sight less wear on a person's backside and, with the window open, you still knew you were covering country. Matt missed seeing it up close, though. The outside seemed like what he couldn't remember. He wondered if Jarms saw it this way, too, and if his driving was a trick to avoid recollection.

They could see Colfax in the canyon below. A few lights burned in the houses below in the canyon's shade. The dog slept in the backseat. Jarms brought a whiskey bottle from under the seat. He drank and sighed and offered it to Matt. The alcohol warmed him and turned the dwindling light yellow and lazy.

"I been gone two days," Jarms said. "You think they'll still know me?"

"I believe so," Matt said.

"I need a reason to stay out."

"How about to help at the ranch."

"Hell, you do more when I'm not around than when I am."

"Tending Roland, then."

"That will just aggravate the both of us." Jarms grinned. "You know, I don't like town any more than you or the old man," he said. "It's just that it likes me so much and I flatter easy."

The town was lighting up with the evening. Cars clattered the street, though horses still outnumbered them. The whiskey made Matt thoughtful. He wondered what it ought to feel like to be his own age, or even Roland's. It surprised him to be considering such things. He had encountered those who lived young to fend years off, and claimed they never contemplated age, though if their conduct was evidence they considered it without end. Matt avoided the subject for a simpler reason. He'd figured on dying. And now that he hadn't, he pondered how one went about growing old. It seemed a worthy aspiration, aging. He'd done so little properly, it might fit him when the time came. Jarms lit a cigarette.

"I heard your cards aren't good," Matt said.

Jarms laughed. "Cards turn around."

Jarms smoked his cigarette, then rolled and lit a second. He smoked like he drank and like Matt imagined he played poker, as if a clock ticked at his mind, faster with each stroke.

They took a meal inside a beef and taters place along with two pints of ale.

Jarms squared the bill. "I believe I'll see a hand or two," he said. "Care to join me?"

"I doubt I could muster an ante."

"You could sit at another table," Jarms said. "No rule against watching. No advantage. There will be plenty of whiskey. I haven't yet seen you drunk. Might be more entertaining than an inside straight."

They crossed the cobbled road and entered a room behind the butcher's shop. Matt hunted a chair out of the main table's orange light. The players' faces appeared brown and their wrinkles were exaggerated under it. Shadows and brows dark hooded their eyes.

Jarms sat next to a man Matt would later discover who had

earned his fortune smuggling Canadian whiskey from the Columbia River into the Snake and farm counties bordering it. He exchanged the money in Jarms's wallet for chips from his own significant stack. No one spoke of his debt to the players at the table. Matt wondered if such conversation was unseemly. Poker here required manners, it appeared. Another player lit a cigar from a bundle and passed the others. Jarms chewed an end, then smoked. The table turned hazy and sleep was closing over Matt, the voices and the chip clack and the rattle of the cards like water's rhythmic rock or the give and take of air in the lungs of the men.

A whiskey bottle arrived at Matt's table along with a glass. Matt sipped it and felt the cloud that hung upon the game envelop him, as well. A smell like stale blankets entered the room and a congested sensation in his heart seemed a little like he imagined dying might until his pulse returned to itself, matching the beat of the card game. Bets and chips followed, lights pulsed at the same tempo, the smoke some other beatless music that matched the hum in his head. He nodded and listened and opened his eyes and studied the bourbon still pitching back and forth in a short glass. Light played on the fluid arcs as they rose; the force had ebbed too much to produce a wave or a crest, so he shook the bottle violently and studied the bourbon, which foamed and pitched and tinked, and settled once more. Matt set the bottle down and drank from the glass. Smoke from the table climbed over him and he contemplated himself within it; no self at all, an existence by absence, like a decayed tooth pliered from a gum. Once that laudanum lapsed and the thorny molar or bicuspid rattled in a barber tray, the others may perform their duties steadfastly, the hole is what aches when the wind whistles through. Solitude, that altar at which the dimestore novelists and moving picture heroes genuflected, held no cross, no chalice, no smoldering incense, no priest; the sanctuary no pews, nor hymnals, nor choir to sing them; no priest led the congregation, no sermons, no holy book to quote. The sanctuary, in fact, contained nothing, as was appropriate.

Garrett appeared at the table. Jarms nodded at him. "Dog killer," he said.

The others glanced up.

"He kills dogs," Jarms told them. "People's pets. Maybe he'll have the nerve to try a coyote one day."

"That's an unusual manner to address your benefactor," the old bootlegger said.

"Garrett hasn't done anyone a favor he couldn't cash ever."

"Paid your markers," the bootlegger replied.

Jarms glanced at Garrett. "You hadn't ought to have done that," Jarms said. The cards passed and Jarms quickly folded. He said, "You ain't ever going to own me. Hard as you try, you son of a bitch."

"If I'm a son of a bitch, who's your mother?"

"My mother is a she-wolf."

"She was a woman just like ordinary. She bore you and left."

"Must have been a Cassandra," Jarms said.

"I know this county," Garrett said. "Greek don't seem much worth to me. Your mother, I know her, too."

"My condolences," Jarms said. He lifted a set of cards and matched the opener. Matt lit a cigarette, hoping to herd every thought to his mind's edges. At the game, chips clacked like plates in a kitchen and Jarms opened a hand with a fifty-dollar bet. Three players called. Two drew two cards, another one. Jarms didn't take any. He raised two hundred. The players glanced at him over the fan of their cards. Jarms closed his hand and placed it face down on the table. The bootlegger raised him a hundred. Jarms countered with a hundred dollar raise of his own, which the bootlegger bumped two hundred. Jarms, at the end of his stack, called.

The bootlegger held three kings, Jarms a straight. The bootlegger pushed the pot Jarms's direction and Jarms stacked the chips in colors; when one column became untenable, he started another. The next hand he won as well, with three nines, and before too long pulled another pot without a call.

Garrett rose but Jarms stopped him. "You do something like shooting that dog again and I'll kill you." Garrett stared at him. Jarms said, "I'll plan it careful as a jailbreak and you will be no more and everything you know will be no more. What you own will still be here. But you won't own it and you won't know who owns it. Because you will be dead. I ain't woofin'." It was clear to Matt he wasn't and to Garrett, as well.

"I believe the subject was your mother," Garrett said. "I'm not a barking dog either."

"Well fight or deal," the bootlegger said. Jarms shuffled the cards and Garrett exited offering no more reply.

Jarms won two more hands in the next half an hour. Matt watched him shuffle the cards lengthwise then the other way, the cards intertwining like fingers, one over the other. He passed the cards across the apron and listened to the bets, calling without much regard to his own hand and asked no cards to draw. He bet fifty dollars and was upped and in return bumped the bet two hundred and the table folded. This time, before hooking in his winnings, he lay his cards face up. He had not even a pair. The next fellow shuffled the cards, but the play insulted everyone at the table. A man with the wind behind him ought to travel quiet, but Jarms was not the kind to permit a successful bluff to go unappreciated, no matter what it cost him. It was less arrogance than the emptiness in a joke absent the punch line.

The next hand Jarms lost with a low pair and the next with one shy of a flush. Two later, he check-raised into a ten-high straight, smiling all the while. He was not playing like a man bored or one with no ken for the game. He apprehended the cards and each player's nature as well as anyone at the table. Matt realized it wasn't money or entertainment he pursued, it was self-annihilation. It came to him that the man had been bent on such a course since they'd encountered one another and was too generous to be humane about it. Maybe with Roland's health declining, Jarms was free to take broader strokes in drawing his own blood.

He pondered it for what seemed like an hour, until he smelled smoke and saw an orange flick bounce in the window glass. Outside, he rounded a corner to Main Street. Flames piled from the Chinese restaurant. A Chinese boy outside clanged two pans together. Two women lugged water buckets from a trough. The fire had overrun the parlor and kitchen. The tables glimmered, cloths curling over them. The Chinese spoke their rattle. They'd bailed the trough nearly dry.

In a top window where bedrooms were, a shadow passed and passed again. The fire had left the back stairs heaped on the ground. In a shed, a bucket of sixteen penny nails and a hammer hung on a nail. Around front was a porch column and Matt pounded a nail into it as a step and drove another for a handhold. He grasped the eave. Heat had slickened the shingles, but he pulled himself up and steadied his feet. Something thumped him from behind. It was Jarms.

"What're you doing?" Matt asked him.

"Putting you out."

They flattened Jarms's coat over the window and cleared the glass. Smoke boiled out the opening. Matt broke the way, Jarms, behind. They knocked through two rooms before discovering an old man huddled in a closet, holding a boxload of photographs and letters.

Matt piled the man's keepsakes into a pillowcase. He headed them all the same direction as the flames. They would be drawing to the broken window. Matt could smell his jacket burn. He shoved Jarms through the broken glass, then the Chinese. He and the memorabilia tumbled across the edge and disappeared. Outside, the cool darkness looked like good water, and Matt wanted to soak himself in it. Faces stared up at him. Matt stepped onto the shingles. They were slick as melting ice and he tumbled off the roof and ended up on the ground on all fours. Burning scraps rained upon him. His back smoldered; his hands had lost their hair.

A fire engine had arrived and soaked Matt with a hose. The water both hurt and soothed him. He bent and began peeling his smoldering boot leather. The pictures lay in the children's laps. They examined the grain images and letters that looked like smaller pictures. Their grandfather coughed and spat and the Chinese women attempted to slake his thirst by ladling water into his mouth.

Later the town's doctor arrived. He covered Matt with bag balm and wrapped gauze around his bare feet.

"Change it every day for two weeks or it'll infect. He'll howl like an Indian," the doctor warned.

"I don't guess he will," Jarms told him. "He never complained while it was happening."

Jarms managed a whiskey bottle and made Matt swallow some before he got into the car. They passed the smoldering fire and the firemen letting it. Matt lay in the seat as they climbed out of the ravine that held the town. Above, the hills stretched and rose and fell and the road was just a gravel line dividing them.

Matt drank and drank again when Jarms failed to retrieve the bottle. He broke a sweat and shivered until he couldn't stop himself.

"Garrett, he was there," Matt said.

"There, hell, he lit the damned place," Jarms said. The dashlight made him green. They rode awhile in the quiet. "He knows I got a stake in the place, but that's not the real reason. He's like a dragon in old stories. He tears things up just by being."

"How come you tolerate him?"

"I'm sentimental concerning dragons."

Matt said nothing more, feeling mostly fear himself, more even than pain. Jarms saw it, Matt knew, and Matt was amazed that the man's vision into the world had won him so little, aside from good cheer. Jarms opened his hand for the bottle. He drove into the night, letting Matt doze until they hit houselights.

Stopped, Jarms eased Matt from the car and led him toward the barn.

"This ain't home?" Matt whispered.

"Stay still," Jarms said. He undid Matt's belt buckle and unbuttoned his drawers.

"Roll," Jarms said. He pushed Matt to one side, then the other until he'd dragged his drawers to his knees. He retrieved the girl from the house. She bent to inspect Matt's nakedness.

"I'm not using my hands," she said.

"He's hurt," Jarms told her.

But the girl was steadfast. Jarms sighed. He grabbed Matt's flaccid workings. He tugged him firm.

"Now just squat down," he told the girl.

"I ain't going face-to-face with him."

"You don't have to. Just look off somewhere."

She straddled Matt and inched herself down. She blotted out the light from the doorway. Straw stuck to Matt's doctored back. Each thrust brought a new pain, until finally, he was falling apart inside her and she was pulling the suffering from him.

"You finished?" Jarms asked.

"I think," Matt said.

"Good."

Jarms set his hand over the girl's opening and hauled her off of him. He guided her to her back and held her legs over her head.

"Now get in there and cook," he said.

Matt closed his eyes.

"You made us Roland's baby," Jarms told him. Matt nodded. He knew he had. He knew it like he knew his own name.

★ 20 ★

THEY DIDN'T BRUSH HIS HAIR, and, though cut, it was less a tangle, his head still appeared a tumbleweed, and his sloe-eyed gaze left him looking half-asleep well past noon. His clothes, aside from the hand-me-downs in which she had dressed him that first night, were thin as a veil where they had not been patched or let out to account for his growth. Beard peppered his chin. Lucky was sixteen, but so strange and uncultured that no number, outside height and weight, could accurately describe him. He followed her like a pup, nodded at what she told him, smiled in submission when it wasn't appropriate, and performed tasks with such vigor he missed their intent then moped when she corrected him. He hummed, though the sound was hardly musical, more like bugs careening about a light. The boy seemed unaware sound emitted from him at all.

He was underfoot at first, but once she'd assigned him a routine of duties he could manage on his own, he proved productive enough. And he was, of course, young and tireless. Wendy realized she must have been strange country for the boy to come upon.

Outside his mother, Wendy had witnessed him speak to no one until his first night on the ranch. Linda was not unneighborly when encountered but traveled wide circles to avoid such meetings. From birth, the boy knew little other than her voice. Wendy wondered if his mother's presence was as oppressive as Wendy herself found God or the comfort believers knew.

On the skyline, a pair of riders appeared and disappeared throughout the day. She recognized them the next day and the one following. Drifters, she figured, sharing part-time work at another ranch or laying over before a push west across the desert and the pass between here and Seattle, or north and west to the dam in the coulee. Perhaps they weren't paired at all, or only out of convenience or necessity, like she and the boy.

She broke from seeding the spring crop and studied the boy drive a nail in a post and twist and loop barbwire over the head, then hook the nail, and wire into the wood. Finished, he started another a foot higher. She wondered if cities were lonely, if a hundred people stacked into twenty apartment floors could remain separate. If distance and geography didn't keep them apart, what was loneliness, what did she share on a hillock, gazing across livestock and grain and a great river, a hundred square miles of country with a thousand others whose vista most days did not extend past a flat's walls or the streets piled with buildings? The boy looked up, found her, and grinned. She raised her hand to acknowledge him before returning to her planting.

Wendy's physical labor piled muscle and sinew upon her like a man's, and she perspired far beyond the restraint implied by femininity. The latter forced her to break her work into two-hour pieces with fifteen minutes between in which she undressed and dried the cold sweat with a bathing towel. When she glanced up and recognized the boy staring, she thought he might bolt, but instead he walked closer, his blinking eyes taking her in. Her chest was beaded with sweat. She told herself it was good practice, her nakedness; there was knowledge in it he required. She put the towel in her fist and dragged it underneath each breast. Her nipples rose with the gesture.

The boy's eyes took her in. Her feet started blunt as quartered wood and her ankles thick, then muscled legs and thighs and boxy hips, and thin again at the waist. Above, she turned blocky geometry that only her breasts' arcs argued.

The boy undid his belt and opened his fly, fingers scrambling.

"What do you think you're doing?" she said.

He looked down at his pants and the disturbance there. "It's misbehaving," he said. The horses' necks bent, their mouths pulling at the grass. She could hear the roots give way.

She turned her back to him. "Pull on it," she said. A few tugs and she heard his zipper close and his belt buckle cinch and hasp.

•

EACH DAY, SHE DRIED HERSELF and he spied on her from behind the sagebrush, and though she never condoned it, neither did she forbid it. The knowledge made her head light. The boy rustled in the high grass like a pheasant or a grouse and soon every wind or insect clatter, any time a rabbit broke brush distracted her. She suffered a broken hunger, persistent and impersonal; she wanted it to be the boy, though any resolution would multiply their loneliness. People's loins could not remain locked forever, ecstasy or not. At some point, sleep and food and drink turned necessary, and then where would they be?

She was ordinary, yet the boy's eyes had lifted her to more. It was she who clipped his hair and shuddered his manhood that first night. A part of her had hoped as much, but now her certainty of it left her uneasy. She knew nothing of the machinations of a body, she realized, nothing of what one's flesh might do to another. It was smoke to her. Once, when she took to rest, he gathered the horse and seed and spelled her. She watched him clear the hill and kept her disappointment to herself.

•

SOON, HE WAS SEEDING MORE than she and putting up the horses at night to boot. When she rested under a lone pine, waiting for her turn—she would have to halt the boy, he'd never surrender a chore on his own—she would watch him and wonder if the boy was using these few days to make of her a rumor to be reheard throughout his life as she'd done with Matt these past years. She and the boy were bound for the same end, she decided. Oblivion. It should satisfy her, and she was surprised to find it did not.

The riders remained, silhouettes atop of the rocky breaks. The boy measured them as they reappeared. They paralleled the road. He said nothing, just tapped the sheathed knife in his belt. The dry weather left the air smelling dusty and full of something. Over the hill, Wendy heard him make water.

The boy killed a pheasant and an early duck, and Mrs. Lawson and his mother plucked and boiled them in a kettle and served the birds with a jar of pickled cabbage. The boy finished before them and left to check on the animals. Wendy was tempted to give him some company. She heard Linda offer her something. More tea or a stale cookie from a box, but she was suddenly too exhausted to jar herself to pay attention. Mrs. Jefferson took Wendy's hand. It was hot and clammy and Wendy would have guessed not very agreeable to the touch. She studied her palm against the woman's, both rough like two pieces of earth colliding.

"Would you like a child?" Mrs. Jefferson asked.

"I don't see much in the way of children in my future."

"If you did, would you want it? Or would it be just another crop to plant?"

Wendy stared at her. "I'd want to want it," she said finally.

Linda said. "I want my child. I always have. It's unfair, wanting your babies. They're much better off chores. I'll bet your parents loved you very much."

"They did, I think." Wendy said. She closed her eyes and felt sleep coming for her, like her father slipping into her room, standing, watching, a thing he had done every night of her life with him. She wondered if he lingered by her empty bed now and dreamed her in it. She worried she was splintering his heart.

"Yet you left them?"

"I am selfish," she said. "My guilt trumped their affection."

"Still?" Linda Jefferson asked.

"Still," Wendy replied. She excused herself and found the boy in the horse corral. He sat a fence post, watching them eat. She could see his eyes shining in the house lights. The river and the house eaves gleamed, as well, like polished glass in the darkness. The full moon glowed and the stars. It reminded her of being drunk on the porch. Everything carrying its own light. She'd cloaked herself in an afghan but was still chilly. She'd counted herself good before, but a good that was only dry country, watching the river course past, going its one way. She shook her head at her thinking. It amused her being so high and mighty once. It saddened her, too.

According to all accounts the coming dam would make the river turn backward until it had filled the broad new reservoir like a washing tub, and no current remained, just flat water stirred only by the wind or a fish swimming through it.

Long ago, she'd daydreamed time backed up that same way. Evenings, she'd undo the rifle shot and watch Matt rise past her window glass and take each gift from her porch to his house like she was the one giving. There, he met her on the hill and put all their awkwardness behind them, drinking from the jug until they were sober and enjoying a long walk. Later, he and Linda journeyed into a snowstorm and found his father and brother, held captive there so long, and delivered them home where they, like two halves, were joined, but she was alone. Feeling good turned as hard a prospect to manage backward as it did traveling ahead. The knowledge left her not wanting anything.

So she quit her daydreaming, stopped any thinking, except what was needed to run the ranch. Winters, she attempted Emily Dickinson a few times, but the cool leather binding felt like saying words behind someone's back and she shifted her attentions to dime westerns and histories, where the doing mattered more than the feeling.

The boy beside her knew none of this. To him she was just the woman who permitted him to watch her undress. She had nothing but rancor for their indiscretions, but it was what he wanted, to know what he hadn't before. She was not thinking of him for those mean purposes, however. It was herself she was readying. The dam would come and she would have to learn to stand in front of a man naked. It was only time that separated her from the boy.

•

WENDY AND THE BOY HAD seen neither person nor beast in the fields for two days when the riders met them on the road. They raised their hands to hail them, and the boy halted the horses.

"Would you have any water?" one asked. He wore a ball cap and looked dirty, as he hadn't shaved. The other was clean-cut and short. Wendy rustled through their gear for a water jug and passed it to the men. They drank their fill though the day's heat was unremarkable.

The small one returned the jug. His face was wet and smooth.

Wendy had watched the boy studying the short man's throat as he drank; his Adam's apple bobbing was somehow obscene. Now the man met the boy's stare, glaring him into boyness.

"You strong enough to break earth with that?" the dirty-faced one nodded at the plow.

"He manages fine," Wendy replied.

The man dismounted and inspected the tines. "Looks like it could use a whetstone."

"Time permits we will get to it," Wendy told the man.

"Man would make time."

The boy fidgeted. He stared at the back of the horses, his ears red.

The man dismounted and took the reins from the boy. "Maybe we could bunk at your ranch. Look after things."

Wendy unlooped the rifle from the seatpost.

"All right," the man said. He returned the reins to the boy but slowly at his leisure. "So much for the Good Samaritan, eh?"

Wendy reported the details to the women upon her return. The boy ate in silence, then posted himself as sentry on the porch. That night, Linda didn't sleep. Instead she propped herself in the rocker and watched the boy outside. The others fell to slumber quickly and she was glad for that. It was cumbersome loving someone and an exercise that required privacy. In the darkness, she did what she imagined every mother did: she listened to the sound of the boy's breaths and watched his calm face. Perhaps it was because she was older and tired and in need of stillness or perhaps it was that she'd relinquished all people except the boy. He was dressed and groomed and productively laboring and looking at Wendy like she was a star fallen from the heavens. Linda recognized that moment in boys' lives. She once fanned it aglow for spelling, poems, or arithmetic. When she taught, she could never comprehend a mother's doting, but she understood that vigilance now. You steered a child through the day safe, and it gave you permission to watch it sleep. It was the sleeping children that still loved you.

She took another sip from the moonshine in her cup. She wondered why drinking did what it did, how the world became a place to get off from. She imagined men grunting over their fires cooking meat or just warming themselves, in fear, whispering a god's name for solace. Folks used liquor similarly, like prayer; the destination was all that differed. The boy was in one camp, hunting his orders from the stars while Linda remained in the other, taking hers from a quart jar.

Wendy rose and sat on the sofa across from her. Linda had switched to tea and offered Wendy a cup. "It's from tules. It's warm." Wendy drank the strange mixture. It nearly scalded her tongue.

"Where is Lucky?" Wendy asked.

"Out there." Linda nodded to the window. "Something's going to happen."

"Seems quiet enough."

"Quiet is what sets him off," Linda said. "Even when he was a baby, he was a prophet. I remember once—he was four or so—he pointed at the sky. It was clear, like tonight, just constellations and planets and the moon. We were going to collect berries the next day. And he started bawling. He wailed and wailed. Finally, I got why out of him. He wanted to make jelly and it was going to rain. I told him there needed to be clouds for rain, but he just kept sobbing."

"Did it rain?"

"No, it was the hottest day of the year."

Wendy looked at her, puzzled.

"It was his first endeavor," Linda said. "He's better at it, now."

She sat quiet a minute. Wendy sipped her tea.

"What else has he predicted?"

"He anticipates the seasons."

"Is he right?"

"Within a few weeks."

"Anyone can come within a few weeks of predicting spring."

"But few spend time trying. Prophecy is in the attempt."

"Did he predict the fire?"

"I suppose so, as he started it."

"He burned the house?"

Linda nodded.

"Why?"

"Because of what he predicted would happen afterwards."

"Was he right?" Wendy asked.

Linda lifted the pot from the stove and refilled both their cups. "I don't think he's finished yet," she said.

It was quiet.

"He really started the fire?"

"He's a determined child," Linda said.

★ **21** ★

A WEEK LATER, WENDY AND the boy broke from evening chores to see two horses strange to the place hitched to the corral. The smell of cooking met them before they reached the barn. Inside, Mrs. Lawson had roasted and stuffed two chickens. Linda perched on the edge of the living room sofa, and the two strangers who sandwiched her were the same that accosted Lucky and Wendy the week before. They passed a jug. The short one nodded. Wendy ignored him.

Mrs. Lawson disappeared into the kitchen and returned with two more glasses. Wendy and the boy sat along with Mrs. Lawson.

"These are my long-lost cousins," Mrs. Lawson said. The two nodded at Wendy and the boy. The dirty one handed the jug to Mrs. Lawson, who filled all their glasses. They were union men hunting new work. Mrs. Lawson had offered them a meal and the tack room for the night and a pair of cots and a stove there.

They all sat for ten minutes in silence, tipping their drinks. The shine was strong and tasted of juniper. Lucky drank quickly and poured more from the jar for himself. Hunched together drinking, they were just faces lit by the glass lanterns. Wendy stared through the window into the dark, until she saw the reflection of the boy, who was watching her in the glass. She gazed back, as if their eyes locking were some puzzle that she might think her way through. Linda looked on, too, a tall and helpless goddess pinned to the earth.

Mrs. Lawson set the food on the table and all but Wendy loaded their plates with a thigh and leg, potatoes, dressing, and canned green beans. The men reached across others' plates for whatever pleased them enough to double their helpings.

Linda watched her son. He'd always been cautious with food, as if eating, like handwriting, were graded for neatness. He was more so now that he wore fresh clothes. The habit infuriated her; he took double the time over a meal she did. But now she recognized his fastidiousness was to be admired. His mind had become circumspect as a hawk's; it left little to error.

The cousins abandoned silverware as soon as etiquette appeared past notice and lifted their meat to their mouths and tore it from the bone. Their lips popped and their tongues lapped the grease drippings that clung to them. They shoveled beans with their forks onto buttered bread. The spatters pocked the gravy and potatoes, lumps as ugly as cancers that they ate as if it were a king's meal. They devoured all the food before them.

Mrs. Lawson cleared her throat. "How come you boys left Seattle?"

"We used to work in the warehouses until companies hired scabs and their own cops who beat any man who wanted a living wage," the shorter one replied. "We busted a few heads to square things and they got the regular law to put warrants on us. So we decided to seek work elsewhere."

"You were communists?" Wendy asked.

"No more communist than you are a professor of literature. Politics don't feed anybody."

"No offense," Wendy said.

"I am offended," the ball cap replied.

The room remained quiet a long while.

Wendy said, "I can't blame a man for making a living."

The man nodded. "It's a mean world," he said. "The politicians are the only ones that can afford a philosophy." He touched his face below the whiskers. "I almost got killed in them places and it turned me owly. One man had an arm he hurt that mended straight and hard as a bat with no feeling in it. He beat me to a hump. Killed several. Suppose I was fortunate. One of the fisherman on the docks sewed me up or I'd've bled out."

"I remember they had themselves a lion at the zoo there. Heard it roar for miles. Then the darkies ate him."

He wiped his hands upon the napkin and so did the other. "We thank you for the meal," the short one said. "Please excuse us while we build our bunks."

Wendy watched them go, then retired to her room. She was dreaming more, or remembering them because she woke with each one. In some she was lifted full size by her father who had turned large as a church steeple. Another, Matt came to her and whispered a word she couldn't make out. "What?" she asked. But he wouldn't answer. It was his face, she knew.

She woke and returned to the front room. There in her night shirt, a blanket around her for decency, Linda rested, awake. Wendy curled on the divan. Midnight, Linda tapped her arm.

"You were crying out," Linda said.

"I'm sorry."

"It's all right. I wasn't sleeping," she said.

Linda stirred the fire. Wendy watched the flames until Linda touched her shoulder.

"Where is he?" Wendy asked.

"Out there," Linda said.

"He's not tired?"

"No," Linda told her. "He doesn't need sleep. Not now."

Wendy realized the boy already succeeded in one respect. He was guarding them and she was allowing it. It had gone too far his way. She saw him thinking of her. It was something she found too pleasant, and she willed herself to study the window. Outside, she recognized a splash of moonlight on a face across the corral. The boy, she thought, but she saw another follow. A few minutes later a pair of long shadows darkened the yard near the house's south side. A tool levered at the sill of Mrs. Lawson's room, but she had locked her window clasp against the weather. They tried Wendy's room, next to hers, but that window was painted shut years before. They circled the house tugging fixtures, prying for loose sideboards, with no luck. Linda found a skillet and broom handle. Wendy pulled the poker from the fireplace hearth,and deadbolted the door.

A few minutes later she heard knocking. They didn't answer. The men pressed the door with their shoulders. The frame shuddered and nailed wood squawked with their weight. One grunted, then the other, then the door gave. A sound like a grain sack hitting the ground followed. The boy's head appeared in the window glass, then was gone. On the porch outside, lay the taller of the drifters tied at the wrists and ankles.

A half hour and the boy returned carrying a saddlebag. He set it on the ground and drooped the tied man over his horse and snubbed his wrists to his ankles. He slapped the horse's croup and it trotted off.

The boy looked to Wendy. "They wanted to hurt you," he said.

Wendy nodded

"There's another and he has a gun," Linda told him. "He'll come back."

"No," Lucky said. He lifted the saddlebag and opened it. Inside was the short man's head. Lucky threw it in the open stove. Blood hissed on the coals, and the boy added an extra quarter of pine to stoke the fire. It kindled, and flames rose. The man's skin blistered, then blackened. His hair crinkled. Wendy could smell it cooking.

"Good boy," Linda said.

Mrs. Lawson stood in the doorway of her bedroom.

"They were not my cousins," Mrs. Lawson whispered.

"No," Linda said.

"They were not family. They were liars."

"Yes," Linda said. "They were liars."

The room was quiet, aside from the sizzling of skin.

"Did you predict this?" Wendy asked Lucky.

The boy looked at her.

She undid her blanket, then tore her shirt in half and stood naked under.

"This," she shouted. "This."

She spun like a dervish, faster and faster, her hair twirling. The severed head came and went under her arm. Its eyes had shut or perhaps its landing in the fire had left them that way. Linda found the blanket and draped it across Wendy's shoulders. Wendy sat in a chair with the blanket. The boy set some coffee on to boil. When it was finished, he poured a cup, then offered one to the rest of them. Wendy took hers, though her hands shook.

The boy was calm as a stone. He'd done the men like good math, plotting a line and measuring to where it bisects the next. He was making angles, dividing people and events and Wendy herself into something he could gauge. Wendy coughed, then vomited bitter bile. It was the smell, she said, but it wasn't that at all. Mrs. Lawson gave her water. She drank and spat and drank again.

"I want to know about my father," the boy said.

Linda sipped her coffee. The boy waited.

"I suppose you do," Linda told him.

The boy looked stumped. He had thought the one question would be enough.

"What did he look like?

"It's difficult to reduce a person to looks," Linda said.

The boy stood and reached into the fire. He pulled out the head. "Did he look like this, goddammit?"

"No," Linda said.

The boy returned the head to the fire, then wiped its grease on his pants.

"I didn't care for him," Linda said. "It was you I wanted."

Wendy finished her coffee and the boy poured her another cup. When he stood over her, she could feel him looking into the blanket, and she knew she'd passed the place she could do anything about it.

"You were fathered a long time ago, if you want the truth," Linda said. "Longer than you know. The other was just coincidence. Your father was just a boy. He could have been any boy."

"Why'd he leave?"

"Someone shot him," Linda said.

"That isn't so," Wendy said.

However in Linda's mind literal truth was too narrow for such matters. Lucky nodded at the mirror in his hands, unaware what he was agreeing to. Soon, Mrs. Lawson returned to her bedroom and Linda to the extra room she and the boy occupied. *What else was there for them to do?* Wendy thought.

When the door squeaked, she knew it was Lucky coming for her. She heard his footsteps pad the floor, his breath in his chest rushing. His naked body was led by an enormous erection, tipping him forward like he was running downhill. The hair behind it was oddly like the mountain's fog, and the root seemed disconnected from the man. She considered looking up and trying to meet his eyes to see if she could find some reason there, but finally, she stared at the business end of him. It was his reason.

He bent on one knee like a noble waiting to be knighted by the queen. His flesh lay against her belly and drummed. She rolled and it was on her hip. It was just skin and blood, she knew. They were all just skin and blood and bone. She stared into its small mouth, waiting for an answer, or a story, or just for a signal to go on and finish it.

"I can save you," he said. "I did it the once already."

"I don't feel saved," she said.

She turned away. The boy waited. He was right of course. He'd done the work to earn her, and she felt odd about not allowing him his prize. A part of her hoped to, larger than she'd ever imagined she would invest in that sort of thing. She longed for a body's warmth to hide her. She knew he'd do whatever she asked, but she couldn't get the question from her chest to her lips. It shuddered between, not swallowed, not spoken, stuck where she could neither digest it nor spit it out of her. Finally, she closed her eyes and willed herself to sleep. If he took her that way, she would abide it, but she could not bring herself to invite him.

When she awoke, she was unstained. The boy had returned to the room he and his mother shared. Wendy opened the door and watched them sleep. His shoulder was large and awkward under his mother's arm, and his tipped head lay across her covered breast.

★ 22 ★

THE NEXT MORNING, MATT LAY late in his pallet and watched the sun rise, something he had not done in ten years. His hands had chapped and they itched. He stroked his singed eyebrows and ragged hair. Smoke clung to his hair. His bandaged feet leaked yellow fluid. He pulled socks over them and donned his work clothes. Walking was a new kind of anguish. The pup glanced at him and turned its head and whined at her own pain.

Outside, the old man, tipped by the cast on his leg, eyed him from the porch.

"You look chewed up and spit out."

Matt rested on the trough's lip and closed his eyes and squinted into the sun lifting from the eastern horizon.

"I don't think I'll be much use for a while," Matt said.

The old man was above him, then, shifting from his good leg to the cast. He knocked his hands together. Matt's own heartbeat picked up, and he felt giddy. He opened his eyes and gazed at the boots, studying the laces. He pulled his T-shirt over his head and undid his pants. He could bear them no longer.

Jarms stood in the doorway.

"Get in the trough, Matt," he said. "I'll bring the ointment and the dressing. We got to see to your feet. There's some fresh linens, too. You can make a wrap."

Jarms returned with sheets and the medicine and spread some on the soles of Matt's feet. Matt winced with each pass and finally commandeered the tube himself and doctored his chest. Jarms greased his ankles and shins, then rifled old bed sheets until he found one long enough and tore holes in it for Matt's arms and head. Matt closed his eyes and Jarms lifted the sheet over him. It was cool and a little windy underneath where it didn't cling to the ointment. Jarms checked Matt's feet again, then crafted gauze stockings around them and anchored them with tape. The birds were scolding, and the sun was trying to warm the morning.

Jarms herded him to one of the bedrooms inside. He delivered his traps on the next pass and Queenie the last. Matt didn't argue.

"We'll tend things," Jarms said. He left, and later Matt heard him lead the cattle to the barn. Roland remained in the doorway, leaning on his cane.

"You think he would've went in?" he asked. "Without you, I mean."

"I reckon he would have," Matt said, though he did not like to lie.

•

A MONTH LATER ONE EVENING when Matt was repairing a fence gate that allowed grain trucks to pass through the pasture, Garrett slowed his truck and let it idle, then opened the door. He poured two cups of coffee from a thermos and offered Matt one. They stood on the peak of a steep hill, the only real promontory for miles. Before them, farmhouses and outbuildings scattered the country, gravel roads like arteries; automobile lights like blood flowing awkwardly between.

"You've got this enterprise tapping like a sewing machine," Garrett said. Garrett pointed his arm south and west. Most of it was darkness. "I bought most of that country up in the last three years. The old man got out of the market like Joe Kennedy and ended up with a fortune and land is cheap. Everybody's going under and glad to have bottom dollar," he said. "Land is cheaper than, well, dirt."

Garrett pointed toward the Jarms ranch. "See that group of lights there. I haven't quite cornered that place yet."

Matt nodded. "I doubt they're selling."

"I know the old man's doctor."

Four miles away, a truck slowed for the grade and shifted down; Matt could hear the whine of the transaxle.

"How come you shot the dog."

"I apologize for that," Garrett said. "A fit of frustration. It was stupid. The dog did no harm."

Matt didn't reply.

"I'm a good aim. I shot her where she could be fixed."

"It was meant to wound me."

"It was meant to wound Horace. Did, too. I've rarely seen him so irritated."

"You just twisting his tail?"

"Trying to square him away," Garrett said. "He's not inclined to break or lead, though."

"What's that to you?"

"I got a soft spot for him. I hate to see him go to waste."

"He seems bound and determined."

"With Roland looking after things he could go on forever, or at least till he pickles his liver and kidneys. That isn't the case any longer. Roland is going to pass on soon. He leaves the place to Horace. Well, it will bankroll some good stories then go belly up. He's a child. He needs looked after." Garrett drew his tobacco pouch from his shirt pocket along with papers. He picked free three brown leaves and rubbed them between his palms and the flakes rained into the papers. Not one missed its mark. He turned the papers until the tobacco settled, then, on the short side, licked the opposite with a darting tongue that reminded Matt of a lizard. He twirled the paper perfectly and handed the cigarette to Matt along with a wood match struck on his pants zipper. Matt smoked. Garrett lit another for himself.

"You ever hear of a trust?" Garrett asked. "A person deposits money or land or gold or the like into it. Like a bank. Except that money, it has a trustee. The trustee decides when to open the purse and when not to."

"You see Roland taking to a bank after all they've undone?"

"It's not a bank that handles it, it's a lawyer."

"I doubt he'd see much difference," Matt said.

"The lawyer, he just signs the papers."

"This trustee, that going to be you?"

Garrett shook his head. "You."

"Until Roland passes?"

"Until Horace passes. When that day comes you'll sell it to me. Fair market."

"How come you don't just take it?"

"Horace is crazier than a billy goat and refuses taking care of himself or his money. You know he's down in the big poker game to men who don't have that sort of money. But they have guns and nothing to lose." Garrett said. "But the man has never bullshitted me. Do you know how valuable that is? Someone who will tell you the truth no matter how ugly or how much it costs him."

Matt said nothing.

"You can't imagine being boss? Is that it?" Garrett asked. "Someone has to be in charge. It might as well be a person that knows how to do the job." Garrett grinned. "The world's a strange place."

Matt toed the dirt with his boot.

"You see I'm attempting to help Horace," Garrett said.

"I never doubted it," Matt said.

They were quiet a while.

"Who owns what is only ink on paper." Garrett said. "Bad and good, right and wrong, more ink, more paper. Whiskey was illegal, remember that? Now they can't sell enough. I follow the bible closer than any priest ever thought to and, God, he looks out for me for it. You could give me some of that about how tough it is for the rich to get to heaven, but I been to New York and I saw St. Patrick's. That place is the holiest thing in these United States and it's a palace. Tell me why they didn't feed a million poor Irish with that money? Because they'd be hungry again tomorrow. But that church will stand longer than any of those paupers will live even if you fed them ten meals a day. God is, above all things, practical."

Garrett stayed quiet a while. His face was green in the moonlight, and his skin looked suddenly like it could slip from his face like a mask and pool in the gravel under them, leaving just the bone and muscle underneath.

"Horace has read more than me and he knows more ideas than me. He can tell you the difference between Aristotle and Socrates and whoever else had ideas about other ideas and he can talk them like a goddamm lawyer." Garrett laughed finally. "You know what the difference is? Horace, he knows a lot of philosophies, but he doesn't have one."

Matt did not reply.

"You and me can look after Horace," Garrett said. "Roland passes and the house can be yours. Horace will just live in it. It's all he does now. Then in months or years he'll turn up dead or drink himself so far rummy, he can't get back from it. It'll happen before me, don't even argue it—you'll have a home."

Matt stayed quiet awhile.

"You think you're siding with him?" Garrett asked.

"Maybe I'm just not siding with you."

"That's a selfish reason. Not liking me is no cause not to do business when it serves everybody involved."

It was simple logic, even if Garrett bent it to his hearing. Roland would listen to it.

"Like I said." Garrett grinned. "The world's a strange place."

"Not that strange," Matt said.

Garrett smoked his cigarette to a stub. "You ain't doing him a good turn," he said. "Fact is, you're killing him dead as a heifer to the slaughter." He clapped Matt on the shoulder with a grip firmer than congenial. "You disappoint me, big man. I was hoping for more from you."

★ **23** ★

Through early summer, Jarms made circles between town and the ranch. He'd traveled that orbit for years, but now he turned the ideas of ranch and town over in his mind like a coin he continually flipped, hunting a pattern from the results. Some mornings, Matt woke and Jarms joined him in the chores before the sun rose and remained throughout the day. Others, he rose early, worked until lunch and after drove the Ford in the general direction of town. Some days, Matt did not see him at all.

The Ford occasionally failed him. Jarms woke to flat tires often enough that he finally purchased a pump; a week after he rose to the tires cut with a long knife. He bought fresh inner tubes, but soon the pistons would not fire. The spark plug wires were snipped. Jarms repaired them and arranged a chain and padlock to secure the hood and engine, though a few days past the Ford died for good, sugar in the gasoline tank pasting the piston to the cylinder walls. Jarms saddled his horse, Ahab, named for the Melville character rather than he of the bible, and made for town. Upon his return he tethered the animal beneath Matt's window open even on the coldest nights.

Matt thought the culprit might be Roland, and Jarms wondered over Matt's complicity. Whoever it might be, however, did not appear willing to sabotage an animal.

The girl hadn't returned for eight weeks, Jarms stopped to talk to her father and verify her condition. She felt weak at the stomach mornings. Jarms inquired about her bleeding, but the man would say no more. Jarms did not speak to the girl. He was certain, though, and after he delivered her meal each evening, he paused at Matt's door every night to report her progress.

One evening on the porch, Matt smoked a cigarette and rolled another. Roland had lost weight and color. Evenings, he listened to the radio serials. Together, Matt and Jarms watched Roland drift into sleep until he snored.

"Wish it was me with the bad heart," Jarms said. "No work would be a cure I could take to."

Matt nodded. "Maybe it's why you're in good health."

Jarms lay back on the rocker and closed his eyes. He was long enough silent that Matt thought he, too, had dozed off.

"You even in your game?"

"Somewhat."

"That like being somewhat pregnant?"

Jarms laughed.

"You didn't say how the poker was working out," Matt said.

"I'm more certain about the girl than the cards."

Roland shifted in his sleep and sucked a hard breath then struggled until his leg freed. Jarms worked his cigarette.

"They're gonna be building dams on the Columbia. Jobs better paying than this're coming."

"And a line to get them," Matt said.

"You and I know there ain't no line you'd wait in long."

"You putting the run on me?"

"Why'd I want to go and do that?"

Matt shrugged. "Maybe inside straights and low pairs."

Jarms shook his head. "You worry too damned much."

"Equals out, you not worrying at all."

"Together, we break even, then," Jarms said.

"Maybe," Matt replied. He yawned.

"Keeping you from your rest?"

"You're about to."

"Well, you're awake, now," Jarms said. "Might as well go for a ride."

"Car is still broke," Matt said.

"Trap wagon runs, though."

"Where?"

"Cemetery."

They traveled in the truck to Roland's tree and the graves of Jarms's siblings. Matt sat and listened to the little stream collect itself and move for the river. Sometimes Jarms went alone, Matt knew. Matt wondered at the headstones for children's graves and if they were not unlike the rose thicket marking his brother and father's bones and if either made a difference one could measure and call comfort.

Jarms offered him a bottle and he took it.

"How long does it take for a baby?" Matt asked.

"Nine months," Jarms told him. "She ought to make it that far. The doctor says she's healthy."

Matt poked a stick in the damp gravel.

"She's got wide hips," Jarms said.

"Is that good?" Matt asked.

"Is in cows," Jarms told him.

They sat and watched the moon rise. He could feel the cold coming. It calmed him. The stars above were so indecipherable that he figured nobody knew for certain anything and the realization comforted him.

They shared a cigarette that left Matt's mouth sticky and sweet with the bourbon.

"That girl pretty?" he asked.

"You seen her before."

"Never up close."

"You were pretty close the one time."

"It was dark."

Jarms nodded. "You particular?"

"Just inquiring."

Jarms lay his head back into the tree bark. Matt heard him chuckle.

"You ain't one to inquire," he said. "Something's on your mind."

Matt watched the cigarette in his hand burn down. He dragged from it one more time then set it in the dirt.

"I was thinking about the baby," he said.

"What about it?"

"I was wondering what it might look like."

Jarms laughed. "Like itself, I expect."

"You don't think it'll favor the mother?"

"If it's lucky."

Matt said nothing. His cigarette was finished. The butt left a black spot in the dirt.

•

HER HAIR WAS THE COLOR of hay, but he'd forgotten most of the rest of her. The profile of her nose he could gather if he pondered enough, but the rest remained a pebble in his shoe that left him raw and doubting. The child weighed upon him, as well. He considered it every night. It would have him in it, and he worried which part the child would draw.

"You think it will know me?"

"You think a calf ponders the bull that made him? It doesn't know anything but its mother."

"You're one to talk," Matt said. "You don't know your mother."

Jarms stared at Matt.

"I guess that came out mean," Matt said.

"I guess it did," Jarms agreed. He sighed. "Old Roland mothered me about as well as any damned woman could."

"Seems so."

Matt vowed to quit thinking of it. To imagine children until they had come was as impossible as to forget them after they had gone. Matt wondered if Roland would make it into another year.

"That baby might perk him up," Matt said.

"He'll know it soon enough," Jarms said. He rose and jingled his car key. "Come on if you're going to," he said.

In the grain truck, Jarms drove the ridge's trail and parked within view of the old place where the girl's family resided. He withdrew binoculars from the glove box.

"That top window's hers."

Jarms handed him the binoculars and Matt gazed into the girl's room. Inside was a chest of drawers, painted white. A brush and comb lay on its top next to a ceramic-faced doll with rose painted cheeks, its hair nearly gone. A tiny mirror had been tacked to the wall above it. Blankets on a cot made up her bed.

They had to wait a while before the girl turned in. She sat in the room in the lantern light and brushed her hair. It was long and thin and he could see the color of the plain wall through it. Her chin was pointed and her jaw a pleasing crescent. Her nose was as he recalled it, and her eyes were small—he couldn't make out their color. He waited for her to do something extraordinary, but she blew out the lantern and was gone.

★ 24 ★

ROLAND REMAINED HOBBLED AND JARMS returned to bring in
the harvest. Matt set him to driving the combine while Matt sewed
sacks. It was the most skilled labor there was. A man had to fill a
fifty-pound sack with grain and hem it shut before the next fifty
pounds of wheat filled the grain bin. The labor was numbing. It'd
taken him a whole harvest to make himself passable at it. One day,
they stopped for water, and Jarms sauntered to the back and stared
at the sacks and twine.

"I'm tired of eating dust," he said. "Let's swap."

Matt said, "You can't keep up."

Jarms grinned. "I might surprise you."

They cut all day into the night without stopping. Jarms not only
kept pace, he got far enough ahead to start a cigarette every dozen
bags or so. His hands and the twine were a blur.

They quit with the end of twilight. Matt nodded at what they'd
finished.

"That's a lick of work."

Jarms agreed.

"More than we'd get if I was bagging,"

"Yep," Jarms said.

"You cut just fast enough to carry me, didn't you?" Matt had run the combine near double Jarms's pace just to try and test him.

"Didn't make much sense to cut faster than you could sew."

Jarms stared at him. It was quiet and damp from the coming evening. The night smelled like bread, and a fog of dust turned the moon huge and orange.

"You let me think you were useless," Matt said.

Jarms was counting the bags and writing the numbers into his notebook. Each night Roland ledgered the totals. He was awake late, figuring. His color was better and his lungs had cleared.

"Old Indian trick," Jarms said. He clasped Matt's shoulder and pointed him to the house. They could see the light shining from it.

He said. "I sewed bags before I was twelve. Neighbors hired me from all around. I was a good boy once. I got it in me."

"I'm glad to know it," Matt said. "I could use the help."

Jarms shook his head. "There's no future in it."

"Work, you mean?"

Jarms nodded. "Roland worked all his life. So have you. What've you got I ain't."

The question stumped Matt. He'd never figured it in a gathering way.

"I got a job," Matt said.

Jarms laughed. "That's a good answer. They're damned hard to come by, I hear."

"Well, what've you got?" Matt asked him.

Jarms smiled. "And that's a good question and I'll consider it deeply, but in the meantime, let's go see if that girl's any fatter."

They traveled the rutted road in silence aside from a static-filled country station until Jarms parked and switched the radio off. Jarms rested awhile, but Matt remained alert. One lantern lit the house below and they could watch it travel from room to room. Jarms put a blanket over his lap. Autumn was approaching and the night turned nippy. Their breath fogged the glass. Matt rolled down his window and watched it disappear. He let the cold air come over him. He enjoyed the way it cleared the sky and made his skin feel fresh-scrubbed. Watching the girl did the same thing to him. She stood in her room. All he could see was her shadow on one wall, and it took the binoculars for that. He couldn't help but feel some anxiety when he saw the new swoop of her belly and milk-heavy breasts.

"You think she knows we're here?" Matt asked.

Jarms shrugged. "It doesn't matter to me what she knows."

"Not at all?" Matt asked.

"Nope. What's in her belly is all that counts."

"I guess so."

"You gone and fallen in love?" Jarms asked him.

"No," Matt said. "I just don't know how to leave her out of it."

"It's easy," Jarms told him. "We'll give her money."

"That don't seem like enough."

Jarms said, "You know how rare cash is?"

"She might change her mind."

"Nope."

"Maybe the baby'll want her."

"What do you want to worry about all this for?" Jarms asked him.

"Seems like it bears considering."

Jarms pointed to the darkened window where the girl's room was. "She's cattle," he said. "Or a ewe, or a brood mare. Nothing more. Nothing that bears considering. Not one goddamned thing."

"Not even the baby?"

"More livestock."

Matt was quiet. He looked at a place where the dark line of the horizon met the night. Night had scared him once. Looking now, he realized it wasn't the sky that made him afraid, it was the dark over the country underneath it.

"Remembering your girl?" Jarms asked.

"She never answered my letter."

"You wrote her?"

"A month or so back."

"Jesus, with this baby coming?"

Matt said nothing.

"You don't see what one's got to do with the other do you?" Jarms's laugh idled and died. "Good for you," he said.

Matt just stared at the darkened house. It seemed to him as sacred as a church, and for the first time since he could remember he felt like praying. He thought for a moment he might ask for Wendy's answer and reconsidered, figuring his best hope was in continued silence.

"She don't need you," Jarms said. "No more than that girl in that house does."

"I don't guess so."

"You know why men make armies?" Jarms asked.

Matt shrugged.

"They got to be together. They make armies and taverns and card games. Women, they stay at home. They don't need nothing but themselves. Don't let yourself think they do. It's men that do the needing in this world."

Matt had been alone fourteen years, but he wasn't inclined to argue. What Jarms said seemed true enough. He'd never quit needing the whole time.

"A baby still seems worth a little concern," Matt said.

"Roland'll concern himself for all of us."

"You sure?"

"He's been doing it for me all my life," Jarms said. "He's doing it for you, too. He's good at it."

Jarms lit a cigarette and started the car. He pinched the butt between his finger and thumb and took a deep pull and released a stream of smoke. Matt watched his hand shake, then still. Jarms stared into the cigarette ember. The car motor rumbled and Matt wished he'd turn it off so they could sit longer, but Jarms backed up and turned them toward home.

•

THE THREE OF THEM CELEBRATED the end of cutting with a spitted lamb, dining from it three nights, squandering the days in the porch's shade, napping. Autumn, traditionally, was slow for farmers, leading to a winter of dormant country and keeping livestock from starvation and the other perils of snow and cold. The air cleared and Matt could see Steptoe Butte, which rose from the grain swells of Palouse like a random bicuspid in a golden and verdant gum. The county, Whitman, was named for missionaries local Indian tribes assassinated outside of Walla Walla—in what became another county entirely. Steptoe was an army colonel who managed to lose enough battles to the Palouse Indians, a tribe so poor they never merited a reservation and existed now only as Yakimas and Spokanes, that he was eventually martyred. The county had planted a dozen radio towers there and constructed a switchbacked road to a tiny park at the summit. The most remarkable aspect of the landmark was the lack of stone and trees. Scrub brush and dirt blanketed the peak to the apex, not unlike the country beneath it, which Lake Missoula, through a series of ice age floods, deposited the richest loam this side of the Mississippi. If a thresher could manage the thirty-degree grade, wheat and barley and canola would line the slopes until August cutting.

Farther east and south, Kamiak Butte sat the horizon, less prominent as it was an extension of the St. Joe Range, which was itself an arm of the Rockies. Kamiak, the chief rebel harassing Steptoe and George Wright, was summoned to the Latah country near what was then Spokane Falls to a peace conference where he was summarily hanged without a trial. Perhaps the butte was justice or at least an admission of something, not guilt, of course, but regret. The slopes of Kamiak were forested with white pine and broken with meadows so fragrant with wildflowers that one almost was sickened by the sweetness, as if the chief's body still rotted somewhere beneath.

In October, Jarms sold a portion of the grain. Five years before, Garrett and his father had constructed two modern siloes with dial scales and grain pits from which wheat and barley could be augured and elevatored to separated storage vats. Jarms had been happy to store with him as it was a shorter distance than town and Garrett charged the same rent. He permitted Garrett to buy and sell the Jarms wheat because he studied the commodities market and could milk a dime more per bushel than Horace or Roland, who more often than not sold on whims or when they tired of fussing over it.

The enterprise had flourished. Grain nearly filled both silos, and Garrett pulled fourteen-hour days to manage the enterprise and harvest his own crop. As a result, Jarms agreed to meet Garrett at the silo to cut his check. Horace arrived with Roland and Matt. A five-man crew swung spouts toward combination truck containers and aligned them with the ports, then tugged a rope that unloosed several tons of grain. A tremendous rattle followed and a wind yellowed the air. Semi drivers idled, afraid to smoke as the grain dust was volatile as nitro.

Roland shook his head and grinned at the operation. Jarms excused himself and walked across the dirt lot for the check. Matt could see them through the office: Garrett's mouth pinched like he was intent on working something from his teeth, Jarms circling his hands and later kicking a desk. Jarms slammed the door and marched to the Ford, Garrett trailing.

"What's the mule in the road?" Roland asked through the opened window.

"The bastard won't write the check," Jarms said.

Roland looked past Jarms to Garrett. "The wheat there?"

Garrett nodded.

"Sales receipts?"

Garrett nodded once more.

"Bank holding the cash?"

"Yes," Garrett said.

"I fail to see the rub," Roland said.

"I hold twenty thousand dollars of your son's IOUs."

"Well, that's not my concern."

"But it's mine," Garrett said. "And I'm not releasing your grain until the note's paid. I don't want to see him wasted any longer."

"Waste or not, the money's due."

"I won't pay."

"Will you write it to me, then."

"You'll pass it on to him."

"That's my business."

"And this is mine. I will not make the check."

"I've got a lawyer who says different."

"I imagine so. He will argue with mine and they will both get paid, but you will not. Not for a long while, anyway."

Garrett nodded to Matt. "I will pay him and only him."

They were silent.

"All right," Roland said. "Write the check."

But Jarms was on Garrett. They rolled in the dirt. Each's arms locked the other's head. Jarms champed Garrett's forearm and his blood spackled them both. Garrett's hand tore Jarms's throat. Matt, out of the car, kicked Garrett in the ribs. He heard one break and kicked him once more, then dragged him by the collar and drove his head into the car fender.

Roland fired the twelve gauge he stowed beneath the seat for an equalizer. Matt loomed over Garrett, who spat and blew blood through his nose.

"Matt," Roland said. "Get in the car, please."

He complied. Jarms eyed Garrett on the ground.

"You, too, Horace."

Garrett remained on all fours. He gasped.

"Seems to me you misplaced your loyalties," Roland told him. "Or thought some of us did."

Garrett laughed finally. "Now how come he's the only one I take serious?"

They remained quiet a long while in the car.

"I could kill him," Matt said.

"So could I," Jarms replied.

"We'd be rid of him," Matt said.

Roland sipped his coffee. "No, we wouldn't," he said.

•

EVENINGS, THE THREE SAT OUTSIDE on the porch and took their meal if the weather permitted. After, they played rummy and con-structed a list for the day that followed. Roland moved about without a crutch, swinging his ossified leg toward his intended course. He was too weak for labor, but too bored to idle, so he employed his energies toward the kitchen where he constructed, with the assis-tance of an old cookbook, elaborate and peculiar smelling stews and sauces that, despite Matt and Jarms's misgivings, ended up better than restaurant fare. Jarms did not drink those days, even when Roland and Matt imbibed. Matt recognized color returning to Jarms's face.

Owls hooted and nighthawks punctuated the night along with the cattle's low or coyotes' yips or the creak of the screen door. All would set Roland in the storytelling mood, evening. The tales contained dead ends and false starts as their plots unspooled, and he told them with trepidation, often reduced to retrieving the volume from his library to make certain of details he had once committed to memory.

Matt and Jarms visited the girl nearly every week. Neither of them said much to the other. They'd clean up and pack a snack and watch the house. Some nights all they'd get of her was a glimpse. Others she'd sit on the porch and allow them to contemplate her growing belly. She waddled when she walked. Her parents rarely spoke to her, though they didn't seem angry as much as daunted, like the child was bad weather.

$\star$ **25** $\star$

FALL, THE LIVESTOCK BEGAN TO disappear. At first, whatever killed the calves had decency enough to drag them away, and Wendy could allow herself the delusion of miscounting. Soon, though, it was taking its meal in the corral and the pasture and once it left a mauled heifer in the barn. She found them with their bellies split and organs spilled, a liver or heart missing, throats savaged and great chunks bitten from their flanks.

The cattle bellowed nights, smelling what was coming. By early winter, it visited nearly once a week, and she was down to a half dozen heifers and a few yearling calves. Evenings, she stationed herself on her porch with a loaded 30.3D. She built great fires outside the yard and torches from rags and grease and tool handles, but the light they shed weighed little against the night's gloom. Mrs. Lawson left for the coast at the behest of a sick cousin. The postman delivered a letter a month later. She opened it with a butter knife.

Wendy—

I believe I'm safe for people now.

Matt Lawson

Linda and Lucky departed the same day as the old woman, for where Wendy had no idea. It was clear Linda had tired of the close quarters and the boy had grown too depressed to argue, his great victory turned empty by Wendy's unwillingness to deliver what he must have thought appropriate tribute. The riders did not return. She knew they would not. There was iron in the boy, the kind criminals would recognize beyond ethics or any kind of law.

"Good-bye," Lucky said to her.

"Good-bye," Wendy told him.

"We are going to live in a cave now. Just like Mother planned."

Wendy did not know how to reply.

"I hate her," the boy said. "I hate you, too. I hate all the people I know."

"I'm sorry," Wendy said.

"I'm not," Lucky said.

One evening, she spied the boy and his mother setting trout lines on the river. The salmon were a month off and the weather too hot for the fish to feed on anything but fly hatches. Linda sat on the hill and directed the boy, who hauled one string of empty hooks after another. Wendy was not close enough to see the boy's face; it was only his walk she recognized: each step chopped like he wore leg irons. Linda looked gaunt.

The neighbors' buildings had been vacated up to the proposed waterline in preparation for the reservoir. The Bureau of Reclamation bulldozed any tree shorter than twenty feet and hired foresters to fell the others. The lumbermen were not permitted to harvest the timber. The government did not want their project to compete with the mills on the westside, lest a Congressman filibuster the next concrete pour or generator delivery Roosevelt was bent upon. Evenings, burning scrub piles and outbuildings scattered like a pox on the country, reflecting against the river and smoking the moon a bloody red. Shadows of people and loaded wagons often crossed in front of the light the flames shed. A few had trucks and she could trace the headlights lumbering along the dirt roads. Mornings, only the old rock foundations and the scorched earth remained. She could sometimes smell the diesel starting fluid, and imagined even the match's sulfur, and, when she couldn't, she retrieved a box from the kitchen and struck one and let it burn until it seared her fingers.

After the first snow skiff, she walked to Hawk Creek. The falls still rushed, the clear water suspended in the cold air before it turned black in the rock pool below. The standing water was deeper than she remembered. It flooded the swimming beach. She picked through the trail to the river. It, too, was overflowed in places. For a moment she wondered if the river was dammed already. A hundred yards farther was a fallen birch. The stump had been gnawed through. Branches lay askew in the thicket ahead. She separated the brambles. Trimmed limbs and fallen pine lay across the creek, and beavers labored in the backwater.

She couldn't remember a beaver in this country. She looked close in the trees and the brush. An osprey perched on a tamarack limb. It was at least what she recalled ospreys looking like. Her father had shown her one as a child.

When she returned to the ranch another calf was dead. She shoveled the guts into a heap and built a pyre. The cow's eye rolled as she dragged it onto the flame. The next day she rode to town, her first trip since spring. She bought a noisy billy goat and staked him to the front gate, then made a bed on the porch and waited under a pile of blankets. It was nearly a week before she woke to a clatter. The goat was kicking at the pie plate Wendy used to feed it, bending the rim flat. It ran and the tether spun it. Dazed, it sat on its knees, shaking.

She raised her rifle quietly and rested her arm on the porch rail to keep it steady. The moon was clear. It lit the corral and the grass-less yard between the house and the barn. She saw the shadow skulk until it was near the fence. It made no sound. The goat was so crazy with fear that it stood frozen at the end of its cord. The beast rose and she held her sight on it. Her finger trembled over the trigger. She stared at it, stuck there. There was a flash of silver, and the goat coughed its dying sounds. Blood covered its chest. The boy, in a bearskin, opened it up. The liver was in his mouth. Blood covered his chin. Wendy watched Lucky eat and returned the gun to its place on the floor.

★ 26 ★

JARMS AND MATT STOCKED THE wagon and bundled Roland and drove him to the cemetery tree twice a month into November until the snow, when Roland permitted them to halt the exercise. The last trip Matt watched them disappear in the direction of the creek and the tree. The sky purpled like a wound. The stars dimmed and retired as sunlight slid a blinding line across the hill-creased horizon. The light climbed the sky and the same ground silhouetted black, then brown and mottled greys. As morning gave ground to afternoon, father and son remained absent. Matt felt alone and awkward, which struck him as even more out of kilter. Finally, he returned to the ranch. After the cattle were fed and watered, he settled on patching a coat. Little else required attending. Finally, he cooked an early supper of steak and beans and played with the ball and cup on the porch, biding their return.

Soon more snow fell. It arrived quietly, not a blizzard, which piled against windward trees and buildings and drifted. The snowfall hushed even the dairy cattle lows. The country blued under the moon and outbuilding lights. North, a planet perched over the girl's house. The rough road's parallel tracks dented the snow cover toward the creek and tree like a pair of seams that stitched one portion of the farm to the other.

He wondered why he had not yet departed and had no intention to. Matt's accrued salary in the house safe had become three, then four stacks of bills high enough rubber bands were necessary to bind them, money enough to make home a fresh start, enough to retire his mother to town if she preferred. Wendy had not replied to his mail and he had stopped expecting she might. He was disappointed but resigned, and the fact made his return less complicated in the manner that would likely trouble him most. Still, he remained.

He looked at the corral and the outbuildings and was pleased with how well he knew them. He rubbed his belly until he raised the old scar. His exit shamed him. For all his size and strength he was a coward. He'd left a mother alone, but moreover in his mind, a woman for which he felt love but could not face. The bullet was his dodge even from himself.

He should've welcomed this quiet like every other, but sitting on the porch alone left him uneasy. He lived in a house and slept in a bed. He listened to voices familiar to him as his own. Exiting would be like his exits previous. He remained because he required the lesson in it: through thick and thin.

That night, Matt fell asleep on the sofa, awaiting Roland and Jarms. He woke to Roland sitting at the foot of it patting his ankle.

"You can't die," Matt said.

"I can," Roland said. "It's going to be easy."

Matt blinked. "Where's Jarms?"

"Town," Roland said. He rose for the kitchen. Matt listened to the rattle of the coffeepot and the water in the basin, then Roland's steps return. Together, they sat and listened to the coffee on the burner plink and boil.

"You'll keep on with Horace? I doubt he'll get through it so easy."
Matt nodded.

"I got your word on that?"

He nodded again.

"He's a good man isn't he?" Roland asked. "I mean despite the evidence."

"He is," Matt said.

"I wish his mother could see him," Roland said.

"You miss her?" Matt asked.

"No," Roland said, "but Horace does."

Roland rose and poured two cups. Matt sipped the coffee. It was brown as axle grease and strong, how Roland always brewed it.

"You know what the shame of it is?" Roland asked. "He thinks she doesn't count, just because she wasn't here."

Roland drank his cup down and went to the kitchen for the pot. Matt set his hand over his cup.

"How can you sleep at all, with so much of that in you?" he asked.

Roland winked. "Guess sleep don't have the charm it once did," he told him.

•

DECEMBER DUSTED THE COUNTRY WHITE. Little was left for Matt but the cattle and they barely filled his mornings. Roland bundled himself on the porch, and Matt filled him with hot coffee and donuts Roland had taught him to fry and glaze with corn syrup. He idled the remaining time in old storybooks Roland loaned him, in which he underlined words in pencil and waited for the old man to rouse from his naps to inquire their meaning. Roland had Jarms deliver a dictionary from town, but Matt had no patience for that kind of search.

Roland began coughing up his insides not too much later. All night, he'd be racked with jags and spit into an old chamber pot he kept under his bed. The metal clanged. In the morning, he emptied the green and yellow contents behind the house. Matt had offered to perform the chore but Roland would have none of it.

He had lost his weight and his color. Occasionally, he opened his pocketknife and shaved a fingernail to occupy himself. Matt stayed quiet while he'd finished off the one hand and started the other. The old man barely had the wind to walk to the barn, and he had surrendered chores. He accepted the worsening of his condition well, retiring to the porch, breathing the cold, clean air. Even days, he fought coughing. Matt had seen him swoon, when it hit him bad, but afterward he'd seem better for it. Sometimes Matt would glance from his book to see the old man asleep with frost in his hair.

Together, they would tarry on the porch for the few times the headlights bounced over the country and turned at the mailbox when Jarms had tired of town and gambling. The trips to the girl's place were fewer, then ceased for good. His debts mounted, growing rumor and substantiated by Garrett, who visited to attempt to bend them to his reason. He still refused to part with the grain money and Roland didn't argue.

"I'm having my lawyer come out next week," Roland said one night. "I'm changing my will. The ranch is going to you."

Matt took a pull from his cooling coffee. The old man watched him, then looked back across the yard. Matt set the cup down and stared at the black liquid inside.

"I'm a hired hand."

"You're more than that, and you don't have Garrett holding a lien on you."

"He don't have to pay," Matt said.

"But he will."

Matt nodded at the truth of it. The cards and the debt would wear him down; something about Jarms invited it.

Jarms rose before either of them to cook their breakfast and left the meals in the oven. He took his alone before the sun rose. All they knew of him in the weeks leading to the Christmas holiday were his footsteps. In those early morning hours, Jarms paced the living room like something in a box.

Finally, Matt rose before first light and found him in the kitchen.

"Roland ain't getting no better."

Jarms stirred some eggs he'd scrambled with bologna. "You expect him to?"

Matt shrugged. "I ain't never watched anyone die. Not so slow, at least. I don't like it much."

Matt went to the cupboard and found the coffee. He unloaded some into the percolator and filled the pot with water and set it to boil. Jarms turned another burner down and sampled his cooking. It was enough to his liking that he emptied the pan onto his plate. Jarms wolfed down another bite. It was hot and he coughed.

"I've took care of him," Jarms said. "I brought him you."

Matt got up to test the coffee, but it hadn't begun to perk. Jarms scooped a forkload of egg into his mouth. He got up and poured a cup full of coffee even though it was only lukewarm. A few loose grounds stuck between his teeth. Jarms let his breakfast lie and looked up at Matt. The skin around his mouth had gone slack and pink. His eyes were watery and red, like someone who'd worked all night and still had the next shift.

Matt lifted a Christmas candle from the middle of the kitchen table.

"You sentimental over the holiday?" Jarms asked.

"I believe Roland is," Matt said. Roland had begun to decorate the house with wreaths and a set of tiny nativity statues Matt had never seen. "We need a Christmas tree."

"There's some nice ones north of here," Jarms said. "Spruce seven feet or so."

"I didn't think any spruce grew in this country," Matt said.

"Roland planted them."

Jarms got up and set his plate in the sink. Matt watched him cross the lot outside and disappear into the barn. Fifteen minutes after, he emerged with a team harnessed to the sled. He'd loaded the axe and fifty feet of rope. He beckoned at the window and Matt shucked on his coat.

Jarms let Matt drive the team. Roland had planted the trees near the west end of the ranch, an hour's ride at least. Matt watched the sun spill over the country and the sky go blue and clear, promising another cold day. He wrapped his buffalo coat tighter and worked his fingers into his gloves. Only his face was exposed and the cold wind of their traveling was just enough to keep him from dozing.

Jarms recalled the direction and led them to the trees despite snow covering the landmarks one might use for bearings. He smiled, pleased with himself. They broke the crest of the hill and surveyed the trees.

"Jesus, we'll never get these back," Jarms said. The smallest of them was twenty feet tall.

"If we did, we'd wouldn't get one through the door," Matt said.

Jarms drank from a flask and spat. "Goddamnit," he said.

They sat a while. Jarms took the reins and began the team south and west. They left Roland's farm and passed others, each house issuing a stream of smoke from its chimney into the frigid sky. It was past lunchtime and Matt wished he'd packed for a longer trip. Still Jarms drove and coaxed the horses over the white hills.

Near mid-afternoon, they hit the Palouse River. It was black and sluggish. Jarms stopped and let the horses drink. Matt could see scrub brush and leafless cottonwoods, but none resembled a Christmas tree. Jarms's face was as blank as the country they were covering.

A mile later, they hit a rise, and on the other side was a farmhouse and shops and barns spread across the river bottom. In the yard was a smattering of smallish spruce.

"Whose place is that?" Matt asked.

"Garrett's."

Matt frowned.

Jarms stopped the horses in front of the house and knocked at the door. A grey-haired woman answered. She spoke to Jarms before she slipped on a coat and rubbers and walked across the yard toward the sled and the trees. She was weathered, but her eyes were blue and thoughtful. Matt took the coffee cup she offered and thanked her. She set the pot on the seat and disappeared to start another.

"Let's get to it or we'll be stumbling around in the dark," Jarms said. His axe blasted the trunk of the smallest tree. Though the chore was not enough work for one man, they hacked at it together, then loaded the tree and laced the rope across the branches to secure it. The woman stood in the cold and nursed her own coffee cup, standing extra straight as if to prove the cold couldn't shrink her. Jarms returned the pot and clucked the horses up the grade. The woman raised her hand, but Jarms didn't return the gesture.

"Where's the family?" Matt asked.

"Old man's dead. Garrett lives down the road."

"She here all alone?"

"As it should be," he said.

"That your mother?" Matt asked him.

"Yep."

"Garrett. He your brother?"

Jarms nodded.

Matt stared into the blankness of the snow. He watched the horses break the crust that had formed with the day's freezing and their backs glowing in the last of the sunlight. The runners sounded like water.

"Them trees at our place were hers," Jarms said. "She loves them. Roland put in a few every year just so she could transplant them into the yard. When she left, he told me the story and when I was big enough to swing an axe I cut them down except those last few." He laughed. "They were a long way and I was lazy even then. Anyway, we didn't have Christmas trees after and I was happy for it."

A hawk circled and dove. It rose with a mouse in its talons. Matt wondered what it would be like to see the country from that high, to cover it on the wing and not see the lines where one ranch ends and the other starts. He wondered how far he'd see and what would look different and what would look the same.

"Roland don't know nothing, so don't you tell him," Jarms said.

Matt stared ahead. The cold burned his face.

"You know, as mad as I was, if I'd known she was in this country when I was little I'd have hunted her until I found her. I'd have looked everywhere."

"I don't doubt it," Matt said.

"But she never inquired. Not once."

He quieted and said nothing more. It was a moonless night and the whole of the land turned black, except the farmhouses that winked with yellow glows from their windows. Jarms steered them through it without fail. It was his country. Matt could not help but feel his friend knew more about it than a man ought to.

•

LATE THAT NIGHT, MATT AND Jarms propped the tree in Roland's makeshift stand. Roland watched them haul the tree into the room with enormous satisfaction. He had found an oak apple crate full of trinkets and, together, they hung the ornaments on the thawing branches and unraveled a string of dried cranberries and circled the tree with them. In the kitchen, Roland boiled some beef hide for tallow and poured candles. He mounted each in tin saucers and drooped them over the branches strong enough to bear their weight. Matt watched as the old man lit one after another, then turned the house lights out. Jarms felt a melancholy come over him in that low flickering light, as if they might be the shadows the candles were licking at, and he didn't know if he feared their disappearing or their overwhelming him.

Roland constructed a pallet on the sofa and Matt brought a pillow and blanket from his room to join him. They drank cider and talked and played rummy until Roland began his nightly coughing spasms and eventually settled down to sleep, and Jarms excused himself and disappeared into the night. It was past midnight when he returned. The candles had burned half down and their wax dripped white across the green needles. "Shhh," Jarms whispered.

"What you got there?" Matt asked.

Jarms's bent to show him. What Matt saw first were the child's eyes. The infant stirred a little and turned toward the warmth of Jarms' arm.

"She gave birth two nights ago," Jarms said. "I thought it would be a week at least, but it took to milk right away."

"You pay the girl?" Matt asked.

Jarms shrugged. "What I could. She didn't complain. It's a girl," Jarms said. "I hadn't counted on that."

Matt nodded. "Still a baby, though."

"I suppose so."

Matt fetched a coat from his room. They lay the child on the soft lining then wrapped it with both lapels. Jarms boiled some milk and poured it into a bottle he'd scrounged from town some time back. The baby fed without waking. Jarms set it between them. He patted Roland on the arm, but the old man just turned like he was having a dream, and Jarms decided to let him sleep.

He turned away from the child and fell asleep too. Matt, though, watched the baby's chest rise and fall, and its eyelids flutter. He realized it had no name, and it troubled him. One of the tree's decorations caught his eye.

"Angel," he said to the girl.

He turned himself toward her and pressed his little finger into her fist, and felt for her grip in return.

Roland awoke in the darkness. The tallow had nearly burned down and soon after there was so little light in the room that he didn't make out the child at all. Later, as he rested, he discovered it through its exhalations, quicker than the rest. He rose again and gazed upon its tiny face between the sides of the coat. He looked at the two who had brought it, one his son of blood, the other a boy he'd constructed.

⋆ **27** ⋆

MATT WOKE WITH FIRST LIGHT, his finger wrapped still in the baby's fist. Her chest thumped fast as a bird's. Jarms snored quietly. The candles had melted to waxy flowers. He touched each one to make certain it had cooled. Satisfied, Matt perked the morning coffee in the kitchen. He returned with two cups—Jarms would sleep till noon—and set one on the end table next to Roland's head. It was then he saw the old man's eyes half open and his mouth slack. Matt sat in the sofa crook and eased his hand to Roland's throat, but felt nothing other than his cooling skin.

Inside the heavy coat the baby began to mew. Matt lifted her, coat and all. She was warm and he set her to his chest. Fresh milk was in the kitchen. Matt boiled some in a pan, weakening it with water like he might a calf. When it cooled, he put the mixture into the bottle. The baby took it and he rocked her in a kitchen chair.

With her belly filled the child dropped off. Matt wrapped her in his coat once more and put her next to Jarms. Outside, the sky had gathered clouds enough to keep the worst of the cold back.

Breaking the bales soon had him in a light sweat. The cattle bustled for their fodder as he broke the thin ice covering the water trough. He listened to them work the hay. He built a fire in the barn stove. After the cattle had their fill, he shooed them aside and shut the door. Their tails switched and their eyes wept with cold. He added another log, and when it took, two more and shut the stove door. He milked the heifers, though his hands ached. Roland had said he'd get used to it, but he had not.

Outside, something puzzled him. At first, it was a low fog, but, as he studied it, he recognized the smell: smoke. He figured it might be a choked chimney spewing but it appeared too heavy. Back in the barn, he saddled his workhorse.

The snow had softened and he made poor time. Halfway, he knew where the fire was and he goaded his horse forward. The house was a blackened skeleton. No wall stood. From the hill where he and Jarms had parked the car, Matt could recognize nothing of the family or the girl. He rode in. Near the porch steps lay the old man and woman, scorched, but not so much that Matt couldn't make out bullet holes in their chests and blood clotting their clothing.

Matt searched through the house's ruins for the girl. He found only chair ribs and a couch frame and a metal bed so hot it blistered his hands, and scarred clothes and fractured plates. The girl's room had fallen into the kitchen. Her brush and hand mirror lay on the stovetop. A magpie squawked. Matt saw it disappear in the high grass behind the house and heard another cuss it. Matt walked their direction. The birds scattered to a nearby leafless elm. The girl was slit from breastbone to her sex. The sack the child had been torn from lay in the cavity, puddled with the liquid it had breathed. There was a placenta and the severed umbilical chord in a pile next to the girl. Matt wondered why the coyotes hadn't gotten off with her, but the fire must have worried them. Matt pondered what he'd put inside her and the ruin it had come to. In the tree, the magpies waited. He waved his arms at them, but they only continued their vigil. He heard the footfalls of a horse and turned to see Garrett crossing the ground between him and the house.

Matt stared up at him. "Your doing?"

Garrett shook his head. "He didn't have any money for the girl. He'd been trying to gamble all week to raise it, but nobody'd even stake him enough to keep in a game."

"You might have," Matt said.

"It would come to no good. You could have done for him for a year and more. These dead are on your head. I've got money," Garrett said. "I told you that. I even tried to help get you some of your own. I own half the place now, maybe more. Every debt he incurred I bought. It's all on paper. I told you I wasn't going to let him waste the place."

"No, you said you didn't want to waste the man."

"The man is temporary; the land is permanent."

"He's your brother but you watched him flounder anyway."

"Blood is thicker than water, but dirt trumps both."

Matt glanced up. "I ought to beat you to death."

"And you could. You'd be better off. But you won't."

"There's been enough blood," Matt said.

He was suddenly tired and argument wasn't going to alter what was. He walked away from Garrett toward the shed where he sorted through the tools for a shovel and interred the freshly dead.

•

HE DISCOVERED JARMS MAKING A coffin in the barn. Hickeys of beat wood surrounded the places he'd tried to drive nails and two boards he'd split by leaving the ends short. The baby rested on Matt's open coat, wrapped in two towels from the bathroom.

Her hand swatted the air above her face. She stopped moving and turned her head and started to cry. Matt rearranged her in the coat, but she still simpered until he lifted her.

Matt watched Jarms set the lid on the plain box. He'd sawed an end off crookedly to fit it.

"Not much of a carpenter, am I?" Jarms said.

"Figure to bury him today while it's warming?" Matt asked.

"Probably best." Jarms wiped some sawdust off his wrist, but was sweating enough for most of it to stick. He patted the box. "Left room," he said.

"Gonna pack him some things?"

"Just that child."

Jarms fiddled with the wooden lid. The barn was dark. Matt couldn't see Jarms's face clearly, just slivers of it in the light coming through. He was set on staring until he looked into it. The stove cackled with the fire taking the pitchy wood.

"You really need to do that?"

"The child is Roland's. Roland's dead. Child has no purpose now. It's a girl child to boot."

"You hate them so much to kill a child."

"My mother killed a child. Killed Roland, too. I don't see no reason to feed and clothe another one."

"You think Roland would agree."

"Tough to argue dead."

"You burn that house?"

Jarms set the saw down.

"I buried them," Matt said.

Jarms paced and his face crossed into the light. Matt saw an eye, a cheekbone, and the corner of his mouth.

Jarms stopped at the woodpile. He knocked off some kindling with the axe and picked his teeth with a shard.

"That sure was a nice tree," he said.

"It was," Matt agreed. "It brought him some pleasure."

"Or it killed him," Jarms said. "It was her smell he was smelling. That might've been enough."

Matt shrugged. "I prefer thinking he liked it." He heard Jarms's tired laugh. The child shifted in the crook of Matt's arm. He jostled her, but the baby wouldn't quiet. It was hunting a breast, Matt realized. He unbuttoned his shirt and gave it his own muscled chest. It found a place and suckled, its moist mouth and teethless gums gnawing him.

"That baby's pumping a dry hole," Jarms said. In the shadows, Jarms's head shook. "You don't know nothing but work, and I don't know nothing period. It's better off with Roland here."

"No," Matt said.

Instead of arguing, Jarms lifted the axe and hurled it at the child in his arms. Matt turned. The blade cleaved the other half of his chest. He looked at it hang from him. The handle's weight pulled him forward. His shirt split and threads clung to the wound. The blood left him in black pulses that Matt felt through his arm and shoulder and neck. The child was still on the other side, snoozing. Matt stood and the axe fell out of him. Muscle and sinew bulged into the gash. He thought of the girl, split open. The blood pasted his shirt to his skin. He set the child down as Jarms made his way toward them. When he had neared, Jarms lifted the axe and swung. Matt's good hand caught the throat and threw Jarms off his feet. Jarms scrambled upright and rushed him. Matt drove the axe handle into his ribs, forcing him into the straw, gasping, on all fours. Matt crossed the barn and opened the doors. The cattle began for the pasture. The light streamed over Jarms. The hair at the back of his head swirled where it came together. Matt turned him with his boot toe. Jarms's eyes were open and rheumy. He looked worn out, but not mean, like he needed another hour of sleep.

Matt's chest ached. The blood slowed, but it soaked his shirt. He worried he'd lose consciousness. The baby was crying again. It would need fed soon.

"It's more mine than yours. It was my idea."

Matt said nothing.

Jarms said, "You'll starve it."

"I can boil milk," Matt said.

"That's not what I meant."

Matt propped himself on the axe handle. He nearly toppled when Jarms pulled it from under him. With one blow, Jarms busted open his own knee. Two more and his leg was nearly off, blood emptying under him. He again took a swipe and caught his other leg mid-thigh. He hacked through the muscle, but the bone was too thick. He gave that up and whacked off his left hand. It skittered across the floor.

"Look at it go," he said.

He was swamped in his own blood. His busted legs dangled. They both sat and listened to the baby cry. "I recall when I was a little guy," Jarms said. "Just two or three. My mother pushing the hair out of my eyes to get me sleeping. After a while I used to fake bad dreams just for her to do that." Jarms lifted his bad hand, then looked at the stump that was left. He shifted himself so he could use the other to imitate his mother's kindness. Pretty soon, he died, hand upon his brow.

Later that day, Matt bandaged himself and built another coffin, one big enough for two grown men. He buried Roland and Horace Jarms together under the tree, all the while listening to the water running and the baby next to him, breathing. After he was finished he carved her name in the tree and his own, too.

•

WENDY STOOD ON THE PORCH as Matt approached and did not move, even when he dismounted. He climbed the steps and she realized he packed a child in his coat like a fresh wound. He looked to have that, too. Blood streaked his jacket and hands.

The baby had awakened. It turned at her approach. It was Matt's, she could see. There was the same bewilderment in its eyes.

PART ★ THREE

When Figures show their royal Front—
And Mists—are carved away,
Behold the Atom—I preferred—
To all the lists of Clay

—EMILY DICKINSON
from poem 664

★ **28** ★

Lucky Jefferson, the Lincoln County sheriff, took his smoke break at half time on the high school gym's back steps. Davenport was down five and hadn't shot a free throw all night. Through the window, Lucky and a dozen or so locals listened to the coach swear and kick lockers. In the morning, they would gather for coffee and determine whether he needed to be fired. Opinion was offered and assayed at the café by twelve farmers with no standing other than land. Once figured, though, it was as sure as yesterday's weather.

A new man silently joined the group. Lucky had sheriffed the county twenty years and it was his business to recognize anyone in it. The man stood in the smoke and waited, neither speaking or spoken to. Lucky finished his cigarette and lit another. This coach ended his harangue with a prayer. He lacked the gall to ask God for victory so they prayed in silence. The temperature had nose-dived to near zero, and, huddled in their flannel jackets and cardigan sweaters like children waiting for the school bus cold mornings, the farmers looked as weak and fragile as their years made them.

BRUCE HOLBERT

Warm air washed over Lucky's face as they stepped inside for the second half.

"Keep Old Dan off another day, boys," Lucky told the farmers. They didn't reply, but he knew each would recall his words before sleep when truths leak into your head you'd spent your waking hours holding back. They were going to die and sooner rather than later. Lucky pulled on his second cigarette and admired the orange ember cook paper and tobacco. The new man hadn't moved. It was cold and clear and Lucky could make out the constellations. They were all that was left of his mother's teachings, stars in the sky that a bunch of ancients thought made pictures. Inside, applause swelled and ebbed as the ball changed hands, punctured by a whistle blast or a yell conducted by the pretty girls who led cheers. The man remaining outside appeared unfazed. He had clout; it was clear the way he carried himself, all shoulders and chest and those slow, deliberate strides that make you hear each footfall.

"Goddammit, state your business," Lucky told him.

Lucky watched a grin slowly stretch the stranger's face. "I want to offer you some work. I want you to find a man. You have a reputation for such matters."

Lucky lit another cigarette. At least it would warm his lungs. He inhaled and let out some smoke and watched it disappear in the cold air. The stranger unlatched a valise and removed a folder. "Name's Lawson."

"Local?"

"A long while back he was. He murdered my brother. Down around Colfax. Before the war. I don't have any photographs, but there's one in your papers from when he was young. Look up 1918."

Lucky shook his head. It was an old, cold trail. Every county had two or three murders unsolved. One sat on his own desk. A boy hung from a roof beam. The father swore it was hoboes, but the boy's pocket still held a walletful of money. There was nothing to lead him. No witnesses. No old grudges. Just grieving parents and a swinging body.

Lucky gazed at the man. He had pluck keeping in this weather with shirtsleeves. But pluck wasn't what disturbed Lucky: it was that sickening feeling he was being steered.

"Why don't you find him yourself?"

The man shifted to face him. "I'd enjoy the looking too much. You get my age you don't want to enjoy anything much. Makes time go too fast."

Lucky chuckled at that. The night was still as could be. "How much?" he asked.

"Twenty thousand," he told him.

Lucky stayed quiet. Inside the feeling would return to his hands, as would the pain. He'd be up half the night with them. The man offered the folder to Lucky. Inside were some handwritten notes: general information, the kind anyone could acquire writing letters and knowing politicians. The man drummed his fingers against the cup rim, an irritating rhythm he repeated a full minute.

"You so close to this brother you let it sit twenty years before looking for justice?" Lucky shook his head. "You're a devoted son of a bitch aren't you."

The man remained unrankled. "Justice has nothing to do with it."

"Why not let sleeping dogs alone?"

The man was still staring off at the light, measuring the nothing out there. "You'll do it. I knew it as soon as I saw you."

•

THE BRAN IN LUCKY'S BREAKFAST the past fortnight made his bowels sluggish as a bear in January. His gut cramped and loosened, and gas swelled his colon while he sat the toilet and pressed his excrement into the bowl. It smelled rich. He reached for the pie tin on the counter and squeezed the last droppings onto it and cleaned himself up and ambled to the kitchenette with the plate. The cafe prepared a meat loaf and sliced it thin. Lucky employed his feces to bind two together, then set them on a bread slice. He covered the meat with ketchup, put another slice of bread on top, and started a second sandwich.

The jail had only six cells. The boy in the last one wore the county's orange overalls. Lucky had assigned him to wash the squad cars in the cold afternoon. His long hair was tangled and his beard stubbled. Lately his skin had yellowed. The boy had immigrated to town with his girlfriend. They lived in the same house. Lucky had suggested alternative arrangements and the boy cursed him. Lucky brought him in for assault, and, though the charge wouldn't stick, the judge only came through once a week and was a week behind on the docket when he did. Three weeks of shit for food and the punk would be in the hospital and Lucky would drop the charges. The other prisoners were a petty sort. Most had heisted groceries or written bad checks. One beat up his buddy with a frozen ham, which might have led to little consequence if the brawl had not occurred in the supermarket.

"I brought you some more of that restaurant food," Lucky told the boy. "Maybe it'll sit on your stomach better than our jailhouse slop."

The *Davenport Times*, a weekly, was a long walk, but he enjoyed the metal sky pressing over the white country. He was pleased to find just young Van Nostrand in the newspaper office. He'd lived in the county only a short time, but was good about making sure he published the names Lucky sent for the police blotter. Lucky sorted the bins for the year. He couldn't recall the date, though he didn't have to hunt long. A boy named Lawson appeared on the front page of the Christmas newspaper. "In Storm Boy, Father Missing Brother Survives" headlined the issue. It contained no pictures of the deceased, just one of a boy who'd survived and one of a young woman who was credited with his rescue. Her name appeared. He stared back at the woman in the photograph.

He recalled his mother teaching him to hunt, and the whole time him knowing it was wrong. There was a meanness in killing that made it pleasant, but she didn't see that. To her it was just food for the table. He recalled worrying over the first rabbit he'd snared. But when he brought the animal back to his mother, she skinned it and put it in a pot to cook, the same as if he'd pulled a carrot from the garden.

He'd read a good deal before and since, but could recall nothing from his lessons about doing in a simple animal. He missed the significance, even now. Hunting season men and boys skinned deer in their driveways and sawed them to quarters for the butcher. Two or three others loitered, drinking coffee or an early beer, all pleased, none nearly as troubled. They had the luxury of eating without killing, and their kinship made him spiteful.

Someplace still in his memory, his mother hovered in the cave mouth. He'd set himself for town and escaped. On the way, he stole clothes from a line and convinced a trucker to share his boxed lunch and haul him to Canada, where he entered the military service.

In the war, Lucky tallied over fifty confirmed enemy killed, most in ordinary ways. One instance, however, found him alone in the Ardennes, looking to reattach. From a thicket, he heard snoring. He hoped he'd happened upon his comrades until he recognized their helmets. Later, they sang lullabies in German, tunes Lucky recognized. Lucky could have circled wide. Instead, he crept to their cold camp and butchered them. Steam rose from their opened necks, and, after he'd finished them, he warmed his hands over it. The day of his orders rotating him home, he donned gloves and put his fists under a tank track transport. The event pulverized the bones of his hands and delayed him in hospital long enough for his papers for the Pacific to process. But Truman sent the bomb and that was that.

Upon his return he discovered his mother had been committed to Eastern State Hospital for the insane. A speculator named Cross-field bargained for the land that included her cave, and, when he couldn't force her to pull up stakes, called the authorities. Lucky put himself up for sheriff next election and, winning, wrote Cross-field so many tickets the man abandoned the county altogether. Lucky never called on his mother, however, and he never heard inquiry from her or the hospital.

For the most part, he'd pounded himself into a hard shape, but, in his infirm moments, he recalled Wendy's fingers measuring and cutting his hair as if they were expert at touching him. She had worked from behind and her breasts listed into his back. His soaped hair wet his skin, and her breath, when she scrutinized her work, warmed it. In his room, tacked to the wood-paneled walls, were magazine photographs, a hundred different faces. The only thing they shared was some resemblance to her.

He had not thought of his mother's name nor heard it in twenty years. Seeing the word in a forty-year-old newspaper rattled him. He hauled the issue to a desk with a light where he could see her better. The pages had yellowed and the pictures appeared trans-parent as ghosts. She was pretty, beautiful even, and the boy, well, he was just a boy.

He walked to city hall and opened the building with his master key and hunted Lawson's paperwork. None appeared to exist, which in itself was not surprising. He had no trouble putting the woman who had taken him and his mother in to the name Lawson and recognized them as mother and son. And she had shared her house with Wendy Worden as well. Finally he found, years later in the records, a scrawled marriage certificate: Wendy Worden to Matthew L. Lawson. He lit a cigarette and chuckled. His visitor had wanted a hired hand, but this work he would have performed for free.

In his office, he called the counties in the eastern portion of the state. He spoke to deputies because at one time or another he'd antagonized each county's sheriff with his unwillingness to extradite prisoners. Most saw law as something of a fraternity and expected assistance from their brethren. Lucky, though, wasn't inclined toward brotherly love. Most every county knew a big man who had raised hell. Lawson's features were plain: brown eyes, brown hair; there was little left for an edge aside from his size.

Lucky drove through town in his squad car. He pulled over a high school boy for chirping his tires. He got out of his car with his citation book, but the air was cool and crisp and the trees white with frost. The streets were small and lined with well-kept houses, lights splashed some windows, and smoke barreled from the chimneys. A black line of state highway cut through town. Cars eased over the slick road, and a yellow county truck had begun sanding. It was a nice place to live, more pleasant than most. He let the boy off with a warning, then went back and cleaned out his desk. It had been a good job, to his liking anyhow.

★ 29 ★

COULEE DAM WAS TWO TOWNS. One, a row of flat single-floored houses that rimmed the river's east side, was inhabited by the engineers who conjured the sorcery required to stop a million years of river and the contractors entrusted to fashion their witchery into steel and concrete. The other, a cluttered array of canvas tents, had been hurriedly erected to house those who performed the labor.

The dam itself was busy as a hive. On both sides of the river powder monkeys drilled and blasted. Their explosions shook the coulee all hours of a day, dust and rock scattering hundreds of feet every direction. Below, loaders filled twenty-ton belly dumpers with unnaturally sheared granite slabs, which they deposited upon the riprap lining both riverbanks. On the cleared cliffs, jackhammer operators dangled by ropes a hundred feet from the top to beat the rock smooth. Drillers in a similar apparatus followed, auguring rebar and conduit into the rock to secure the structure. In the river, another crew drove enormous squared pylons into the bottom until they had constructed a watertight circle a quarter acre or so. Pumps pulled the water clear and steam shovels clawed the mud to bedrock. Then more jackhammers and rebar, and then forms, then concrete.

The quartermaster offered Matt and Wendy a blanket and sheets and assigned Matt bucket duty on a cement crew. The job consisted of waiting for the crane to dip a bucket into wet cement; he then straddled the boom cable, his feet balanced upon the bucket lip until over the pour site. The crane operator could hydraulic the bucket shut with gears, but once filled, the pressure couldn't manage the weight and a man was required. The bucket jockey kicked the latches until the concrete fell from under him. The chore required booting both the bucket sides free at once. If not, the bucket wobbled and the man hung on one foot, or worse, dangled by his hands on the boom cable. Or, the jockey could split and end up straddling both halves. Fighting for balance swung the cable, which caused the bucket to spin or buckle.

The hand opposite Matt was named Mills, a gaunt fellow with a weathered brow and a beard that saw a razor once a week at most. A ball cap hooded his eyes, and he would screw it to his ears before each pass. They didn't speak; even their lunches had been staggered to keep one crane in operation.

•

HIS FIRST PAYDAY, MATT DID not have time enough to draw. He saw to it that Wendy and the child were fed and down, then toted a cut log in front of the tent for a stool and started a fire. A few campfires glowed: lead men; the lines of lackeys, like Matt himself, climbed the beaten trails to Grand Coulee's B Street. Dawn, they returned. A lantern or flashlight occasionally bobbed, leading their way, the men shadows and laughter. Some wretched. The night was like so much water, a few feet in front or behind and the rest was a mystery. It was not unlike day in that regard.

Each man fought to his bunk, shackled to his lot. Matt had no call to lord it over them. They would wake in pain, but so would he. Alcohol wouldn't be the source, but drinking didn't form drunks either. Matt remained sentinel at his self-assigned post all day Saturday and through the night once more, ceasing only to fetch meals or retrieve firewood. Sunday morning, the low fog socked itself inside the coulee then burned off. Most of the men lingered in the tents even after the breakfast call. Matt listened as they groused through late morning until they emptied their whiskey jugs and resorted to concocting cocktails of gasoline and milk called Heat.

The only consistency was the river. Its hum continued despite the plans and toiling of the hundreds on its banks. Behind Matt, inside the tent, were a wife and a child. He wanted to be filled with them like the drunks with their bottle, like the channel with its river, but he was too leaky a vessel. They might fill him and fill him until they were empty and still he would be, as well. Wendy saw that and, as the months passed, kept Angel with her nights. Children loved so hard they inherited their parents' wounds, and Wendy hoped to suture the child before she bled out.

For a while, he and Wendy sipped the hot, bitter coffee. Church bells clanged, and motors started throughout the town. Matt watched cars back from their driveways and cross the bridge down-river in procession.

"You ever go to church?" he asked Wendy.

She nodded. "For a while. I didn't care for it and I was stubborn."

"I wished I'd gone," Matt said.

"You did," she told him. "You used to come get me right after."

She worked her coffee and spoke nothing more. Matt listened to her breaths. He saw her lingering, owning the words to soothe him but not the sentiment. After nineteen years, Matt had encountered her once again on the porch of his mother's house. The evening was soundless, not even cattle lowed in the pastures. Old Peach was silent, just foundations and burned wood. A deer herd explored the streets and browsed lawns. Matt peered toward the knoll where he'd buried Luke and his father.

"Them roses must be hardy."

"I tended them," she said. "I lived here."

Here?"

"With your mother," Wendy said.

This stopped Matt.

"My Lord," he said. "You took care of her and the place."

She nodded.

"I can't leave this baby," he said.

"I wouldn't expect so," Wendy replied.

The Justice of the Peace was an old deputy. In lieu of a pension, he earned fifty dollars a month to arrange the burials of those too poor for the trimmings and marrying folks too godless for church, he stared at the ruffian before him and the poor woman and child he would marry him to.

"You want to do this?" he asked the woman.

Wendy didn't reply. The land was gone, but her father would invest in another business in a town on higher ground. Considering what the government offered on the ranches, a business would fetch enough to start clean, with inventory. In time, Wendy would likely manage the enterprise. Her father trusted her. But that path required a retreat, if not stated implied, and she did not yet have surrender in her. It was poor rationale for marrying a man but it was hers.

"The country is drowning but that don't mean you got to marry the first deadbeat that asks, child or not. I can find you work and a bunk."

"I do," Wendy said.

"I haven't asked yet."

"Well, when you do, that's my answer."

The man delivered the vows and they repeated the parts meant for each and signed a certificate.

As for Matt, his mother had abandoned her land, which was only a memory anyway; the money for it was in her purse, where it should be, he figured. Like an animal, he reverted to instinct. He worked through the mountains the next three days. The snow was four feet high in places and travel slow. Queenie bounded gamely through the drifts for an hour but eventually abandoned them for better prospects. As they climbed, the tree shapes turned poorly drawn cones, abstractions of trees as if snow had commandeered the Earth's contours, scooping and piling horizons with the wind before freezes until the thaws clotted them into new forms. Twice the horses stepped into deep hollows beneath the hoary cloak. The wish of the horses' hooves punching through the snowpack and the creak of their saddles and possibles and the occasional clang of the bridles against their metal hoops were all that punctuated the silence. Matt remained on the glean for a sign he could recall or a site to weather night. She followed like a tired soldier. He couldn't guess what she thought, so he made no attempt.

Camps, they rolled themselves together under heavy blankets in a snow cave, the child between them like a stove heating two rooms. That Wendy remained mornings when he woke and stoked the fire and boiled the coffee still confounded him. He guessed she'd set off any time and a thing in him welcomed her parting; her silence, agreeable at almost any other time in his life, served to remind him only now of the stilled voices in his head.

They discovered a Forest Service hut for the summer fire watch. Inside were a stove and a single bed frame. The child fussed and Wendy opened a leather satchel and offered her a frilly shirt. She fisted the lace and rubbed it in her hands and finally chewed it to a grey mush. Evening, Matt returned with an elk's hindquarters. The rest he had lashed to a high tree bough to deny the coyotes a share.

A half jug of milk remained, and Matt fed the baby while Wendy turned the elk steaks, substituting a tin plate for a skillet. Frying the meat evenly was impossible so what they ate was both seared and raw, and the black blood slid down their chins as if they were animals ten thousand years before when fire was as much a threat as a boon.

Wendy reclined on their pallet and gazed at a gap where the mud hadn't stuck between the log walls. Matt stood and undressed himself. He bent himself and knelt at her side. She lifted her hands to fend him off, then stared at them there. She shook her head in surrender and undressed.

Matt saw her privates under him, just a hair-covered mouth swallowing his own makings. He felt like the air had thinned. Wendy's eyes closed and her face clenched. She whimpered. After, Matt dressed and stood sentry outside, staring at the moon. He wondered if he could ever touch a person without busting them open.

The baby began a wet hack the second week. Matt hooked his little finger into her tiny throat and dragged green phlegm from her. When she went feverish, Wendy employed cold rags and steamed water, but it did little good.

"Are you going to let us die?" Wendy asked. She needed him like food. She'd taken his name and his watery seed not for what she felt or even what she remembered of him, but for his presence. He could find food and keep a fire. He could frighten others. It wasn't desire blocking her way to Matt, but it did not move her his direction either. The mistake of the boy embarrassed her and it had worn a track into her memory.

"Would you like it better if I did?"

She smiled. He had returned her faithlessness with his own. He commenced to prepare the horses and after a time, she disappeared into the cabin to wrap the baby. They rode that night into the village of Kettle Falls. The ferry was closed and they forded a narrow place below the kettles the Indians scaffolded for the salmon run. Their wet clothes froze to them as soon as they left the river. Matt had tied Angel into a bundle and strapped her to his back, which kept her dry. The doctor's wife answered the door. The doctor put a plastic tent over the child and a machine pumped treated steam into it. Three days later, Angel was well enough for travel and they headed to the coulee and work.

And now he had work, but little more. Wendy offered him the baby, now four months old. He took her and dropped his face close and allowed her tiny hand to tap it. Her eyes blinked at him like he was the sky. She rarely cried; Wendy often cited her worth on such matters. Matt figured it differently. Crying did no good; it was wasted time. The child was only being smart.

"I don't know what to do," Matt said. "I got no idea."

"Me neither," she told him.

The next night, straying rounders insulted each other with bawdy language outside his tent. Matt tolerated it until a tall fellow with legs thin as a kildeer's pissed on the canvas. Two steps and Matt tore the tent flap open and two more and he was on the man before he buttoned his trousers. The rounder's cheekbone broke with the first blow and the blood warmed Matt's hands. A second cost the man an eye socket and a third a half-dozen teeth. The man's companions pinned Matt's arms, but he wrestled loose, throwing two into a ragged locust. Half a dozen more were required to end the beating. The rounder lay on the cold ground, pants still undone, walleyed as a pike. Matt had split two other lips and broken a nose. No one spoke. Together, his cohorts carried their man off. Matt returned to his pallet. Angel cried and Wendy tended her.

An hour later a Bureau security officer opened the tent flap. He held a notebook.

"What'd he do to instigate this?" the man asked.

Matt shrugged. "He's got no manners," he told the man. The man wrote the answer on his pad and nodded to himself.

"Nothing else?"

Matt shook his head.

"Well, it's a dangerous world for the discourteous," the man replied.

★ **30** ★

No houses were to be had in town. A weedy field beyond B Street sat unused, though, and Matt pilfered pallets and gleaned salvageable plywood sheets from the scrapped forms. When he had enough, he began a wooden foundation and, after, framed, quilted the plywood scraps into a square floor. He hijacked the sheets he found nearly whole for walls and sawed one hole in the front and stapled it over with clear plastic. Nothing anywhere was sturdy enough for a roof beam, so he settled on draping tent canvas over a two-by-four frame. A scrapped Franklin stove from a dump kept heat after he welded the back plate and strung new pipe.

He presented the lodge to Wendy hoping she would be relieved to escape the community tents, but her response was unenthusiastic even when he unveiled the washbasin he'd pilfered from the Bureau surplus. Each day, Matt rose early and carried the day's water from a pump a half-mile away. He repeated the tasks daily. Some mornings, when the early hour turned particularly bright with frost or pungent with bloom or the coulee flattened the dawn to a hard red line and the liquid light arced and sprayed from it over the shabby town and the vacant lot in which he and his family resided, he ruminated upon the progress of lives. His own appeared a thrown stone; he had no idea the arm that directed it. Its path remained invisible to those without his history. And rather than concluding on some dirt road or resting beneath a crag's shadow with several hundred similar stones—the former constant, and the latter at least among companions—he was, instead, in a lake or river, descending invisibly, the only evidence of his passage ripples wrinkling the water. A similar description might apply to his wife: the sweep and innocence of it, her muffled fall and slow descent at the mercy of the current and gravity. Some moments the notion threatened to turn philosophy or a resigned sort of religion. He was content to be at the will of a greater force, whether it be nature or fate or providence or gravity.

The spring warmed and, for a while, the weather was pleasant, but no trees shaded the hovel, and when in May an early week of summer descended, the tenthouse was stifling. Matt bought ice by the block and set it whole in an army surplus footlocker to keep the food from spoiling. By summer, Wendy was soaking the child's clothes in the cold pools. She herself went about in undergarments and doused her head with a water glass at regular intervals.

Evenings when Matt returned, he and Wendy undid the tent flaps for the breezes that proceeded up and down the coulee each night. The three of them perched upon shipping crates Matt fabricated into crude furniture and enjoyed the cooling evening. Matt's white T-shirt glowed in the setting sun. He began to construct a hobby-horse from the shelter scraps. Nothing to admire, but he curved it enough Angel could boot the stirrups and gallop. In the meantime, Wendy stitched army surplus blankets into pajamas and purchased discounted fabric bolts to cut shirts and blouses and trousers. Light flooded through the plastic into the room and warmed her and the girl during day. Angel turned circles in the glow as sunshine fell on her as lazily as rain.

Early in June, Wendy recognized she had become pregnant. She applied the early hours each day to washing and hanging clothes upon the rope Matt tied between the shack corner and a spindly birch. By nine, sweat dappled her blouse; the cheap fabric clung at her arms and chest and, when it was past tolerance, she would collect Angel from a cool place in the morning shade and drag her in a rusted wagon to the city park.

The willows cut the sun a little and she had discovered a grassy place under a piece of basalt that offered shade most of the afternoon. At the entrance, the county erected a cinder block lavatory, which included a shower. Wendy undressed the girl and together they showered two or three times a day. Angel danced and Wendy sang "The Ballad of Bonny and Clyde" or "The Old Gray Mare."

Afterwards, they dressed again and ate sandwiches and traded lemonade in a thermos. Often other children joined them with mothers, some doting, some so distant they hardly noticed their charges. Angel remained content to entertain herself. Wendy had struck up conversations, but most withered into graceless silences. Maybe years could pass in the same way.

Angel drew circles in the dirt. Over and over, she followed the same track, trying to make it good. Wendy reclined in the shade with a book. She felt reading a secret luxury, one she kept so because it was a frivolity. She snuck books like Matt's mother had drinks, hiding them all over the house, taking to their clean pages only when she'd put Angel down or when Matt worked the late shifts. It was over a novel she made her first acquaintance. The woman's name was Ardith and the book *Appointment at Samara*. They talked of John O'Hara and Katherine Porter and Edna Ferber. An hour of talk passed without Wendy's notice; to lose oneself was suddenly liberating. She gazed at Ardith, who was smiling—she most times seemed to be on the edge of laughter.

Angel kept in a large oak's shade. Her mouth straightened. That was her father in her, or perhaps her mother. Her womb had never carried Angel and the girl seemed to know it in that animal certainty that children possess. The thought embittered her, but she couldn't restrain herself as her baby approached. Wendy rubbed her belly and felt the child rising to meet her.

"I so enjoyed being pregnant," Ardith said. Ardith's sleeping infant lay between them. Wendy reached across him and took Ardith's hand. She lifted it and set it over her tight stomach. Ardith rubbed it softly. They sat like that a long time in the quiet, until finally Ardith gathered her son to leave.

"Come with me," Ardith said.

Wendy nodded. She and Angel followed Ardith across the park to her car in ragged line. Ardith opened the door and Angel piled in. Inside the car, the wind riffled Wendy's blouse and blew her face dry. Ardith halted the car at a split-level house, with the grass neatly trimmed. Inside, a swamp cooler chilled the house. They put their faces in front of the vents. Angel giggled and spoke a broken word into the air whir. Ardith ran water into the bathroom tub. She offered Wendy a towel as thick as her pillow.

"Take as long as you want," Ardith told her and shut the door.

The water was fragrant with rose petals. Suds whorled near the spigot and lifted from the water. Wendy touched them. The temperature was cool and it surprised her until she considered the weather. It seemed a bath could be about more than getting clean. She undid her worn blouse and trousers, unrolled her stockings and stepped into the tub. On her knees in front of the spigot, she drank, then lay back. The water climbed past her ears, stopping sounds. She thought nothing and wondered at the relief it brought her.

Ardith dropped a drink for her on the tub's edge. It was fortified cola, full enough of whiskey that her head lightened. She remained a long while. The window light had burned enough to know late afternoon had descended when she finally forced herself to rise and dry. She noticed a second drink and her clothes missing. She rifled the drawers and the hamper, but they were nowhere. A new outfit with tags lay on the counter. She sipped the drink and stood naked and dried with a plush towel. The clothes seemed of the same material. She touched them and realized they were a gift. Underneath, she saw fresh underwear and a brassiere and even stockings. She dressed slowly and with great care. Outside the door was a pair of new sandals.

The living room was still cool, like the bath. The mahogany buffet held china and the thin shelves tiny Hummels. A picture of a mountain hung upon one wall and a gramophone lined a cabinet. Wendy caught her reflection in a long foyer mirror. She appeared for a moment like this could be her house, save the stunned expression on her face and the raggedy little girl who had moved across the room to see what the woman she knew as her mother found so compelling.

★ 31 ★

LATE AUGUST OF 1942, IT rained a week entire. Each morning Wendy rose to a mist draped upon the river. The ground turned dark and rich like fresh wheat country, the weeds silver with dew. She regarded it with a pleasure rare in the bone-dry summer. The weight of the child stretched her abdomen and she made water nearly every hour in the tarped outbuilding Matt constructed. Once, upon seeing Wendy's T-shirt rise, Matt inquired about touching it. She'd not allowed it. He said nothing, and she wondered again about the womb that had carried Angel before.

The girl slept fitfully, cutting molars. Her cries woke them two or three times before each dawn. Matt attempted to soothe her with a bottle, but she usually spat the nipple because it irritated her gums. He soaked a rag in cold water to help her gnaw tooth through gum, but it did little good. Wendy finally rose from their pallet and took the child from him. Matt watched as she whispered songs to her and Angel calmed. She rocked, and the baby cooed. He emptied the bottle and wrung the rag over a pail, then lay on their bed behind

Wendy where he could see Angel's face. Her eyes had closed and her hair dampened with sweat. Wendy hummed, tabbing it a little victory. She had wrested a bit of the child for herself.

Matt's routine mornings commenced with building his lunch and arranging his family's breakfast: for Angel, cereal and fruit, and a soft boiled egg for Wendy. Yet Wendy woke the following dawn to their makeshift kitchen clean but with no meal. Matt returned late that evening. The Bureau offered overtime and he was recruited first because he finished the pressing jobs in less time than others. He had transferred from the buckets when the ironworkers required his size to sledge tie rod. He was exhausted the first week, but cleaned out by the third. At the end of the fourth, no one could stay with him. The labors creased his arms and chest with muscle and sinew.

Late, Matt pieced together dinner in the dark house from what they had left him, and warmed a kettle and washed in the bathtub. Too big for the house, he'd put it outside. Through the plastic window, Wendy saw steam meet the cool air. He and Wendy had not been with one another since she announced her pregnancy. He perched at the tub's edge a long while following, but she was asleep when he finally lay down and so was the child.

The next day he lingered for overtime again and the one following the same. He added weekend shifts, as they paid double. Weeks pushed the year into autumn; Wendy felt rent from him and all that was outside herself, and she realized the sensation was not all that different than when he was present. Each day, she and Angel sat and Wendy read aloud from a box of books she purchased at a library sale. Angel often as not hauled the book behind her while Wendy performed her chores. Seeing the child move toward her was satisfying. She had constructed an ally.

The following night, Wendy watched Matt through the plastic. He was by himself in the cold, standing under a streetlight. She tucked the child into her blankets and turned out her light and her own. She heard Matt arrive and undress and lie next to her, though he never offered her a word, nor she him. The next day he did the same and the one that followed. Evenings, she would glance up from cooking or reading and recognize him at his post across the street waiting for them to end the day so he could, too. She thought of him studying her those years before and the gifts he'd left. They changed her life. Not the possessions, but the receiving of them. She wondered now if they were injuries he'd inflicted upon her, or she on herself, each present a limp or a polioed arm until she was weak enough to take him.

She shook her head, and the child glanced up at her quizzically. It exasperated her, this kind of thinking. She'd hoped she might be above it. Her life was her own doing. She thought of him in the cold. He'd smoke more than he ought to, trying to keep warm. It wasn't healthy. The streetlight barely made his shape from the shadows. That was where she loved him. It frightened her. She realized it must have him, as well. That the best in him she could only see from a distance, that up close it disappeared like words from a page if you tried to read a book sitting on your nose.

Her hands twirled Angel's locks. She pursed her lips for a kiss, and Angel, who knew enough to press hers together, made a smooching sound. She looked at the child. She'd once again taken the best from him and left him with just the shell.

That night, Wendy put the child down and turned out her own light. She waited at the door for him. His heavy boots clattered the earth and his huge shadow blocked the street's light. He was blinded by the dark room and collided with her. His force pressed her a step back. She had planned to take his hands and speak to him. She could see his eyes reflect the only lantern she'd kept lit. He turned slowly with one open hand raised, as if for balance, and clouted her. She landed on the floor, stunned, but unhurt. The wind blew cold. When she'd focused her eyes, he stood over her and glared into his palm and its fingers like he'd rid himself of them at first opportunity.

"It's all right," she said. "You didn't mean it." But he had cleared the steps and galloped across the vacant lot. She saw him cross through the streetlight glows as he loped, a man, then a shadow, then gone, then a man again, then shadow until he was out of sight completely.

•

MATT SLEPT IN A PARK and walked four miles to work. Two or three of the fellows offered him a lift, but he just kept to his fast gait. At the shop, they chatted fishing and quality tobacco, and, though he never did partake, their voices grated him, so he packed metal sheets two or three at a time onto a flatbed. When he had loaded the truck, he wheeled it to the forms and hammered each into the ground with blows that would stagger an elk. He didn't take lunch and by one-thirty had beat enough metal to occupy the framers and cement crews for three shifts. The foreman approached him.

"That's the whole of it."

"Get them to cut some more."

"You've done two weeks' work in two days and you been doing it a month straight. There isn't any more to do." The foreman rubbed his jaw. He was a red-faced Scot, veins splintered from drinking, less boss than goat herder. He'd order men to perform a task and they would do it or do something else, depending on their moods. Matt had little use for the man.

"These other men. They have families, too. They work regular, union work. There's no work left to do, and if them bigwigs find out, they'll shit can half the crew. Play a hand of cards in the rigger's loft. Come in late. Go home early."

Matt undid his gloves and set them on the saw table. "I guess I'll have to quit you, then," he said.

The foreman drove his hands into his pocket. Matt could see the gaggle of men behind who had put him up to it. An unsociable man is hard enough to take; one who worked them out of a check was intolerable. He stared at them. They scattered like children. He punched his card into the clock.

At the river, he perched over the rock bank. Across the water, they had blasted the end from a bluff to fit concrete; upriver the engineers constructed parks they envisioned as campgrounds for visitors. The State laid asphalt and merchants threw up shops at the bottom and top of the hill.

He wondered if he could light out now, if he had enough of family to sustain him. Most of his life he had squandered with men alone. In sentimental moods, they would recall wives or children, but each remembered only long enough to glimpse what they could not make real in a thousand years of trying. They shared the same primitive illness. He smoked and wondered what kept men like him from entering into a peace with their lives, what trick of being had they not mastered. He worried whether Wendy had enough firewood, then recalled he'd split and stacked a pile next to the front door a few days past.

He climbed the big hill the locals called Millard Grade because Walter Millard flew a Plymouth off it into a state trooper's living room. Atop, he bent and sucked breaths until his wind returned. The small town's lights scattered between him and the Bureau of Reclamation plant, blue against the snow, and, beyond that the black, blocked river. West was only darkness. He'd passed the last house and considered the only road that led into town from here. He left it for the brush. A mile or so and there was a box canyon and trees and a spring.

He climbed a fence. Cows lowed. He could see their bulky masses in the moonlight. On the field's other side was a granite spill; with no discernible trail, he covered the distance in a straight line. He'd sold his good horse to a banker who worked a few cattle. The pasture was near and Matt found it. He whistled low and the horse trotted to him. He led it to the gate. Inside the barn were a bridle and a blanket.

He swung himself aboard and started the long climb from the coulee. There was enough wood, he told himself, and an axe to bust more. Four miles and he arrived at a lone pine on a cattle path and under it built his pallet. The fire he started was a weak one. He fed it with sage limbs and leaves and needles to keep it from notice.

•

HE HAD DETERMINED TO SEE the Jarms place once more, but misjudged his bearings and two nights later recognized he had reached Garrett's ground. He shot a rabbit and roasted it on a driftwood fire, the fuel remaining from last spring's runoff. He drank from the Palouse than spat. The water tasted of metal and smelled dead with fertilizer leachings. He melted some snow, and settled himself for the night.

Morning, he tied and hobbled the horse, then climbed from the river's cut and hiked the three miles to Garrett's home. At a hilltop eyebrow too steep to plow, he examined the house below. Across the drive a giant machine shed loomed. The open sliding door revealed a rodweeder and harrow and, behind, a combine, the header detached. Metal clanked against metal inside. Two gangly boys fetched tools from a trap wagon. Garrett scolded them for a wrong-sized wrench. The boys blamed each other. The disagreement nearly ended in blows. An hour later, the pickup ignition cranked and Garrett directed both boys from the cab. They huddled in the truck bed as he traveled the road toward town.

Matt descended to the house. A dog bounded toward him and Matt readied for an attack, but when he feinted a kick, the dog cut and circled. A woman in a plain dress met his gaze. She looked like a girl in a statue, and her face, though drawn, was the kind in magazine stands.

"I'm an acquaintance of your husband's," Matt said.

"He went to town for parts. He'll be back shortly," the woman said.

Matt nodded. The woman measured him. "Would you like to come inside?"

He stamped his feet on the porch boards. She waved him to a chair and he perched at its edge letting the furnace heat bloom over his hands. Her brown eyes passed over him. She returned from the kitchen with a cup holding coffee and brandy. He sniffed it, and drank. She poured him another. A spinning wheel stood in one corner of the room. No grease in the joints, he saw; it was a decoration. He sipped his fortified coffee. The woman sat, examining the grain of the pine table. She tapped her cup with her nails, like a clock ticking. When she stopped, the quiet seemed louder than the sound.

Matt approached the hearth and rotated the burning logs. He added another. Pine, it went up quickly and sap popped embers at the screen. He watched the woman extend her hands and stocking feet to the furnace and listened as she sipped her drink.

"Are you married?" she asked. She held her cup with both hands.

Matt said, "I don't know if I am anymore."

She returned her cup to the kitchen and offered to tour him through the house. The kitchen had views up the valley and the bedrooms were as large as sitting rooms. She discussed paintings on her wall by her father from whom she had not heard in some years. The Depression broke him, she said.

"They're fine pictures," Matt told her.

She let her hand pet the frame of one.

"My husband envied them. He didn't want me to have family except him. And the children, of course. I used to ask him to make inquiries, but they came to nothing." She led him to her sewing room. A photograph of one sister with whom she had not spoken since she left home for college and, eventually, Garrett. Though the girl was only grammar school age, Matt recognized the mouth and the shape of the jaw. She was Angel's mother.

Matt excused himself and retired outside to smoke. He sat for an hour watching the sun set, enjoying the coffee Garrett's wife freshened, then excused himself before Garrett and the boys returned.

Near the hill's crest, he recognized the moon was at his back. It was full and bright and clear. He could see the creases and folds and rounded humps of the country underneath it. He did not sleep until he'd covered the three days to Grand Coulee. He would catch on with the dam again even if he had to bust rock. At home, he'd split wood and build them a crib for it, so Wendy wouldn't have to venture into the snow to feed the stove.

In town, he left the horse and bridle with their owner. It was day, but no one noticed. He found the pawn man in the cathouse and swapped his good coat for a loan. He'd be back for it in a month, he told the man. At the hardware, he bought a simple Colt automatic pistol with the lightest trigger in the store. It cost forty-eight dollars, which left him enough for a box of shells. With the last fourteen cents he added some hard candies. His clothes were a mess, but the gun merchant said nothing to him about it. They were afraid, he figured, either because he was big or because he was strange. It didn't matter. It had once, he knew. He'd tried to convince himself otherwise, but it had. It was a pleasant sensation leaving that behind, one he fastened himself to on the walk to the house.

He knocked on the door then opened it. The baby turned; so did Wendy.

"What happened to you," she asked.

He opened a paper bag and dug out the gun.

"Here," he said. He showed her how to undo the magazine and held a bullet into the light. "It's to use. If I ever hurt you, again." He clipped the magazine and set the loaded pistol in her hand.

She pointed the barrel down and offered it back to him. When he wouldn't accept it, she laid it on a high shelf above the oven where Angel couldn't reach. Matt walked to the bed to peel his things. Wendy had built a curtain around it. He pulled it shut, but, when he turned, she'd opened it. She gave Angel one of the candies. It would occupy her a while, she said. Matt shivered. She lay her coat across his shoulders and bustled him under the blankets. She undressed and joined him. She attached herself to his chest like she meant to pull the chill from him. It was familiar, and he realized it was not unlike the storm. She was guessing right, he decided. Just guessing and hoping. That was all faith was.

He went to sleep in the middle of the day, thinking it was simple as that. He woke to darkness and Wendy's breath and the child between them. He thought for a moment what had passed was a troubling dream they were just now rousing from. He slipped his finger in Angel's still tiny palm and felt its grip as he had at first. He wondered at her need for him, even in sleep, and was grateful for it. He let her go and watched as she turned, trying to recapture the warmth of someone's touch. He found Wendy's back, and pressed gently, hoping to draw the same sensation from her. She set her hand on his chest. He felt her pulse race. She patted him like she'd touch some new animal, one she doubted, like it was herself the touch reassured.

★ 32 ★

LUCKY NEVER ENJOYED INVESTIGATIVE WORK. F.B.I. men all believed themselves wily, but they frittered days begging handouts from others not far removed in ethics or intellect from those they tracked. If he wanted information, Lucky asked: once. If he preferred another response, he twisted the question or the respondent until satisfied. With nothing to go on, he decided to look into his employer to peel the orange.

He selected a booth in Jack's Chinese Restaurant's Kicking Mule Cocktail Lounge. A beer light behind the bar and the lamp over the cash register were the only light. A Chinese boy delivered him a T-bone steak—the menu's only American item—four evenings in a row.

Once a youngster in a suit who peddled for the furniture store complained about farmers so tight they still had their mothers' feather tick mattresses. Well into his vodka tonics, the man cussed Garrett. Those listening stared into their drinks silently, and the young man stopped mid-sentence until the bartender dialed the black-and-white TV to baseball and his companion switched subjects. A day after, an old pensioner in worn shirt and trousers attempted to connive more tab from the bartender. Lucky sent him a round. The man tipped the drink, and Lucky rose to join him at the bar. Lucky mentioned Garrett. He had once been Garrett's partner in drink. The man offered a few tales of whipping Indians and the old Chinese restaurant they once frequented, but Lucky could cajole no more he could call useful.

Finally, Lucky told a hospital clerk he needed names for a family reunion and that he required the birth for the county between 1890 and 1920. She would not permit him to check out the official hospital records, but agreed to allow him a records cubicle and a legal pad. He found Garrett easily. Born to Helen and Webster, first name James, middle Henry, but learned no more from the hospital. He visited the county clerk and tallied the land plots with the family name. They expanded steadily from the first filing in 1872, but, in the thirties, the family's holdings doubled. Garrett was wealthier than Lucky had surmised. Lucky scribbled road names that bracketed and intersected the newest acquisitions, then returned to his cruiser and drove. It took him most of the day to cover all the roads. The country was rolling hills, nothing but tilled ground; none scrub but the little that banked the river and creeks.

Lucky saw that a number of houses were occupied. He had no idea which was the family home, so he waited for the mail truck to pass and after plucked grocery circulars from each mailbox. Two didn't have Garrett's name on them. The first was the drunk he'd encountered at the restaurant bar and the second shared a last name with the first. Lucky drove the long driveway and discovered someone in the shop rebuilding a truck transmission.

"Looking for James Garrett," Lucky said.

The shop was dark besides the light from the open door. The man shoved himself from underneath the wheat truck, wiped his hands on an orange rag and blinked, then gave directions that Lucky ignored.

"I figured this house," he said. "It's a nice place."

"It'll do."

"Must've been in the family awhile."

"I believe it belonged to a man called Jarms. This piece is called that."

In the car, Lucky traced his homemade map. Garrett had acquired a vast amount of land in his Depression-era sweep. The sky slipped to dusk. Lucky drove on. The first two houses were Garrett's sons. Neither were off crawlers, but he heard kids in the yards. The last house was Garrett's. Lucky chanced the road in, determining to play his cards, until he recognized the track looped up the valley. He cut his lights and coasted past the main house. The road hadn't been graveled and a fog of fine dust forced him periodically to pause until it settled. It was reduced to tire ruts when he broke over a hillcrest toward the river. Below, one house light was burning.

He parked and listened for a dog, but heard only coyotes down-river. The garden was turned, but the willow branches touched the grass. An old woman answered his knock. She stared at him.

"I'm glad you've come," she said.

She asked him in and served him lemonade. "It's fresh," she said. "He brings it to me from town."

"It's nice your son takes care of you," he said.

She said, "he won't let me out."

"Well, maybe he just likes to do the shopping for you."

"Do you see an automobile out there? There's not a fit animal to ride. I walked once to the barns. All it has is cows. He comes once a month with the groceries. That's all of people I know."

"You've got grandchildren and great-grandchildren, though."

"He tells them I'm dead," she said. "He doesn't allow me to light the house except when it's dark enough they won't be working. Is that any way to treat your mother?" she asked.

"My mother's dead," Lucky said.

The woman stared into her hands. Underneath her coffee table were National Geographics and a book of crosswords, open. Lucky stooped to pick it up. It was a hard puzzle and she'd not missed a word.

"How about your other children? They might be nicer to you."

The old woman sat for a moment. A crocheted doily draped the chair arm and she plucked it from its place and stabbed her fingers into the holes.

She nodded. "Perhaps he would have," she said.

"He?" Lucky asked.

"Yes," the woman said. Lucky didn't interrupt. She had determined to confess, and, as her voice scratched on, he grew more certain it was as close to truth as any of them could manage. She'd abandoned a child, she said, and her fate was justice, plain and simple. She apologized for complaining about what she deserved. It was late when she finished. She sat exhausted in her chair. What pressed Horace Jarms to madness didn't appear clear. He was dead, that was all she knew of the end.

As he rose to depart, she grasped his hand. A cataract clouded one eye, but the other set on him like a weight. He gazed into it. The years had unraveled the woman, and she saw her own hand responsible. Blaming others was a simple track, though it went round and round and round. Laying it on yourself at least gave you peace from the chase.

"You must go, I know," she said.

He felt tired. He decided he'd sleep in tomorrow, sleep till noon if it suited him. It would strengthen his resolve.

But that night he did not sleep. He reclined in the tiny bed and listened to the radio playing country music. The street lamp outside shone through the curtains, a reddish kind of light, the same as when he closed his eyes and stared into the lids. His head hurt.

Early morning, he woke the clerk and bummed two aspirin, then pocketed his badge and drove to the police station. An hour in the basement and he discovered the file on Jarms's death along with several others. The murders appeared a killing spree, but absent motive, weapon, or bodies. The name on the report was the current sheriff's father.

Lucky climbed the storeroom stairs and inquired directions from a deputy, who turned out the old man's grandson. He thanked the boy and wrote the address on a paper scrap. Bertrand Heitvelt napped on a porch swing, the steps to it lined with tulips and gladiolas. Their scent lingered on the stoop. Under the swing, a cur pup raised its head and sidled through the propped screen door into the house. Lucky heard a food bowl. He kicked Heitvelt's foot and the man started.

"I'm from Lincoln County. I'm the sheriff up there."

"I know who you are."

Lucky nodded. "I'm examining a case, a murder with no weapon, no motive, and no body. You want to tell me how that can be."

Heitvelt squinted. Lucky showed him a list of names. "I don't have to tell you nothing," the man said.

"You ever heard that in your travels? A lawman hears that, he knows to quit looking, doesn't he?" Lucky leaned against the porch rail. "I guess I could ask your boy about this. Maybe his police work's better. Maybe his conscience is, too."

Heitvelt sat for a long time. The dog waddled out the screen door and licked Heitvelt's hand. When he didn't pet it, it tried Lucky, who kicked it across the yard.

"I never saw it. Garrett told me."

"You believed him?"

"It seemed prudent," Heitvelt said. He looked at Lucky's face the way a cop does, trying to remember enough about you for the next time.

"They really dead?"

"I believe so."

"The hired man do it, this Lawson?"

"He worked there a few years. Lived and worked. They treated him like kin and he seemed to feel similar. I don't know what happened out there, but he'd be on the second page of any list I made." The old man coaxed the dog. It circled wide of Lucky and returned to him, and dropped its head into his lap.

"You're a damned sorry policeman," Lucky said.

"My boy is better," Heitvelt said.

●

LUCKY WAITED AT JARMS'S DRIVEWAY until dark and Garrett's truck lights bounced on the washboarded road.

"Lawson killed no one, including your brother," Lucky said. "Why are you putting me on a wild goose chase? In fact, why are you chasing the same bird?"

"Because if Lawson had listened to reason, he could have saved them all," Garrett said.

"Your reasons."

"Does it matter whose if it rescues lives?"

"I got a feeling lives don't mean much to you."

Garrett looked off to where the black sky met the blacker earth. "Most don't, I admit. Some did. Horace was my only kin, the rest were just blood. Lawson didn't kill him, but he forced my hand on the matter."

"You killed your brother. That's why you're packing this grudge."

"No more than Lawson did."

"No less, though."

"That's true," Garrett said. "I suppose you're going to quit me."

"I'm not employed by the people any longer. Seems to me who did what to who is someone else's business."

"That's so. I hired you to get Lawson. You got some reason yourself."

"That's where you're mistaken. The man is in a photograph with my mother forty years ago. That's not enough reason for murder, even for one inclined toward blood."

"I'll add five thousand," Garrett said.

"That might wet my whistle." Lucky told him.

Garrett wrote out a check and passed it to Lucky. Lucky examined it. "Just so you know," Lucky said. "I'd've hunted him for free."

"Why's that?"

"Love," Lucky said.

"That's a word I did not expect was in your vocabulary," Garrett told him.

"That remark might offend me if it hadn't come from a man with the mark of Cain all over him."

"Fair enough," Garrett replied. He dug a paper from his pants and offered it to Lucky. It was a paycheck stub from the Grand Coulee project.

⋆ **33** ⋆

A WHOLE BOOK OF HISTORY passed in the next five years. FDR's heart clogged, Hitler and his minions ate a handful of poison, Truman melted Hiroshima and Nagasaki with a nuclear sunrise, and the Soviets turned Europe into a chessboard and cut loose the queen in Eastern Europe.

None of this was more than newspaper clippings to Wendy Lawson. What occupied her remained within a few miles of her, and most within hearing. She thought it a woman's lot to tend first those around her, and if those like her herded nations the newspapers might write more about swap meets and less about armies.

Wendy was more interested in the boundaries in her home than those in Berlin. She had once thought Angel the balance between herself and Matt. As the time for the new child approached, however, the girl alternated from distant to clinging. After Luke split her womb, Wendy was slow to mend. It was June before she could resume their park ritual. Pushing the pram tired her and required both hands so, on their walks, Angel was permitted to wander. The girl, a kindergardener now, closed her eyes and ordered Wendy to direct her. Occasionally, Wendy would fool her into a sprinkler or a puddle, which tickled them both. Wendy encountered Ardith at the park, where they continued to talk books and children. Ardith spoke of her husband, Ray, at length, though Wendy wasn't inclined to do the same.

Evenings, Angel asked Matt questions while Wendy prepared meals or cleaned them up in the trailerhouse they could finally afford. She didn't hear their words, just their sound. Matt scooped her into the chair beside him and pressed his finger to her lips. He set his head across her little chest. His huge head in her arms rocked like he heard music inside her. His eyes closed, and when they opened, she knew they would see nothing but the child. Morning, she'd turn to him gazing at her the same way. It broke her heart, that kind of seeing.

As Luke grew to crawl then toddle, Angel trailed him across hill or dale, and if she didn't the boy would grow confused and howl for her. At first, Wendy considered Angel's devotion to Luke nothing curious. The oldest looked after the babies, especially girls. She'd done so herself. Later, though, she recognized more in Angel's constancy. Wendy had always thought Luke's sleep steady, until one morning she woke before dawn and discovered him in Angel's bed. He visited almost every night, Angel admitted, returning to his room at first light. He never cried, just wrestled into the place Angel made for him. Angel recognized Wendy's distance, even concerning the child of her blood, and she saw the boy's fears and put herself between them. Wendy knew it should have shamed her, but all she felt was gratitude.

She began to leave for long evening walks after dinner, not gambols or meanders. Shoulders forward, her forehead leading her like the prow of a ship, she hiked to distant points and returned, sometimes marching through rock-choked canyons or arid brush

if it provided a direct path. Occasionally, her route would pass
Ardith's home and they would exchange a few words, but Wendy
soon pressed on. Her thoughts stacked in her mind like cordwood,
rounded, split, and quartered, too much to clear if she had ten winters to burn through. And her thoughts required flame, a conflagra-
tion, though she had no idea how to strike a match and ignite the
blaze. Instead each step the pile grew. She considered the bullet she
put into Matt and her years laboring on the Lawson ranch in pen-
ance and deliberated on her parents and sisters, as well; she had no
idea where they had emigrated after the grocery's drowning. She
pondered Linda Jefferson in a cave and Lucky half-naked next to
her, neither able to move—more fodder for remorse. Though she
did not regret their inaction, she reproached herself for what led to
it. She worried over how Angel had come about and worried that it
mattered to her. She became angry and then was angry at her anger.
She feared Matt and feared his absence. Once she put the pistol
into her purse and carried it with her a week. The weight finally
annoyed her. Her walks were slow-burned, and upon her return she
would be more fueled than when she departed. She added her miles
to four or five, barely reaching home before the children retired.
Finally she lit into Matt.

"You know you never once inquired about my day?" she told
him. "If it went well or poorly?"

"How was your day then?" Matt asked.

She laughed.

"That isn't what you want?"

"No. Tomorrow you'll ask and it won't matter. If I asked for
flowers and bows the house would be filled with them and it still
wouldn't be what I want, because it will mean nothing."

"You mean nothing like before."

"Yes, nothing like before. That was when you knew how to give
to me that way."

"Maybe it was then when you made me feel welcome to," he said.

Wendy found the bourbon bottle in a cabinet and uncorked it. "We are going to get drunk," she said.

"I've got to work tomorrow." He had been rehired and promoted by the Bureau.

"I'll call you in sick." She brought two glasses to the table and filled them. Wendy nodded at his glass. He sipped at the bourbon she'd poured him. She drank down half her glass, sighed and waited for the numbness to reach her.

"Why did you send me that letter?" Wendy asked.

Matt shrugged and put his chin in one of his huge hands. With the other he lifted the glass and peered at the light through it.

"Was it because Angel needed a mother?"

"No," Matt said. He closed his eyes.

"Was it to make me happy?"

"Well, I'd hoped it might."

"But that wasn't the reason? I mean the main reason?"

"No," Matt said. "Should it have been?"

Wendy finished her glass and poured another. "It doesn't matter what should or shouldn't be. I want to know what your reason was, not what you think it should be."

"I didn't ever figure on anything but you and me or me by myself."

"So you married me just because I was first?"

"You were only."

"What if I wouldn't take you?"

"I'd have been in a fix."

"Nobody ever meant anything to you besides me?"

He shook his head.

"Then how did you end up with a daughter?"

Wendy concluded her drink in one swallow. Matt said nothing, just watched her refill her glass.

"I'm raising the child. I've got a right to know what happened."

"It wasn't like that."

"Do you know how many men must say that to women?"

Matt said. "I'm not other men."

He went to the sink and filled his glass with water. He wolfed that down and poured himself more and broke ice from a tray to cool it. He set a chunk in her drink. She watched it turn waves in the brown, oily liquor.

"Why'd you marry me, then?" he asked.

She'd come to believe their coupling was an old, poorly conceived plan that each of them followed out of stubbornness or lack of another.

"I waited," she said. "I waited all those years."

"You happy you did?"

"I don't know," she said.

He nodded. "At least that's honest."

He rose and stretched; his great muscles rolled like ground moving. It didn't often strike her anymore, his size. It was the last thing she took into account. He was who he was every day, simple and injured and firm in will toward what he would not name, just as she'd remembered him.

"You forgive her?" Matt asked.

"Who?"

"Angel."

Wendy considered the question. She drank again, but remained clearheaded. She stared at the bottle and envied the time when it did more for her.

"I try," she said finally.

"That's too bad," Matt said. "She hasn't done nothing wrong."

•

THE SUMMER BEFORE ANGEL ENTERED fourth grade the park service finished Spring Canyon Park. Each morning, Wendy delivered Matt to work, then, after Angel and the boy performed morning chores, boxed cold chicken or lunch meat, potato salad and fruit left from Matt's lunches and drove them to the reservoir where they lunched and swam. Angel devoured classwork. She was ready for good books, Twain, Steinbeck, and Willa Cather. On a blanket reading with Wendy, she felt as if she had some gravity in this world.

For Wendy reading had turned desperate; she grazed popular mysteries and frilly romances along with the classics, then the Old Testament, where she remained. She studied how its people responded to crisis or victory and the boredom between. She held little regard for deity or philosophy. No matter which was true, you were at the mercy of a tale. She had come from such stories, though her parents' strongest wishes—like all parents—were likely that the narrative stop with them, that their children, liberated from stories, would know real freedom. As for herself, she didn't want to know more; ignorance in Wendy's life had been her only bliss.

She gazed at Angel next to her. Her dark hair was long and straight and parted in the middle, and her face had begun to take on the angles a young lady's does. Her high cheekbones belonged to her grandmother, and her full lips, Wendy could only guess, were her mother's. She'd been silent a long while, looking out over the water, farther than the children now, toward the canyons and ridges and rockfill left from the dam's construction. Wendy tipped her head back on the blanket and closed her eyes. She enjoyed resting in the sun, seeing the red light through her lids.

"He doesn't talk to you," Angel said.

Wendy glanced at the girl's face. It was still as a porcelain doll's. "He doesn't talk much to anyone."

"I know," Angel said. "But with me it's different. He is sure of me."

"Talking about your dad like that," Wendy said. "I'm not accustomed to it."

"I do wish he'd say more to you," Angel said.

"Why don't you tell him so?"

"It would hurt his feelings."

"It would," Wendy agreed. "There are things he doesn't want to say, and it seems they outnumber the ones he does."

"He's a donkey," Angel said.

Wendy laughed. "Why's that?"

"It's something we want and he doesn't, so he makes it hard."

Wendy combed her hand through the girl's hair and stroked the little bones that made her mouth move. Angel turned her face into the warmth of Wendy's palm and Wendy embraced her. "I never thought I'd end up like this with you," Wendy said. She recalled fairy tales from her youth. Fathers broke their children's hearts with stepmothers. She could recall not one that fared well.

Wendy picked a stray thread from Angel's T-shirt and wound it around her forefinger. It looked like pictures she'd seen on catalogs reminding you to remember to order. The oddity of it struck her cold. In school, memory was all they touted: dates and spelling words and the Constitution's Preamble. They taught it all wrong. Forgetting was more useful. "I figured I'd make you this way or that. You'd be my child, then."

"But I am your child," Angel said.

"No," Wendy said. "Though I'd love it so if you were." The girl blinked, but her face was still. "You mean I love Daddy more?"

"It's natural, I always considered it so anyway. You're his."

"But I'm yours, too."

Wendy shook her head.

The girl stood, then bolted for the shower rooms. Wendy followed, but Angel refused to speak, and when Wendy made another pass at explaining, she began humming to drown her words. Wendy remained outside the door, not willing to leave her. When Matt arrived, it was near sunset. He'd paid the town taxi.

Wendy nodded to the bathroom. "She won't come out."

Matt glanced at the word on the door. "Are you by yourself in there?"

"Yes," she said.

"Can I come in, please?"

Angel cracked the door. Matt unfolded his wallet and put money for the taxi in Wendy's hand and she handed him the car's keys. He went in. Wendy returned herself and Luke to the trailer where she fed the boy but couldn't stomach food herself. Near ten, she heard Matt's steps on the metal porch. The door opened and Matt carried Angel, asleep, to her bedroom.

When he returned to the front room, he was shaking. She took a step toward him, and when he didn't rear up, another. She crossed the room and took his elbow awkwardly, and he looked at it in her hand.

"Can we sit outside?" he asked. She nodded and they opened lawn chairs. The bugs were bad, so they switched the light off. In the dark, she could hear sprinklers tick and the crickets scratching. He shifted, preparing to speak. She ought to love him more, she thought. She ought to love them all more. It was all she wanted to be able to do.

"You aren't ever going to hurt us again, are you?" Wendy asked.

"There's other ways of hurting."

"It's the only one you know, though," she told him.

"The rest is all accident. I promise that."

"Me, too," Wendy said. "I shouldn't have said it. I thought it might help. Help me at least. Will she ever speak to me again?"

"She will," he said.

"I wouldn't blame her."

"She said that sometimes, she'd wondered if you wanted her."

"Lord. What did you tell her?"

"I told her it was me you wondered if you wanted."

"Did you tell her the truth about her mother?" Wendy asked.

Matt shook his head. "I told her she hadn't got your meaning straight," he said. He drew back where he could see her face. "I'll tell you, though."

Wendy nodded, and he went on. It was early morning by the time he finished, and they were both goosepimpled by the night. One of his legs had gone to sleep. He stretched, then banged his heel on the bottom step, and she watched him waiting on the feeling to return.

"It seemed to me telling it to her, she would be losing two mothers."

She closed her eyes, and lifted his cold knuckles to her cheek. "I didn't mean to be cruel," she said.

"I know," Matt said. "Me neither. It just turned that way."

⋆ **34** ⋆

LUCKY RARELY DRANK, THOUGH HE held no opinion concerning drunks, pro or con. The few times Lucky imbibed left him nearly tender. He listened to music and conversation of others or just watched lights and cars passing and was perplexed by melancholy. Doubt was too high a tab for drink; he refused to pay it. Often in his early years copping, his sexual apparatus distressed him similarly. Inclined to emotions he himself had vowed to correct, the appendage often made exiting the house an embarrassment, and, once, vexed him at work so, that he squandered the shift pretending to shuffle papers. Finally, at the hardware, he purchased a roll of bailing twine, snipped a piece and looped it around his leg and his nemesis and tied it off. He intended to halt it from jutting like a poker, but the string thinned the circulation once he maintained a certain girth and his penis retracted on its own. Its antics had ended years ago now and it left his life tidy, the way he'd chosen it to be. That he was traveling the highways between Colfax and Grand Coulee, then, with an open pint he'd nipped past the neck and shoulders, disconcerted him. He worried for what else might be amiss. He seemed in the throes of what drink stirred in him anyway, and hurrying the sensation seemed the proper way to pass through such country and emerge on the other, where he assumed he'd find sense once again.

The wheatfields passed like so much chaff: rowed acres and fences and sprinklers and rock and a few poplar starts for windbreaks. He navigated the Rocklyn cutoff to avoid Davenport, where a fair number would enjoy an invitation to his comeuppance. At Wilbur, he went north. Twelve miles out, the highway swooped into the Grand Coulee that appeared in need of water despite one of the largest rivers in America pressing through it. The rock looked rusted anywhere it faced weather. The thirsty pines remained dwarfed and spindly. Sagebrush and cheat grew best. The towns along the bottom were noted primarily for their transgressions.

He recognized the lighted string that marked the dam's backside, a single luminous row a mile wide. Maintaining the project still employed much of the county. Though his childhood unraveled in those places drowned behind it, Lucky felt no nostalgia for what had been lost or bitterness toward those forces constructing the structure. When he looked to the speedometer, he realized he was traveling only twenty-five miles an hour, and he tapped the accelerator toward the speed limit. He turned at an intersection and drove a short stretch of highway past Delano, a town that thought so little of itself it took a president's middle name, and mispronounced it to boot, to Electric City, whose city fathers appeared to possess no more inspiration. Lining the highway were Scott's Service and Norm's Cafe and two taverns that changed hands so regularly sign makers ran them a tab. Lucky eased into a lot, checked the address and sipped more whiskey. He'd seen a hotel vacancy lamp a mile back. There, he could sleep and maybe wake hungover enough to hone an edge for whatever the next morning delivered.

The road descended a long hill past a single row of houses, darkness sliding over them. Porch lights glowed and streetlights above them. Lucky himself watching the shadow of his car and the shape of his head and shoulders in the window. When he looked up, the road had swerved and he plowed over lawns, passed near stoops and under windows. Wendy, bent in the front window of the house, scrubbed dishes and stared outside vacantly. She did not notice him. Lucky jerked his car to the gravel then u-turned in a wide spot and halted across the street, a hundred feet away from her. In the glove box, he hunted his field glasses. He put them on her. She'd grown heavier in the face, but Wendy it was. He checked the address on Lawson's paycheck and the mailbox numbers: they were identical.

He took one long breath and listened to the air collect inside him.

He sipped at the last of the whiskey. It had been right to drink. He was flesh and bone, like any other. He saw children in the living room, a girl near the age to turn out, maybe the age he was when Wendy happened onto him. They would be fine children. Lucky would father them well; though they may be of another's seed, they were as much his as she was. They'd been orbiting him like the satellites the Russians claimed circled the world. But gravity had its laws and his family was falling to him as justice had deemed it. He looked up into the skies and nearly cried. *Finally*, he said and listened to the word.

He put the glasses to his eyes again. The first he saw of the man was a great passing shadow. The front door opened and heavy steps clobbered the metal porch. The shadow maker sat, his legs dangling to the walk and his arms resting on the top step. A match flashed and disappeared. The man sipped the cigarette. Lucky's payment for what the hard world owed him: twenty-five thousand dollars and them. It struck him that when the world turned peculiar, it rolled all at once, like a big fish that was suddenly there swimming when before it was only water you were seeing.

•

INSIDE THE BY A DAM Site Tavern, pool players circled the tables with cues. Others waiting lined quarters underneath one bumper and added their names to a chalkboard. Lucky went to the board and erased it. A few looked up. At the bar, he ordered a Coke. The bartender collected his money. He offered Lucky a can and a frosted glass. Lucky poured and drank.

"Who's toughest here?" he asked.

The bartender pointed to a man who was medium-sized. His biceps and chest tugged his T-shirt taut. He shared a pitcher and a table with an attractive brunette. At the table, Lucky stopped. The woman had a nice complexion, Lucky thought. She was thin where it didn't count and broad were it did. The man, Parker, glanced up. His face was deeply creased. Lucky pointed to a beer glass. "This hers?" Lucky asked. Parker nodded. Lucky unzipped his drawers and deposited his pecker into the glass.

Parker sat, stunned. For a moment, Lucky thought the man would disappoint him. The woman gasped.

"My Lord," she said. "My Lord."

Parker upset the table standing. The pitcher hit the woman in the chest and her soaked shirt clung to her body like skin. Lucky's penis remained damp with beer. He tucked it away.

Parker's first blow caught him at the chin, depositing Lucky on the floor. The man wore boots. Lucky stood, inclined to avoid real damage. Parker clouted him again. The woman scurried to a booth. The next blow lit Lucky's head with color. It felt like sleep, then a boot clobbered his ribs and he was awake and hurting. He scrambled to avoid the boots and Parker wailed at his head with a beer glass until it broke. Lucky could see the glass pieces on the floor. Blood warmed his neck, a slow trickle, nothing serious. Inside his jacket he found his holstered pistol and steadied it with both hands. Parker's T-shirt was spattered with Lucky's blood, the broken glass still in his hand. Lucky stood, leaving the gun on him. His ribs ached, but they weren't broken. In the bar mirror, a bruise purpled his cheek. He touched the swelling with his free hand. It would blacken nicely.

He set a twenty on the bar. "See he drinks that up for me," Lucky said. The woman hadn't moved from the booth. Lucky could see the line of her bra in the wet shirt. Parker sat next to her looking stunned.

"She his wife?" Lucky asked.

"Was going to be," the bartender said.

Lucky drove the car again to the address in his pocket. His watch read past midnight; the trailer windows were dark. He shut the car door quietly and limped across the street and lay in the grass that bordered the trailer, the lawn's coolness soothed his swollen eye. He looked at the trailers and clapboard duplexes that lined the block, places people lived whole lives as unremarkable as the blades of grass surrounding him.

★ **35** ★

WENDY'S EVENING WALKS CONTINUED THROUGH the 1950s. Her forward-leaning figure in the evening shadows traveling the road shoulders or park trails or reservoir banks became as ordinary as old man Vlachi's daily vigil in front of his makeshift museum or the school buses that clotted morning traffic. Slowly, the exercise became, if not therapeutic or relaxing, at least a meditation that evolved toward restful. Even when her parents pressed her toward religion as a child, she had felt as if she observed the hymns and prayers and Eucharist through the stained glass. She never recognized a ritual's values until she acquired her own.

For her husband, every day, every act was a sacrament, the firmament above was his chapel ceiling, the ground the floor, and the light needed no colored windows to make itself holy. She once thought him simple, but simple was not a choice, and he decided every morning to rid the world of complications that might distract him from herself and the children and the labor required to provide enough of what they hoped for to trust they had earned such gifts from the world and deserved more of a share than he himself possessed. She had learned to admire him and enjoy him. It was more than she had offered anyone else, other than the children.

Toward the end of the decade, Wendy read of her father's death in the newspaper obituary. The funeral was a half hour away in Wilbur. She was determined to attend alone, so Matt organized another ride. Dawn, the highway climbed steadily through the Grand Coulee and up the rocky wall and highway leading out. Above, the ground was open and bare aside from crops. Enormous wheel tractors made short work of the earth, turning vast amounts in a single pass. It didn't seem far enough past horse and plow that a man could think up such monsters.

She had a strange urge to smoke. Wilbur was a few miles ahead and she stopped at a grocery for a pack of cigarettes. On the highway again, she lit a cigarette and clamped it between her lips and inhaled. The smoke left her hacking and dizzy. It settled nothing, and she dashed it in the ashtray and tossed the pack in the backseat.

She arrived early at the church. Inside, she watched the minister and mortician wheel the casket in for viewing. The minister perched on a metal chair and studied his notes, and the funeral man laid flowered wreaths over the shined cedar. He opened the top side and took a second arranging her father's suit. Half an hour, her family arrived. Her sisters appeared healthy, their children in ties and slacks. Their husbands draped their best coats over the pew's back. Her mother peeked a few times, then made her way to Wendy in the back pew. "Come," she said.

Her sisters said nothing to her, though they did whisper to their husbands, explaining matters, she presumed. The service was short. The minister joked that that was the way Harold preferred his religion. He read some scripture and closed with a prayer and a hymn: "The Old Rugged Cross." Wendy sang what she could recall. The family rose to view the casket. When her sisters passed, they set into their father's pocket folded papers; notes, she would later discover, suggested by the minister to allow for whatever remained unsaid. Her father's sightless eyes looked just that. Wendy patted the box's edge, found her father's hand and stroked it until the cool skin unsettled her.

The community building hosted a potluck served by her sisters' friends. After they fed their children, the girls approached Wendy.

"How are you?" Rachel asked. "We haven't heard in so long."

"I'm married to Matt Lawson," Wendy said. "He works at the dam."

"I wish we'd known," Amy said.

"You would have if she had wanted you to," Wendy's mother replied.

Her sisters didn't know how to continue, then Rachel laughed and Amy joined her, and then for no reason she could apprehend, Wendy found herself in tears, as well, laughing and crying simultaneously.

They rested on the folding chairs a while longer, squeezing each other's hands or elbows or shoulders as their conversations started then lagged like dogs in the sun. Amy and Rachel excused themselves to mind their children. To Wendy's surprise they steered their families to their cars and returned. The four of them cleared tables and washed casserole dishes until dark, then, when there was nothing left to clean, embraced each other and walked to the gravel parking lot together.

Her mother drove her back to the church and her car. They sat in the dashlight's glow.

"Your father understood," Wendy's mother said. "In fact, he was proud in his own way. The man admired a sacrifice. He'd have made a wonderful pagan."

"Why didn't they mention you in the eulogy?" Wendy asked. "You were his wife."

Her mother shook her head.

"You left him?"

Her mother rolled down the window and let in the cool air. She stared outside as Wendy gazed at her face. The light was gone, and she looked suddenly old. "It was your dad who left." She went on. "I'm not suggesting he didn't have reason."

Wendy closed her eyes. A truck passed. She heard the heavy motor whine with its load.

"I loved him," her mother said. "But by the time I happened upon the knowledge, he was past convincing."

Lights burned above the street and in each house down the block. A sprinkler ticked on the church lawn.

"When I said your father never felt slighted by your going, I wasn't speaking for me. I was angry the whole while. I think that's to my credit, don't you?"

Wendy smiled. "Maybe so," she said.

"I think it's time for you to go," her mother said.

Wendy opened the car door and crossed the lot for her own. She raised her hand to wave, but her mother's grim face had turned toward the windshield and the lights cutting the darkness in front of her.

Wendy drove. The centerline passed in rhythm like a heartbeat she couldn't hear. The deafness was her own. The children asleep in their beds would smell fresh as clean laundry. She loved to listen to them. They talked a pure language while adults only picked at conversation like a magpie over a carcass. Perhaps they would still be awake enough to wish good night.

Before she entered the trailerhouse, Matt had poured her fresh tea and set the cup next to a book of stories from New York she'd been enjoying. In the living room she drank it, and soon he delivered the dish of fried donuts. He'd iced them like cake. They were still hot, and the white cream pooled on the plate.

"My," Wendy said. She plucked one from the plate and took a bite.

"Do you like them?" Matt asked her.

"They're awfully good," she said. "Where in the world did you learn these?"

"Some ways back," he said.

Matt offered her another donut. Wendy took it.

"They've grown fast," she said.

"Too much so," Matt said. "I'd like to keep them babies longer so I could double check my work."

Wendy laughed. "It's not the kind of work you patch, I hear."

They were quiet again, finishing another donut each. Matt let off, saving the rest for the children.

"They'll wonder why you're treating them," Wendy said.

"I believe I'll let them wonder."

Matt went to the kitchen and returned with two glasses of milk.

"Boys will be coming for Angel soon."

He scraped the plate for the last of the frosting and put it on his finger. He turned the finger Wendy's direction and pressed it to her lips. She licked the frosting until she could taste his rough skin.

"It's not natural to keep her from them," Matt said. It was Angel who stilled him when he needed quieting. She'd sit at the foot of his chair reading, and he'd watch her from above, just gazing at the part in her hair, imagining what was happening in the mind underneath it. Matt could reach Angel without measuring his heart in doses.

His hand was still in hers. She stood and lifted it with her. They had a radio on the mantle and she turned the knobs until she found some band music. He looked puzzled.

"Just put your hand right here," she said. He took her by the waist and she him. Their left hands stayed locked together, and Matt stared at their clasped fingers like they might be as far away as the moon. Wendy recalled her father. When she was barely six, he'd shown her the same constellations she'd taught to Luke and Angel. All that air and light above, and you could still find pictures. What she wanted to learn seemed much less, and that left her hopeful.

She felt Matt's grip on her hand and returned it. They stayed how they were a long while, not even moving their feet.

★ 36 ★

WENDY SHOUTED FOR LUKE TO hit the ball on his first ups. His head swiveled and he stood outside the batter's box blinking at her. She reclined on a blanket with a cup of wine, up the right field line with Matt and Angel where they shared a picnic dinner. Luke beat the ground with his cleats. The pitcher threw two strikes, then, after a pitch so wide he couldn't reach it, he got fooled on a third. Wendy watched him jog to the bench for his mitt and cap.

Ardith and her husband were in the small bleacher behind the backstop. Their boy was on Coulee Dam Savings, the opposite team. Wendy circled the field to say hello between innings. Ardith smiled and her husband said it was nice to see her. His face was shaved close and he wore his hair high and tight, like locks and a beard were threats to his notion of order. It had been clear for some time that Ardith and her husband saw Wendy as a charity case. They fell over one another to be helpful, once offering to loan her a car, even cut a separate key for her.

When she returned to the blanket, Matt offered her a sandwich. Angel read her book. Luke glanced over. Angel waved, knowing it would embarrass him. The two of them remained close. He talked to her first when he was vexed. The girl was reading *The Catcher in the Rye*, a book Wendy purchased for her. They would argue about the meanings when she finished. Matt left the house when they talked books. It wasn't their intellect that disturbed him, it was their vigor.

Luke's team took its at bat then returned to the field. He was a strong boy, but his only other athletic asset was determination. He played harder than the other children. After practices, he would labor with only the street lamp to see by, swinging his bat the way his coach had instructed, or throwing a ball into the sky and tracking it through the light. The thwack of his mitt put the neighborhood to sleep nearly every night.

The coach turned him catcher because he played like every ball was hit to him anyway. This game, he had blocked a wild pitch and flagged two pop fouls. Wendy had held her breath while he took the steps to get under them. An error and he wouldn't sleep and neither would Matt. Luke would mope in his bed and Matt would fret over his moping.

Matt shifted on the blanket. Most fathers, if they were interested at all, hollered at their sons. It embarrassed the boys. Matt, though, had lost interest in games early on; after his father died work filled most his waking hours. Their son, though, took to balls as a toddler, and when the interest stuck, Matt sought out mitts and bats and practiced in the park with him. Wendy had never seen Matt coach him, though Luke would inquire if he was holding the bat or throwing the ball correctly. Matt only laughed. Wendy wondered what he found so funny.

"That there can be a wrong way to play anything," Matt told her.

Luke came to bat again in the last inning. The score was tied. Matt closed his hands over one another. Angel dog-eared her page and leaned into his shoulder. The first pitch was a ball, outside. The opposing team chattered in the field.

Luke stepped into the box and the pitcher delivered another pitch. The ball thumped the catcher's mitt and the umpire called it a strike.

Luke settled into a crouch and steadied his bat. The pitcher threw one in the same spot. Luke's eyes grew large at the same time the bat whacked the ball over the left fielder's head. Wendy watched him give chase, Luke lumbering past second. The fielder dropped the ball then retrieved it. He heaved it to the cut-off. Luke rounded third. The cut-off was their best player and he threw a strike to the catcher. The ball arrived at the same time Luke did. He slid and upended the catcher, which separated him from the ball, his mask, and one knee pad. They landed together on home plate. The umpire waved his arms and signaled safe.

Angel stood and screamed. Wendy's hands hurt from clapping. Matt, though, headed for the field. She thought he was going to congratulate Luke until she saw Angel cover her mouth with her hand. Luke stood over the base, a trickle of blood between his eyes—the catcher had crowned him with his mask and after stood, taunting him, Ardith's son. Luke swung his fist and the boy dropped to all fours. Ardith's husband hurried in from the bleachers, Wendy thought to retrieve his boy, but instead, he tackled Luke. Both of them skidded across the base. Luke rose first. The bat still lay on the infield grass. Luke took two steps for it before Matt met him.

"Bully," Ardith shouted. Matt bent and hoisted Luke in both arms and hugged him there in the middle of the game. It was quiet, except for Luke's sobs, and Ardith and her husband's rants. Angel rose and went to them and Wendy followed. Matt turned the family toward the bench and began walking. Luke was heavier than Wendy, but he held to her like a breeze might take him off if it decided to.

"Your boy's no good, Lawson." Ardith's husband still stood at home plate, his face red, his finger pointing.

Matt looked to the umpire, but he was just a high school boy in a mask and pad. He and his family continued the other direction. Ardith's husband followed. Matt collected Luke's cap. Ardith's husband circled them and swore. Luke shivered as if in a cold wind. Ardith's husband finally ran past what words could do and spat on Luke.

Matt was into the husband quicker than the man could lift his hands. They tumbled then rose together. Matt held the husband's throat. Ardith screamed and thumped Matt's ribs with a bat. Her husband attempted to box Matt's ears. Matt lifted him higher. The man was gasping. His face went white; his eyes closed and his limbs quit struggling.

"Matt," Wendy screamed.

Matt threw the man ten feet into a chain link fence. Ardith gave up her bat for her husband. She lifted his head until he began breathing again. She looked at Wendy. Her mouth opened and she seemed to be working at a word, but it did not get past that.

At home, Luke retired to his bedroom and Matt followed. Wendy heard the bed groan with his weight. Angel perched on the mattress next to them. She had Luke's hand and stroked it softly. Blood pasted the boy's brow. Wendy hurried to the bathroom and wet a washrag and returned to Luke's doorway. Angel took the rag from her and began to dab his cut. Matt sat, looking confused, then he began to speak. "I recall hitting when I was coming up," Matt said. "I don't remember if there were any reasons. I just know I did."

His words were halting, and he paused between them, like he was hunting the next. "There's nothing wrong with it. If you've got cause. Like if it keeps another safe, but it's a waste of time otherwise. You had a right," he said. "I'm not saying you didn't."

He let loose of Luke's hand and touched the boy's chest. Silver light poured over them from the porch lamp outside. Matt glanced up and recognized Wendy watching. He scooted to one side and patted the boy's bed to make a place for her. They waited for her to join them. They waited for her to join them as they had for years, all three of them. The floor was wood and her stocking feet slid, making her feel light, like she was a ghost of herself, the good one, that was doing the things she'd hoped she could do. She could hear their breathing, see the light play off their wet eyes. Below were her feet taking her into that undiscovered country that was her family.

The boy leaned forward and she hugged him, a mother and her child simple as that. To know their sounds so well seemed a gift she had left unwrapped.

★ 37 ★

IN JANUARY 1954, A GENERATOR in Powerhouse Number Two took on a wobble smaller than a person would notice. The engineers had installed sensors and alarms to monitor such problems, but a power surge no one noticed blew them. Early June it suddenly shook like a failing top. Vibrations rattled the entire dam's structure until the generator shaft snapped and the generator wedged askew in the penstock. Water flooded the powerhouse. Insulators exploded and anyone a half-mile or closer with hair looked like he had suddenly been put upside down. Alarms clanged throughout the surrounding towns and volunteer fire crews trundled the highway toward the disaster. The remaining safety measures held, however, and within a week the powerhouse was pumped dry and the turbine stoppered. The concrete, though compromised, held, aside from a black trickle seeping from the powerhouse wall.

The bigwigs took a lesson from the Dutch Boy, though. August, when the river flow was weakest, they drew down the reservoir to the original banks for repairs. Matt was not required for the work and he found himself with a week's vacation. At the children's urging, he and Wendy drove them to the site where they grew up.

Miles Road descended from the wheat and scablands into a series of canyons cut by creeks that emptied into the river. Inside the car, the radio played news and advertisements. The windows were open to battle the heat, and the air's hum halted any conversation. They were, instead, pressed by their own thoughts into reverie or nostalgia or anticipation of both or neither as the dry, yellow country passed beside them.

The road followed a wide bluff and the river appeared and disappeared behind the outcroppings, water flashing like coins in the light. When they broke finally into the bottom country, Matt felt first disappointment. The river appeared to have simply shrunk; the current throttled by other dams, upriver, that Canada had constructed in the last twenty years, but moreover, it simply appeared too small for its channel. On each side a quarter mile above the old bank grey mud cracked in the sun. Scattered stumps marked the courses of creeks that once more held aimless trickles. Depressions held standing water too stagnant for the ducks to light or idle. The white sun beat through the cars' front window and bleached all that was before him the color of bone.

Wendy's hand touched his. "Look," she said.

The road had put them a half mile above Peach. Rectangular and square foundations lined former streets, creating a strange geometry in a place that appeared otherwise without lines, straight or otherwise.

"There." Wendy pointed. "The store was there."

The kids peered through the window. Matt slowed the car and pulled out when a wide shoulder permitted. Up the asphalt he recognized others doing the same. Twenty cars, he counted, parents, grandparents, and children following their extended arms and pointing fingers. His own did the same as Wendy described streets where she had lived and foundations that held the homes of her friends and her father's customers. Matt was impressed with her memory. He had willed himself to discard those years. It seemed chore enough to steer each day across the rails; now, gazing over the vessel that held those years, he wondered if perhaps his fears had multiplied the labor required and subtracted the pleasure he might have taken otherwise. The notion depressed him further.

"Where are my grandpa and grandma from down there?" Luke asked.

Wendy remained quiet awhile. Matt wanted to hear her answer. "Your grandpa is dead. Your grandmother is in Wilbur."

"The town?"

Wendy nodded.

"It's so close. Why doesn't she come see us?"

"She hasn't been invited," Wendy said.

Matt chuckled at that.

"How about on your side?" Angel asked.

"My father passed when I was little."

"How did he die?" Luke asked.

"In a bad storm. Him and my twin brother both."

"Were you somewhere else?"

"No," Wendy said. "He was in the storm, too."

"But he lived," Luke said.

Wendy nodded. "He did."

They stayed quiet awhile, then returned to the car. The new road traveled near the school site, which was on high enough ground to have survived the reservoir and instead collapsed upon itself through neglect. They walked together past the foundation to the bluff. Matt directed them to the ranch and the graves next to its foundation.

"You can't leave them flowers on Decoration Day?" Luke asked.

"I don't need to," Matt told him. "Your mother planted rose bushes there. They had flowers until winter every day."

"You've known each other that long?" Angel asked.

"You think we just met and had you?" Wendy asked.

They chuckled a little.

"Do we have a grandmother down there, too?" Angel asked.

Matt shook his head. "She moved to the coast. She'd be past eighty if she is still among us."

"Does she not speak to you?" Angel asked.

"No, she doesn't, but don't dig into to it. Like most holes, there's just more of the same. It's not her fault nor mine, or maybe both ours, but blame is beside the point. I hope she's comfortable and I'd wager she'd like the same for me." He went on. "None of this matters. I'm not sorry we come, but it's you all in the here and now that counts," he said.

"Amen," Wendy said.

"We're like a country with no history," Luke decided.

"Makes less to study, though, doesn't it?" Matt said.

They returned through the long twilight, quiet once more, though none dwelling on their wounds present or past. Luke fell asleep and Wendy found a station with bobby sox music for Angel to hum with. They passed again through Creston and Wilbur and descended into the coulee. Wendy patted his thigh.

"My old workhorse," she said.

★ **38** ★

THE CHILDREN GREETED MATT'S RETURN from work each late afternoon as great sport. He had assigned Luke the lunchbox. The boy hurried off the lid for whatever treat Matt had for him. Angel traded him a quart jar of ice water for his coffee and he stood and drank it all, then bent and smooched Wendy on the cheek before going inside to clean up.

It was these moments Wendy began to recall during her walks: the grass and the cool of the sprinklers and the children and Matt and her within it. It appeared to her that when she subtracted the weight to press meaning from days the more she was inclined to enjoy them, and for some time her days had turned lighter and easier to bear. She realized she was in some ways growing young again, attending to what existed rather than what used to or might not. Once, she had considered such a perspective the capitulation that turned people bitter, but recently she determined the opposite might be the case.

The children both worked as soon as they were old enough to ride bicycles. Angel, in high school, tended neighborhood children and cooked harvests for the family of a boy she'd been keeping time with. Luke delivered papers, cleared driveways, piled leaves, and cut lawns, depending upon the season. The children kicked half their wages to Wendy, who kept the family books tight as a stuffed goose. She would ration their savings back to them when she saw fit, which wasn't nearly as often as they did.

Matt watched this with some worry. He'd worked from childhood and, reflecting, it seemed part of what wrecked him for laughter and play. He hoped the children's lot would be better. On occasion, he would pass on to them extra from what Wendy allotted him. Once she set a crate with all their business on the coffee table.

"Maybe it's time you keep this family square," Wendy told him.

He picked out a tax form and looked at it. "We'd be busted."

"With a houseful of toys." Wendy said.

"A live giraffe probably," Matt chuckled.

"It's not all that funny," Wendy told him.

"I'd get whatever you wanted, too," he said.

Matt considered Roland. The old man couldn't help himself regarding his children and it seemed Matt was in the same fix. Wendy attempted to instruct them, while he cheated them all out of the lesson to enjoy the children's good cheer. And, like Roland, he was keeping them from her.

The children, though, saw him as their patron, and it was with this knowledge that, in the early summer of the year of Sputnik, they approached him requesting a car.

"Tell her it's practical," Angel said. "She likes things practical. She's always having to haul us places. This would save her from it."

"Maybe she likes taking you."

Angel rolled her eyes. "It would be fun. That's what we were thinking."

"There's fun to be had walking, too," Matt said.

"I've been walking a long time," Angel told him. "I think I've taken all the fun there is from it."

"I could buy a horse. You could drive him."

"I'd like a horse," Luke said.

"How about a horse, sister? That's what I did all my driving on."

"I'm not a cowboy," Angel replied.

Matt patted her shoulder. "You're not a car driver, either," he said. "And I doubt that will change."

•

WENDY LAY IN BED WITH a book by some Frenchman named Camus. Matt rested next to her studying the last of the morning paper.

"She's going to be married before you know it. They both are," Matt said.

Wendy feathered her book and turned to him. "You worried for them?" she asked.

"No more than usual," he said.

She covered the ground between them and dropped her head to his chest. She could hear his heart and lungs through his breastbone and thick skin like the generators underneath the dam, spinning and cranking without end, the steady hum of work. The book was on her lap, still and open. She closed it, thinking how little words could really do. She lifted her face to Matt's and he kissed her and she handled him in the manner that had become her invitation. He switched the light, and they readied each other for a while. Finally, he put himself over her. She pressed her hands into his chest. He rocked above her like a stone she was trying to find a place for. She listened to his breathing and let hers match it. She wrapped her sex to his until they became one thing moving instead of two and she was able to break loose and finish for herself.

After, she lay next to him. His eyes were open and blinking at the light from the window.

"The children want a car," he said.

She laughed.

"I think they're serious."

"I'm sure they are," Wendy said. "Could you imagine us with a car at that age?"

Matt said. "I don't guess I can."

"You'd have brought me a Ford rather than a gelding."

"I'd never even have to train it," he said. "Just go to a mechanic." He laughed, too. "And it would never have kicked you."

"Even if it did you could've just changed its tires or something, you wouldn't've had to kill the thing. And I'd never shot you off the roof."

Wendy found the scar on his stomach. She made circles around it with her fingers.

"I probably never would've come down and bothered you," he told her. "You'd have had a fine life."

She shook her head. "You'd've come." She thought of Angel and Luke. They were just arriving at living.

"A car," she whispered.

•

THE FOLLOWING SATURDAY, MATT DROVE Wendy to a farm that stood on a sagebrush knob of the scab country west of the river. Rock and no rain made it useless for even the sturdiest crop. Instead the family owning it collected scrap iron. The patriarch was a bald fellow whose shuffling walk led them to a '48 Ford. Wendy wrapped her jacket close to fend off the gusting wind.

"She's due a little cleaning," the man told Matt.

The car was boxy shaped and an unsettling green. The grill had rusted. The junk man opened the door and the ignition chattered until the motor turned over, though it sounded like a washing machine full of shoes. Rat turds pebbled the floor.

"What'd you say again?" Matt asked.

"Twenty-five dollars."

Matt glanced at Wendy. "It runs," he said.

"I can hear it."

"Tires got air."

Wendy pulled her coat tighter. "Seems a bit neglected."

The junk man pressed the accelerator. The motor whined. "It's a goer," he told them.

"But is it a stopper?" Wendy asked.

"I don't know," the man said. "It ain't moved in a good while." He looked at the dash and fingered a crack there. "I thought I was doing business with your husband," he said.

"The children driving this belong to both of us."

"Well I'd hope for their father's manners instead of yours," the man said.

Wendy stepped back from the car to let Matt take up the bargaining. Matt spat on the ground and shook his head.

"You seemed ready enough a minute ago," the man told him.

"Minute ago you hadn't talked coarse to my wife. I believe it will cost you twenty-five dollars."

The man opened his mouth, but Matt raised his hand. "You ought to stop while it's just money."

"You threatening me on my own place?"

Matt said, "I'm done talking. That just leaves doing."

Matt steered her for their car. She took his hand. They returned to town with the heater going. Wendy warmed her hands over its vents.

"It's not often a woman gets her husband to take up for her like that," Wendy said.

"I didn't think much of the car was all." Matt waited a moment then winked at her. She laughed.

"Don't seem we can spend much more," he said.

"Yes we can," she told him.

"I thought you'd fight this the whole way," Matt said. "Now you're wanting to put up more than I'm willing."

She smiled. "Maybe I'm turning unpredictable."

"You've always been that."

"I have, haven't I," she said.

"You going to take in ironing to pay for this car?" he asked.

"Look at you arguing for thrift."

"I guess it's my turn isn't it?"

She laughed again. "There's a rainy day account I've been keeping."

"What if it rains, though?" he asked.

"Rain is just weather," she said.

Matt turned them onto the highway dividing Grand Coulee. B Street still had its dark reputation but clean businesses lined the highway thoroughfare. Wendy wanted real car lots. There were two. They stopped at the first. The sun was warmer and the wind had relented. Wendy pointed to a fifty-six Chevy, blue as evening sky. It appeared to have never seen the road. The seats were clean as restaurant plates and the untarnished ashtray metal shone.

"It's twice what we drive," Matt said.

"I know."

"See the price?"

Wendy nodded. The sun reflected off the paint and it looked to Matt to glow, like those pictures of Christ assuming the throne.

"It's as pretty as a good horse," she said.

He smiled at that.

"Well, they'll be tickled. I can tell you that."

Wendy paid with a bank draft and the dealer threw in the first fill-up free. Matt offered her the keys. He followed in what would be now known as the old car. The power steering wheeled Wendy out of the graveled lot with a quarter turn of her hand. She felt graceful as a doe. When she eased into the accelerator, the motor lifted her like air itself was all that was underneath. She closed her eyes and thought of the children driving off from sadness instead of slogging through it.

Matt parked on the street. Wendy opened the door and Angel and Luke tumbled from the trailerhouse. They stood for a long while in the driveway without moving. Luke was open-mouthed. Angel finally turned to Matt.

"Oh Dad," she said. She wrapped her arms around his neck.

Matt undid Angel's hug and put her hands in front of her, between them. "It'd do you some good to appreciate your mother," he told her. "This was her work all." He walked inside, leaving them alone.

Wendy watched Luke and Angel, who approached the car like it was an animal they were trying not to spook. Luke touched the fender with his hand, then bent his face to the warm metal.

"I never saw anything so pretty," Angel said.

"I'm pleased you like it," Wendy told her.

She handed Angel the keys. Luke hurried through the passenger door and waved from behind the glass. He uncranked the window. "Hey Mom," he asked. "You want to go riding?"

She surprised herself and did, leaving the front seat for them. The radio worked fine and they found some modern music that couldn't even succeed in annoying her. When her children glanced back, Wendy's eyes were closed and the wind was spanking her hair and jacket and she was smiling at the pleasure of their travel together.

⋆ 39 ⋆

MORNING, LUCKY LAY PROSTRATE ON the grass and studied the sunlight through its dew. Each breath clanged his lungs against his ribs and he decided at least one was broken. His clouded right eye leaked blood and yellow fluid. Through it, the horizon seemed upended. Blood pasted his tongue to his mouth. Sleep and the beating bent his thoughts and, for a moment, he couldn't recall what put him on the grass this early morning. A car hushed by, and Wendy's voice turned audible through an open kitchen window. He comprehended the words separately, but in a sentence they confounded him. She spoke of sandwiches and a fresh peach and being short of bread and coffee and Lawson answered, the voices gonging inside Lucky's skull.

The door opened and Lawson lifted him with an ease that he was unprepared for. He stared up into the jaw, clean-shaved but still peppered with what would be beard and the nostrils and thick shock of hair. He had never seen a man's face as close. Matt's calm eyes gazed ahead. Lucky watched the face pull away until he could see its whole shape.

"What happened to you, hombre?" Lawson asked him.

Lucky moaned.

"Okay," Lawson told him. "What is hardly the point."

Matt stared into the sky. "What am I going to do with you?"

Lucky wrestled his badge from his shirt pocket.

"Law?" Matt asked.

Lucky nodded. "Got jumped hunting a fugitive. Slunk off while they were drinking. Caught a lift and got dumped here. Couldn't manage any more."

"Your man close?"

"Coulee Dam. He'll want to close the deal. A load of warrants got his name on them."

"You want me to find a cop?"

"He is a cop for the county," Lucky said.

"I can give you a lift toward the dam."

"I'd say that's the wrong direction for me."

"I imagine so."

"If you could let me lay up in your place an hour or so, I could get some help and turn the tables."

"There's a thousand ways that's a bad idea."

"I know," Lucky said. "I'm asking."

Lucky lifted the man and lugged him into the trailerhouse and dropped him onto the sofa. Wendy joined him. She wore a house-coat, but most of her leg showed before it buttoned. The darkness above made Lucky giddy.

Lawson said, "He was on the grass."

Lucky propped himself on one elbow and peered past Lawson. Wendy stared from a face softened and fleshy with the years. Her cheekbones no longer carved her face into a clear shape. She'd lived too long comfortably. Her eyes were the same brown; there remained a little desperation left in them and when he struck upon it, she squinted and recalled.

"Put him out," she said.

"He's in no shape for that."

"He can't stay."

Lawson bent and his face became large again. "You want to go the hospital, buddy?" Lucky could smell the coffee on his breath. He shook his head. Lawson shrugged. Wendy's eyes darted from the couch to some spot in the kitchen. She didn't look at her husband. She was already hiding him, Lucky knew.

"He's a cop," Matt whispered. "Some criminal bunged him up and wants to do more. He just needs an hour to get squared away," Lawson told her.

"Can't you see this bothers me?" Wendy asked.

Lawson collected his lunchbox. "Probably puts him out, too."

"What if I say no?"

"Do you want them to kill him? I doubt he can take a second whipping. Where's my coffee?"

Wendy held to the thermos. "Matt!" she pleaded.

"Should I set him at the end of the driveway for the trashman?" Lawson asked. He took her hand and raised it in his. Wendy pressed her lip under her front teeth, a fresh gesture to Lucky. She'd kept learning after him, and he'd stopped with her. He was inclined to lay a good slap on her.

The children rose ten minutes after Lawson's departure. Lucky smelled pancakes and listened as Wendy piled them onto plates. The children were an inconvenience to the chore ahead. He supposed he could rise and shoo them himself, but he didn't desire a battle. Lucky dozed and Wendy fed her brood and collected the breakfast dishes.

"You've eaten double what you're allowed already," she said to the boy. "You and Angel get along," she said. "It's too nice a day to waste indoors." Luke went to his room for a basketball. Through the window, Wendy watched him amble toward the concrete hoop and backboard at the park.

"I don't have a basketball," the daughter told her.

Wendy opened the cabinet above the refrigerator. She offered Angel a leather-bound book. "Tell me what they mean," Wendy said.

The door shut behind her. Wendy remained at the window, watching her. When her attention returned to the room, Lucky sat up, rubbing one shoulder.

"I'd have a cup." He nodded at the coffeepot.

Wendy brought him one.

"They're fine children," he said.

She nodded.

Lucky winced raising the coffee.

"Does your visit have a purpose?" Wendy asked him.

"Right to the point, same as I recall." Lucky smiled. "I'm sheriff," he said. "For Lincoln County. I'd say that's some improvement from the last we saw each other."

Wendy studied her fingers through the holed afghan.

"I'm going to take Lawson for a long walk off a short pier. I've been paid good money."

"What do you have against him?"

"You," Lucky said. He blinked, speaking in monotone, as if he might be translating some language difficult to decipher. "Things just got into a line and stopped here." Lucky stood and lifted her at the elbow until she was upright, then steered her toward the bedroom. She halted in the hall. He backhanded her, but she held her ground.

"All that's over," she said.

"It hasn't ever been done on my end."

"What you feel is no longer my concern," she told him. "I'm sorry to put it that way. It's cruel, I know. Maybe all of it was cruel. I'm cruel, maybe. Me letting you think it was more. I'm sorry."

He undid her housecoat but she closed it and tied the wrap. He was a child, as she'd left him. He put his gun to her head.

"Take off the clothes." She did and stood in front of him, a naked woman, yet she looked as composed as if she'd dressed for winter.

"Nothing will be different if you do it."

"Everything will change."

"No," she said. "You'll have raped me. That's all."

"You love me."

Wendy shook her head. "We were confused," she said.

Lucky stood. His head ached and so did his chest. Each breath tried him. He was still confused, he realized.

"Go on into the front room," he told her. He followed her there and rested on a chair. He directed her to the sofa. Wendy sat with her legs and arms covering herself. They stayed quiet a long time.

"When's Lawson get back?" Lucky said.

"I thought you were here for me."

He shook his head. "I just happened onto you."

She looked at him. "You're here for me."

"You're just begging for him now," he told her. He chuckled a little. "I listen to them old country songs. Nobody knows, but I hear when they come on. Them boys can sing. I figure I been wounded like them maybe. By you and by Lawson, too. But I can't carry a tune." He shook his head. "It's a shame," he said. "I could sit here and serenade you until he gets home. Maybe if I was sung out I wouldn't need to kill him."

"What good will killing him do you?" she asked him.

He smiled. "What good does it do them cowboys to sing?"

"He'll turn the tables on you," Wendy told him.

"I doubt it," Lucky said. He thought he needed killing, though. It would be some rest finally. He imagined it as peaceful as sleeping late. He set his gun on his lap and waited. When the children returned, he stripped them and put them next to their mother. The girl was heavy-breasted and thin at the hip, but his loins were done. The boy was thick bone and muscle and skin and a confused pair of eyes.

He felt drowsy and ordered Wendy to perk coffee, then drank the entire pot, but it did not wake him. He stood and circled the room; the colors went to mud and he dreamed waking dreams that smelled like fresh meat and fire and tasted of iron and smoke and he heard his name whispered, a silly name, yes, but the voice spoke it like it was from a book and equal to other words and if he repeated it long enough, he would mean what books meant and end as books ended.

The boy on all fours crawled into the kitchen, a good boy; he had attempted to resist, and might have accepted a bullet for his mother and sister, if Wendy had not scolded him into submission. Lucky watched him climb the counter. The boy dropped to the floor, a gun in his fist. Wendy and the girl stared at him. Lucky realized he had been speaking, but had no idea for how long. He raised the pistol and shot at the boy. It was a small caliber gun, but the report rang for long enough to break the cadence of thoughts in his ears.

Wendy had gone to the boy despite Lucky's weapon.

"He's all right," she told Angel. The gun lay on the floor.

"Leave it," Lucky said. "Please."

Wendy returned to the sofa with Luke. Lucky thanked her, thanked all of them as if they'd done him a service. He listened to the stove clock tick; as it wound off minutes, his breaths joined the rhythm, then his thoughts, until it was just a clock in a room, and he was once more able to discern what was outside his head from what was within. He could hear their breathing, too, and he nearly shot them just to gain himself silence.

At half past four, Lawson parked in their driveway. Inside, he saw the gun on the floor. He bent to examine it.

"Don't."

Lawson blinked adjusting to the curtained room. He recognized his family on the couch, unclothed.

"You and me have business?" Lawson asked.

Lucky nodded.

"This business require them undressed?"

"No. I just wanted you to see them this way."

"Well, I have."

Wendy held the children's hands. All their eyes stared at Lawson.

"It'll be all right," he told them. The boy nodded and Angel, too. Wendy, though, began to weep.

"There somewhere else may be more fitting we can settle up?" Lawson asked.

Lucky shrugged. "Suit yourself." He stood and followed Lawson to Lucky's car. Lucky sat in the passenger seat and held his gun on Lawson as he drove. West of the towns and into the rocky country that surrounded Banks Lake, Lucky ordered him onto a secluded, two-rut road that led to Northrup Canyon, where a creek ran year-round. He drove as far as the road allowed, then braked the car.

"We getting out?" Lawson asked.

Lucky nodded.

Lawson stepped out of the car. It was still light. He looked up the steep rock of the coulee.

"I don't suppose I could argue you from this?"

"I might enjoy hearing it."

"I'm not a convincing speaker, anyhow." He took a few steps toward the rocks. "Will you leave my family be?"

"I'm done with them," Lucky said.

"Okay, then." Lawson turned to face Lucky.

"You don't want to know what for?"

Lawson shrugged.

"Garrett," Lucky said. "You know him?"

"Yes."

"He wants you dead. Or in jail."

"You prefer dead."

"Less work," Lucky said. He unzipped his pants and showed Lawson his workings. "I knew your wife." Lucky leaned on the fender to relieve his labored breaths. "I don't anymore." He shook his penis with his free hand. "Now I unknow her."

"Let's get this done with," Matt said.

"You're sure in a hurry for your demise."

"I don't care for waiting."

"Well, then I'll see to it you do a little longer."

Lawson reached into his shirt pocket for a cigarette. He offered one to Lucky who lit it with a matchbook from his pocket and drew until the cigarette end caught. He exhaled a lungful of smoke. Lucky paced a circle around him.

"Linda Jefferson. You knew her?"

"She rescued me once a long time back." Lawson said. "There was a storm. Is she not well?"

"She's my mother and she hasn't ever been well, goddamnit."

"I'm sorry."

A half-mile away, a car passed on the state road. They waited until its sound moved off.

"What's this got to do with my wife?" Lawson asked him.

"I knew her before you," Lucky replied.

"Before she was in grammar school?"

"You were acquainted with her as a child?"

Lawson nodded, and Lucky saw it was as true as a condemned man's words were said to be. Lawson knew her before Lucky himself had and married her after. Lawson had known his mother before his birth: everyone that mattered. Lucky gazed at the gun in his hand. He had thought his living was on the edge of making sense, when it had really just quit logic for good.

He held the gun on Matt with both hands, like it was a fish he feared would squirm from his grasp. Matt pulled up his shirt. "See this scar?"

Lucky nodded.

"Wendy shot me a long time ago." Matt poked the scar.

"She did that?" Lucky said.

Matt nodded.

"I guess she give you a hard time, too."

"I guess so," Matt replied. "If you got to shoot me, I'd appreciate you doing it here."

"It'll leave you gut shot. Head is quicker."

"I'm sentimental," Matt said.

"I suppose if I'm going to go on and shoot you, it's only fitting you pick the place." He put the barrel next to Matt's ancient wound. "You prepared?"

"You'll leave off my family?"

"I'm a lot of things, but I don't lie."

Matt nodded and clasped his hands over the gun and turned the barrel downward at what he thought was the same angle. Lucky tugged the trigger. The bullet's blow shoved Matt backwards into a sagebrush and spun him onto his side. The pain started dull and familiar. Blood warmed his chest and back. He lay with his eyes closed waiting for his organs to come apart.

Lucky stood over him. He rolled Matt and stared at the wound, and shook his head. "Goddammit," he said.

A few seconds and Matt heard the car door shut, then the engine turn. The tires rattled the gravel and joined the sound of the highway. Matt lay, waiting for death. The sky darkened with coming night. He thought nothing and remained where he was. After half an hour, he realized he'd quit hurting as bad. His bleeding had slowed, as well. His lungs took in breath and without sputtering fluid. His eyes worked. He heard the highway. He wondered if this was a trick dying played on a man, one that let him leave life easier. His watch read a quarter past seven and an hour later, it read a quarter past eight. He tipped himself to sit. The wound punished him for movement, but not as much as it could have. He stood. His legs remained unsure, but that was because they'd gone numb. He unbuttoned the shirt to examine the wound and knew then he wouldn't die.

The bullet had exited his back. He heard something sounding like coins rattle. He untucked his shirt. Two bullets fell against the hard ground, one fresh metal, the other black and tired from forty years inside him.

He walked home. At the door, he yelled his name so the boy would put the gun away. Inside, they had all dressed. It seemed as strange as seeing them naked a few hours previous, and he recognized the strangeness came from being alive. Wendy was at the phone. He put his hand over the cradle and she gazed up at him.

"What happened?" she asked him finally.

He shrugged. "I got shot," he said.

Wendy tore the shirt open and saw the wound. She blinked and touched her fingers to his belly where she had marked him. He dropped his hand to hers and inside placed the bullets, first the one that meant to end him, then the other.

Wendy pressed the bullets into her fist and opened her fingers and gazed at them. Angel found the gauze and alcohol in the medicine cabinet and cleaned the wounds. Matt sat with his shirt off, letting them doctor him. Angel cooked dinner later and they moved to the porch to eat, and remained a long while after in lawn chairs, enjoying the cool of the evening.

Soon, the children drifted off. Wendy went inside and returned with blankets to cover them. She stood over him for a long time with another. He took her hand when she offered it.

"I have to tell you something," she whispered.

"Shhh," he told her.

"No," she said.

"It doesn't matter," he told her.

She felt guilty at first, like she guessed a woman might who has taken a new lover, and then realized, that her new lover was her old lover and the good fortune in that discovery. She lay her head upon his chest listening to the sounds he made and following them to her own heart beating, alive, as it had been all along.

★ 40 ★

Lucky reached Colfax in the dead of night. He left his car in a supermarket parking lot and hitched with a truck driver four miles up the highway toward Lacrosse, then walked a gravel road toward Garrett's country.

Garrett owned so much land no one had reason to travel the roads bisecting it aside from himself.

The sky was still grey with dawn and Garrett's pickup trundled slowly toward him, the way farmers ride their own country, gawking and enjoying what owning land means. Lucky stepped into the headlight's glow. Garrett braked his rig and stepped out.

"You look worse for the wear," Garrett said.

"I am that." Lucky took the gun from his pants. He had no idea why he had left it there rather than his holster.

"You use that on him?"

Lucky nodded.

"He's dead then?"

"Creased good. I didn't stay for the funeral."

"I'm not paying until I am certain."

"I guess you'll know soon," Lucky told him. He raised the gun. Garrett lifted his hand, but the bullet folded him in half. Lucky kicked him into the ditch weeds, then dropped to one knee to look at him clearly.

"Get me to the doctor, damn you. I'm bleeding bad."

Lucky walked to the truck and parked it on the roadside. He cut the lights. Alive still, Garrett attempted to drag himself through the cheat grass. Lucky walked with him until he collapsed. He listened to him fight for breaths.

"I'm dying," Garrett said.

"You sound surprised," Lucky told him.

The sun was on the rise. It blanketed the hills gold, the wheat was ripening, and a breeze moved it in ripples. He'd spent hours trapping rabbit or stalking pheasant through mornings like this, but he'd never thought of enjoying the light.

Garrett said no more. Lucky remained beside him until he'd quit breathing and his pulse had faded. He lugged the body back to the truck and put it in the passenger seat. Lucky drove the truck to an abandoned shed. He checked that it was empty and pulled the truck inside, latched the door. The harvest road was dry and overgrown. He kicked the loose dirt that held the tire marks, then walked himself toward town, ducking into the ditches whenever he heard a car's approach.

That evening, Lucky drove to the Rockford Rest Home. In the lobby, his mother was bunched into a wheelchair. The other patients babbled or cried or sat with stone faces aimed at the black-and-white television. She alone looked like she understood where she was.

Lucky pulled a stool to her and sat. He drew his badge from his pocket and placed it in her hand, where she examined it. He felt his debt but had no idea how to pay it. The bill was, he realized, an owing you needed to accept to be a man in this world, one you had to leave outstanding. He took his mother's hand. She spoke his name, and he returned, "Mother."

"There was a storm," she said.

"Yes," he replied.

"There was a storm," she said again. "A terrible storm."

Lucky bent to her. Her fingers touched his face and wound his coarse hair. She looked up, and in her face was all he knew of family, all he'd ever know, and, though it wasn't near enough, he would deny her no longer.

⋆ EPILOGUE ⋆

Because I could not stop for Death—

—EMILY DICKINSON
from poem 712

FOR TWELVE YEARS, CLOCKS AND calendar pages turned without consequence. It wasn't a long span in history, Matt knew, but it was more than he'd permitted himself to hope for. He gave Angel away to a farmer boy after a stint at a junior college, and watched Luke acquit himself well in both his studies and summer work. The boy graduated from Washington State University four years later and took a structural engineering position at the dam. Matt served as best man when he wed, and they took lunches in the riggers' loft when Luke's schedule allowed.

Angel delivered their first grandchild, a girl. She bore a remarkable resemblance to Wendy and this set Matt and Wendy to chuckling so that Angel gave them odd looks. Not long following, Luke's wife, Ann, bore him twin boys. He named them Matthew and Lucas, and this concerned Matt, tempting the fates.

Matt retired in mid-June of his sixty-seventh year. He recalled standing in front of the shop, looking over the Bureau of Reclamation complex. Someone named Slats passed on a forklift and another called Otto, who fished all summer and turned back everything he caught, was whistling while he waited for the new powerhouse shuttle where he operated a boom crane. It was no different than any day that had passed; he simply didn't need the routine any longer.

Fall of the following year he and Wendy culled the husks and stray leaves from a spot Wendy intended for more roses. Wind gusted from the north and geese sliced ahead of it through the sky. He had decided to retrieve his jacket, when Wendy stumbled to one knee. Before he reached her, she collapsed. Her mouth hung open and gasped for breath. He said her name. Her eyes went wide.

He ran for the car, carrying her and through her sweatshirt felt the leap of her heart wrestling loose from her. Driving to the hospital, he spoke her name, recalling reading that the dying lost their ears last.

The funeral was three days later. The casket was draped with roses. Angel and Luke and their families maintained a vigil next to him throughout the service. Matt had bought a suit for the occasion. Angel had put Wendy in a summer dress, as that was her favorite season. The family followed him home for a potluck the neighbors prepared, but he shooed kith and kin away once all had eaten.

But the next morning, some of the cars returned. The glass door slid and his grandchildren raced over the yellowing grass toward the house. They knew little of grief and he held out his arms and smiled, hoping to hold that education off a while longer. It was Sunday; he heard a church bell peel. Inside, Angel found the pans and scrambled eggs and bacon while Luke's wife turned flapjacks. They waved, but Matt was rolling on the grass with the grandbabies. It was bright and cool, the same as it was on the Sunday next, when they returned and again shared breakfast, as they did the Sunday after that and the one after that, as well.

•

EIGHTEEN MONTHS LATER, THE LOCAL doctor sent him to Brewster for x-rays and the pictures returned with a smear on his left lung that indicated cancer. The surgeons removed two lobes and stitched him up then took more pictures and returned to their scalpels and tore into the second lung. Finally the old general practitioner visited.

"I'm carved as Christmas goose," Matt said and lifted his shirt to reveal the sutures. "I'm out of lungs, doc, but not out of cancer. That's what you're here to tell me."

The doctor nodded.

"Well, if there's nothing more, I guess I'll head home."

"You had two of the worse surgeries there are one on top of the other," the doctor told him.

"There's infections, bones mending."

"I'm going to be back here sooner than I'd like and the next visit will be the last of it. I aim to put as much time between this one and that one as possible." Matt eased his legs onto the floor and used his arms to prop himself until he stood. "If I don't make it they can put me back. If I do, I'll sleep in my own bed."

He called his children on the telephone and asked them to visit without children or spouses so he could deliver the news. Neither tried to talk him into returning to the hospital. Both cried. He told them not to and then to go ahead. He said he wasn't worried and found that strangely true, and when they left he slept a deep sleep with bountiful dreams of childhood and his wife and vast country.

He asked the children one favor. In November while the weather remained mild, Luke and Angel took him into the Palouse country.

The old house was still occupied. A new shop held a red International combine and a pair of diesel trucks. The man who answered looked in some ways like his father. His name was Ellis Garrett.

"Do you know that lone oak by the creek?" Matt pointed north where he remembered it being.

"That the one with the carvings in it?"

"Do you think it would be all right to go out there?" Matt asked.

The man nodded. "It's a half-mile farther then west on a harvest road. Mind the chuckholes."

Luke opened a barbed wire gate and Angel drove through it to the tree. It was larger, though parts of it had shriveled and died and it needed to be pruned. Matt saw no sign of disease, however, and the fallen leaves still gathered against the trunk appeared healthy enough.

Matt circled it and stroked the cold bark. The names were still there, though barely legible—just white scars. Angel discovered her own and gazed at it. Matt unsheathed his buck knife. He found each name and hacked the letters deep into the old bark. After he'd finished retracing what was there, he cut Wendy's name and Luke's and the grandbabies'. His arm ached from the labor and his chest burned, but he continued until the whole of his family and Jarms's was there to be read.

•

MATT'S FUNERAL WAS FIVE MONTHS later. Angel recalled him lying in the hospital bed, smelling like fruit gone bad. He asked to visit the grandchildren alone. He whispered to each, but when Angel and Luke inquired later, the children allowed only it was a secret. He'd grown weak with cancer and needed to be tipped to sip water, but he latched on to Angel and Luke like he had when he lifted them whole in his hands as children. They stayed with him until he'd drifted off, then quietly both kissed him and left the room. He died that night alone. It grieved Luke horribly, but Angel recognized it as his intent.

The chapel service was short. Angel and Luke watched the pallbearers unload the casket and listened as the winch motored it into the grave. Angel kissed Luke's hand in her own. After, she gathered her children to her, and bent her head back into her husband's warm stomach. She closed her eyes and listened to the minister recite his lines. The mourners stirred and rose to leave, but she remained a little longer then finally stood and joined her family in the procession to the parking lot.

A man in a black suit, heavy and stooped with age, passed her the other direction. She recognized him, a demon from a bad dream long ago. The man dropped something gold and flat and metal onto the casket and then began to wail.

ACKNOWLEDGMENTS

MANY THANKS TO JANET ROSEN, Sheree Bykofsky, Julia Drake, Judy Klein, and Dan Smetanka for their generosity and care for my work. Thanks to friends and family for their patience and wisdom, especially Holly Holbert, Jackson Holbert, Luke Holbert, Natalie Holbert, Jody Mills, Max Phillips, Elizabeth McCracken, John Whalen, Charlie McIntyre, Chris Offutt, Bob Ganahl, Jim and Lisa Van Nostrand, Rick and Kim Simon, Dave Koehler and Desi Koehler—whose grandmother midwifed my father into the world and it seems like we've been joined at the hip since—Pat Holbert, Barbara Holbert, Bonnie Hogue, Margaret Moore, and especially Vince Moore, a one-time resident of Peach with a wealth of knowledge about the country now under the reservoir. Also, thanks to Mt. Spokane High School for its generous flexibility and support, especially Jim Preston, Darren Nelson, and John Hook. Finally, thanks to *The Iowa Review*, which published the first chapter of this novel as a short story many years ago.

Printed in the United States
by Baker & Taylor Publisher Services